What people are saying about Golden Heart Winner Mary Strand and her books:

From Amazon readers:

"The Romance Genre has a strong, unique Voice rising within its realm. And that Voice belongs to Mary Strand!"

"A fun, fast-paced, smart reimagining of a beloved classic."
"…will keep you turning pages, laughing until the very end. It starts out with humor and ends with love."

"This story is laugh out loud funny and full of heart."

From GoodReads reviewers:

"Breezy reading and fun humor throughout."

"…filled with laughs and tears."

"Laugh out loud funny, this book will make you love Mary Bennet and feel for the overlooked middle sister as she takes control of her own life."

DEDICATION

For Mary Faist Pekala,
who asked me to play in a band with her ...
and when I said "Absolutely not!"
kept asking until I said yes.

THE BENNET SISTERS:
Book 4

Livin' La Vida Bennet

Mary Strand

tripleberry
press

This book is a work of fiction. Names, characters, places, and incidents are either the product of the author's imagination or are used fictitiously. Any resemblance to actual persons, living or dead, business establishments, events, or locales is entirely coincidental.

triple berry press
P.O. Box 24733
Minneapolis, Minnesota 55424

WITH HUGE THANKS TO:

Mark Wade, who taught me guitar and how to play in a band and was amazing at both, and who answered Way Too Many pesky questions about guitar and bass guitar for this book. He's also an absolute blast on stage with his bass guitar and vocals ... and his dancing feet.

Michael Oachs, my first guitar teacher, who shares my love of the Eagles (which is not shared by any of my heroines) and was always far more patient with me than Jazz was with Lydia in this book.

Randy Sinz, a musician friend since my college days and a bass player I've happily spent many hundreds of hours listening to, who answered my questions about bass guitar when I first started writing this book.

"Swave" Dave Schrader and Dave ("Dusty") Engedal, two more musician friends since my college days, who let me torture them about garage bands (and, in the case of Dusty, guitars) for this book and this series.

Laura (Hewitt) Colombe, who loves bands the way I do and who gave me great advice about high school bands.

Kind souls who provided critiques, edits, beta reads, or brainstorming help, including Kate Fraser, Tom Fraser, Ann Barry Burns, Just Cherry Writers, and Romex

My own high school teachers at Eau Claire Memorial, a few of whose names I used in this book out of great fondness. In the name of Lydia Bennet I again took teasing liberties in this book in particular with Mr. Skamser, who was a fantabulous English teacher. I'd also like to thank Dick Bennett, who is much better known as a great basketball coach but who introduced me to Pride and Prejudice when he taught our 10th-grade English class. I've loved The Book ever since.

Pam McCutcheon and Laura Hayden, collectively also known as Parker Hayden Media, LLC, who are fabulous. And nice. And helpful. And patient. And all sorts of wonderful things.

Jane Austen, who is simply the best

Chapter 1

Lydia was Lydia still;
untamed, unabashed, wild, noisy, and fearless.

— Jane Austen, *Pride and Prejudice*,
Volume III, Chapter Nine

"I'M BACK! LET the parties begin!"

Dead silence. My gaze flickered over the frozen faces at my old lunch table, then around the cafeteria. Kids at other tables were staring at me, too, and I heard a buzz of recognition, but the kids at my own table didn't say a word. My *crowd* didn't say a word. Was I speaking Swahili? I mean, it wasn't like they didn't remember me. Everyone at Woodbury High School knew me. Half of them worshipped me.

A year away at reform school didn't change that, did it?

Frowning, I glanced across the cafeteria, zeroing in on my sister Cat, who was sitting with Jeremy Fisk, who'd never been part of our crowd. No wonder Cat wasn't at our old table: she was either shut out or too embarrassed. I knew she'd been dating

Jeremy for six months now, but it was still weird. I'd been home for ten days, and she hadn't bothered to warn me how things stood with our crowd. With *my* crowd.

"Lydia. You're back. It's been *ages*."

"Hey, Tess. Yeah, they finally sprang me."

My mom and dad told me not to put it that way, not even to friends, but Dad was the one who shipped me to reform school a year ago, and Mom didn't exactly stop him, and I didn't give a rat's ass what either of them thought.

Grinning, I glanced at Tess O'Halloran and set my tray down in the empty spot next to her. Finally. Someone I could talk to, really talk to, despite all the snotty things Cat said about Tess in all her emails last spring. We'd always been close. I could count on Tess.

She turned back to Amber Tomlinson, though, on the other side of her, which put me right back where I'd started: with no one talking to me. Or acting like I belonged here.

What the fuck? I owned this school, and every one of these kids knew it.

I ran a hand through my hair, still thick but short now, thanks to a year in Shangri-La. It almost killed me to cut it, but I would've done anything to reduce the odds of that repulsive witch, Shannon, yanking it out by the roots. Shannon didn't last past February, but not because they sprang her for good behavior. She torched the headmaster's office.

But Shannon wasn't my problem anymore. When I flew home from Montana, I thought I didn't have *any* problems except Mom and Dad, who should really get a new phone number, 1-800-LECTURE, since that's all they did these days. And, okay, Cat avoided me, which qualified as a slight problem, but it had to be because she had this loser boyfriend. After three classes and now lunch on my first day back, though, I realized Cat wasn't my problem. Mom and Dad weren't my problem.

It was the whole entire school.

"Lydia. Hey."

I glanced to my right, where Drew Mitchell was smiling at me the way Cat used to smile at *him*. On the other side of Drew, a girl with bleach-blond hair was watching me like a hawk.

"Drew. How're you doing?"

He patted the girl's arm. Whatever. "Good. You know Chelsea?"

I shook my head as I sized her up. Beady eyes, too much makeup, one arm draped over Drew's shoulder now. Yep, definitely Drew's girlfriend.

She snorted. "You're that girl who spent last year at reform school? How did *that* work out for you?"

I frowned as her snotty giggle was joined by a few others, including Amber's. None of the guys laughed, though, including Drew, which told me one thing hadn't changed. The guys all still wanted to go out with me.

They just didn't realize I didn't have much interest. Still, I wouldn't mind spending a little quality time with Drew, just enough to wipe that snotty smirk off Chelsea's face.

And maybe teach Cat a lesson while I was at it.

As I pondered exactly what I planned to do with Drew, preferably with Chelsea watching, I gave the little witch an evil grin of my own. "It worked out just fine. But I see Drew hasn't done so well for himself lately."

Chelsea's fat mouth formed a perfect "O" of bright-red lipstick, probably the only perfect thing about her, as Drew gave her a comforting pat on the arm. Tess and Amber stopped giggling, since they knew me a lot better than Chelsea did. They knew I played to win.

At least when provoked.

As I fluttered my eyelashes at Chelsea, I couldn't help noticing that Drew was totally checking me out. As if he knew exactly what I planned to do with him and didn't even want to wait until the end of lunch period.

When I touched the tip of my tongue to the corner of my mouth, Drew swallowed hard. Chelsea grabbed her tray and stood up, jerking Drew along with her.

"See you l-later?" Drew's voice cracked, probably for the first time since eighth grade.

"Definitely." I gave Chelsea a little finger wave as her face turned green. "Can't wait."

♫

I CURLED UP on my bed after school, the window open wide to let in the September breeze. I still hadn't gotten used to seeing an open window and not wanting to make a lunge for freedom. But I was home, back in my old room and—almost—in my old life, and the only wardens in sight were Mom and Dad. Who weren't even in sight right now.

Mary's mangy old cat, Boris, padded softly through the open doorway, and I wondered again why Mary hadn't taken the stupid thing with her when she left for MIT. If she thought this reject from an animal shelter was the perfect homecoming gift for me, she had to be kidding. I knew I should've slammed my bedroom door the instant I came upstairs, but I hated closed doors even more than closed windows.

Boris's orange-and-puke-striped tail swished in the air, almost like he was happy to see me. Doubtful. If I didn't count the slobbering guys, no one in Woodbury, Minnesota, was happy to see me these days.

Boris, though, took a flying leap and landed his sorry mongrel ass on my bed, then moved into my arms and purred on cue.

Stupid cat.

Another Cat, my twin, walked into the room with the same wariness I now aimed at everyone in Woodbury. Despite myself, I hugged Boris a little tighter. "What happened to your old boyfriend, Drew?"

She just frowned as she crossed to her own bed and started emptying her backpack onto it. Like she was going to start studying. On the first day of school, when no one gave homework, or at least no one did it.

She pulled out a sketchpad. No wonder. Little Miss Art Freak probably planned to draw a portrait of a former convict who'd gone straight.

Ignoring Boris, I lay back on my bed and held my pillow in front of my face.

When she still didn't say anything, I peeled back a corner of the pillow. Her sketchpad was nowhere in sight, and she wasn't even looking at me. She *was* doing homework. The Cat I knew only read beauty and gossip magazines. Just like I used to do. Before I spent a year in Shangri-La.

I tossed my pillow aside, which sent Boris shooting off my bed and skidding across the floor to take cover in the closet. With one eye on him, I propped my head on my elbow. "Is that for school? Like, you actually do homework these days? What happened to the Cat I knew and loved?"

Cat's eyebrows went up, but she didn't say anything.

"And I asked you about Drew. What's up? Why aren't you with him, and who's that skanky chick he's with?"

Cat's book was propped open, but I knew she wasn't reading. I mean, she couldn't be. I was *talking* to her.

Finally, she sighed. "She's Chelsea Anderson, and I never *was* dating Drew."

"Practically."

"Besides, I'm going out with Jeremy. Like I've told you a

million times."

"Yeah, I don't get that, either. He's not part of our crowd. We've always stayed within the crowd."

Okay, I hadn't, but the guys I'd gone out with at Woodbury High always moved on. Like, quickly. It wasn't tough to find new guys, but it was a little squicky to hook up with a bunch of guys who were all friends.

Which was why Justin had seemed so great. Even though he hadn't been. As it turned out.

"I told you." Cat abandoned the book, but she perched on the edge of her bed as if she was about to leave. Without telling me, let alone inviting me along. "I dropped that crowd, and I'm glad Jeremy isn't part of it. Really glad."

"You're just saying that because Tess and Kirk busted your chops. I can't believe you fell for that."

Cat shot to her feet. "Yeah, well, whatever. Catch you later."

I jumped off my bed and followed her to the door, but not before she grabbed the handle and yanked it shut. When I whipped it open again, she'd already reached the bottom of the stairs and headed out the front door. By the time I got my shoes back on and ran after her, our electric-blue Jeep rumbled to life and peeled out from the curb. Leaving me here alone.

It had to be a first. But after I got done with Cat, it wouldn't happen again.

WEDNESDAY AFTERNOON, AFTER another boring lunch punctuated by Tess's random giggles at pretty much anything anyone said—except me—my nose wrinkled as I read all the activities notices plastered on the bulletin board outside the principal's office. Why I was standing outside Mr. Paymar's office, I had no idea, since the thought of him always had a ring of detention to it. Volleyball, the fall musical, Spanish club, Robotics, Gender & Sexuality Alliance, Super Smash Brothers, whatever that was. My eyes flickered over SADD: Students Against Destructive Decisions. I could be the President of it.

It was all stupid. Boring. Pointless. Besides, a year at Shangri-La hadn't exactly turned me into a joiner, unlike a certain twin sister of mine who didn't even seem embarrassed to hang with her boyfriend at the art freaks' lunch table.

My gaze kept scanning the activities, maybe because I wasn't in any hurry to get to Accounting I. It was mind-numbingly boring, even if Dad said it would come in handy for a girl like me. Whatever that meant. I saw a notice for gymnastics tryouts, but they didn't start until November. I bit my lip, considering, but flushed the idea. A year and a half ago, I'd spent two months in the weight room and on the gymnastics equipment, working out to get in shape to join the circus for the summer. It had actually felt great and paid off when I got the job.

Too bad I lost the job on my second day, then left town with Justin Truesdale and, by the end of the summer, lost everything that mattered.

The warning bell for fourth period rang just as someone's arm wrapped around my waist. "Are you signing up for something?"

Turning, I found myself in Drew's arms. The only surprise was how he'd ditched Chelsea so quickly.

I winked at him. "You?"

I could swear his heart rate jumped. "Why me?"

Because it would piss off Chelsea and maybe even Cat? Because I was bored? Because hardly anyone else was even talking to me?

"Because you're cute?"

He was, actually. Cat had been madly in love with him since

forever—another reason why the Jeremy thing didn't make any sense—so I'd always left him alone. But I had to admit his ripped biceps were mildly drool-worthy. I could also see why Cat would want to run her hands through his tousled dark hair, and his smoky eyes hinted he was a guy with secrets.

After knowing him as long as I had, though, I thought the only secret was why he'd hook up with a skank like Chelsea.

Not that I was bitter about her "accidentally" slamming into my chair at lunch today and spilling her lemonade on my arm in the process. Not at all. Especially after I tossed my Coke in her face.

Accidentally, of course.

Drew glanced over his shoulder, almost as if he was thinking about Chelsea, too, before he turned back and gazed into my eyes. Like he wanted to be romantic. Lucky thing I don't gag easily.

"Hey, let's get together. Do you want to—"

"Drew? Aren't you coming to class? Like, *now*?"

At the sound of the snotty voice behind us, Drew and I both whirled. Sure enough, Chelsea. Not happy. Go figure.

Still, he had the guts to glance back at me. "Later?"

My eyes glittered as I did a head-to-toe sweep of Chelsea just to amuse myself. She wasn't worth looking at more than once, if you know what I mean, and she actually looked stupid in that miniskirt and killer heels she sure hadn't been wearing yesterday. "Or sooner?"

With a last glance at the bulletin board, I headed down the hall in the opposite direction from Drew and Chelsea. I had a feeling "sooner" would happen sooner than I wanted.

I DRAGGED MY butt into Accounting class five seconds after the bell rang, but Ms. Frey didn't skip a beat in her scribbling on the board, let alone yell at me. Cool. I stifled a groan, though, as I slid past her and found my assigned seat. More homework. They'd piled on homework at Shangri-La, too, but there the teachers, counselors, and other hired thugs found even more creative ways to wreck a girl's day.

"Welcome to Torture 101." The goth chick leaning across the aisle to slide something underneath my notebook gave me a smirk. "Lauren. Lauren Kjelstad. You look like you could use a little pick-me-up."

I started to reach under my notebook, trying to guess what the goth chick would be giving me. Chocolate? But she didn't seem like the perky, have-a-nice-day, cheerleader type. Understatement. "Lydia Bennet. Thanks. I—"

"Girls? Are you writing down tonight's homework assignment or already making weekend plans?"

I grinned at Ms. Frey, who seemed to have a sense of humor, even though her English accent reminded me of those no-nonsense teachers in English boarding schools in the movies. Besides, I hadn't actually done anything wrong, and Ms. Frey didn't look scary as she glided up the aisle between Lauren and me. Seeing her long flowered skirt and flowing peach top, I lifted an eyebrow. She was a bit ruffly for an accounting teacher, even one straight off the boat from England.

When Ms. Frey was five feet away, Lauren suddenly lurched to her feet and knocked all the books off my desk. What the hell?

"Lauren?" Ms. Frey halted in front of my desk as I stooped down, scrambling to pick up my books with no help whatsoever from the goth chick. "What are you and Lydia doing?"

As I grabbed the pen that had rolled under the guy's desk next to me, I straightened my spine. I was used to taking crap from teachers, but only if I deserved it. "Hey, I wasn't doing anything. She knocked over my books." I twisted sideways to glare at Lauren, whose face looked chalky white against her ratty black hair and black lipstick. "And I don't have a clue why."

The guy on the other side of me snorted. Whirling on him, I whipped him the bird.

Ms. Frey frowned at me, but I stared her down. I was *not* going down on the second day of school, especially when it was the goth chick's fault. Finally, after a long moment, she turned to the goth chick. "Lauren, do you have something you'd like to show me?"

She shook her head furiously, and the smirk on her face was gone. So was half of her black lipstick, since she seemed to be chewing her lips off.

Ms. Frey held out a hand. Toward Lauren, luckily, not me. But Lauren kept shaking her head. What was it? Gum? Candy? She slid *something* under my notebook, but it hadn't been on the floor where all of my other stuff landed.

My mind raced. She must've grabbed whatever it was when she sent my books flying, but what was it? And why did half the kids in class seem to think I knew?

When Ms. Frey kept standing there looking grim, Lauren suddenly shot out of her seat, dodged the hand that Ms. Frey held out, and flew out the door. When I looked back at Ms. Frey, her lips were pursed.

And she was staring at me.

"I swear I don't know what's going on."

Her nostrils flared, not too attractively and not exactly what I'd pictured from the English rose she'd seemed to be up until now, but she finally gave a small head shake and walked back to the front of the room.

"Class, we're going to work on checking accounts today. Keeping a checkbook, balancing your account, etc. Eyes toward the front of the room, please."

That last bit was actually for my benefit, because until that moment every kid in class was staring at me.

But not because they thought I was cool.

♫

THAT NIGHT, AFTER Cat finally deigned to grace me with her presence, I leaned back on my pillow, watching her. Totally for lack of better things to do, I also cuddled Boris. He had to be the ugliest cat in the universe, which must be why Mary adopted him from that animal shelter.

"Do you know Lauren Kjelstad?"

Cat wrinkled her nose. "I heard. Since when do you hang out with *her*?"

I frowned. "I don't. I just asked if you know her."

"No one *knows* her." She made little quote marks in the air to emphasize her point. "At least, no one wants to. I mean, except for the other druggies. She—"

Cat broke off, clapping a hand over her mouth and suddenly staring at the floor.

"She what?"

Gaze still fixed on the floor, Cat just shook her head.

I let go of Boris, who curled into a mangy ball next to my backpack on the end of my bed. Crossing the room, I willed Cat to look at me. She grabbed a book—*Catcher in the Rye*, which I had to read for English 12, too—and pretended to read it.

I grabbed it out of her hands. "Spill. I don't know Lauren, just met her today in Accounting class before she shoved all my books on the floor. For no reason."

Cat ran a hand through her long hair, making me wish mine still looked like that. Not that guys seemed to care one way or another as long as they thought a girl put out. "You haven't been

11

gone *that* long."

"A year." I shrugged, even though it felt more like five years. "Not long at all."

She rolled her eyes. "Lauren has a reputation, and it's bad. I heard she was dealing drugs to you in class today."

"She was not!" I glared so hard at Cat, my eyes actually hurt. "Who said?"

"Everyone?"

"And you believed it? Even though I don't do drugs?" Alcohol was cheaper and more predictable when it came to what it did to me.

Cat looked around the room. At everything except me.

"You *know* I don't do drugs. Never did."

She finally met my gaze—and then looked away again. "The thing is, I *don't* know you anymore. After what you did that summer—"

"Believe me, it wasn't a good summer." Understatement.

She rolled her eyes, but I hadn't told her everything. I hadn't told anyone. "Then you were at reform school with all those kids, and God knows what *they* do, and everyone figures you'd probably do anything at this point. Including hang out with a girl like Lauren."

I sucked in a harsh breath, choking on it. "Even . . . you?"

Head down, she picked at a loose thread on her bedspread, almost like she wasn't going to answer.

"I guess. Yeah. I do."

Chapter 2

*"Have you seen any pleasant men?
Have you had any flirting?"*

— Jane Austen, *Pride and Prejudice*
Volume II, Chapter Sixteen

THURSDAY MORNING, I woke up with the sun, a nasty habit I acquired at reform school. It wasn't so bad in January, when the sun never really woke up, but in early September it sucked. Over an hour before I had to start getting ready for school, and I didn't have a thing to do.

Except maybe suffocate the newly sanctimonious Cat with my pillow. Talk about a one-way ticket back to Shangri-La.

I plodded downstairs in my boxer shorts and T-shirt. Mistake. Dad was already on his yoga mat, either chanting or groaning. I couldn't tell which.

He smiled at me in the middle of his salute to the sun, but it came out more like a grimace. Still, he tried. No one else in my life even bothered.

"Want to join me?"

"On a yoga mat?" I shook my head, shuddering. "I was, uh, just wondering if anyone made coffee."

Dad frowned. "You didn't used to drink coffee."

"Yeah, well, I used to be twelve years old." A lifetime ago. "I started drinking it in reform—" He hated it when I said "reform school," even though he'd been the one who sent me there. It was pretty phony of him, the more I thought about it. "You know. In reform school. Shangri-La."

He flinched, but too bad. Moving past him, I headed to the kitchen. No coffee.

I cursed under my breath. Dad, unfortunately, has excellent hearing. No longer saluting the sun or anything else, he joined me in the kitchen.

"How's school?"

"Sucks."

"Cat tells me—"

I whirled on him. "She tells you what? And you *believe* her?"

"I usually do." Dad padded in bare feet to the coffeemaker, where he took his sweet time starting a fresh pot while I stood there fuming. "Especially when she tells me what she's reading in English class."

My jaw dropped.

Dad shrugged. "Is it supposed to be a secret that she's reading *The Catcher in the Rye*? Are you reading it, too? I always loved that book."

Dad had a way of pissing a girl off and totally deflating her annoyance at the same time.

I crossed to the fridge and pulled out a carton of OJ, grabbed a glass from the cupboard and filled it, then sat down, all while ignoring Dad. Or pretending to.

"Why does school suck?"

So much for peace and quiet in the morning. Next time I woke up early, I'd smother myself with a pillow until the urge to get up went away.

I finally glanced at Dad, who seemed to be focused on watching the coffeemaker do its thing. "Don't tell me it didn't suck when you were in high school."

"It didn't." He smiled when I rolled my eyes. "But I confess it was always more about friends and activities than classes. Are you catching up with all your friends again?"

I could've sworn his nose wrinkled on the word "friends," but he already said he tended to believe Cat, and she'd probably spent the last six months blasting all of our friends. Great. *Thank you, Cat.*

I nodded, even though my friends—including Cat—had all changed so much, they were unrecognizable. *I* hadn't gotten weird, and I was the one stuck for a year in a breeding ground for criminals and terrorists.

"What about activities? Are you interested in any of the clubs or sports at school?"

"What is this, the Inquisition?" I extended both hands toward Dad, palms down. "Wanna yank out my fingernails one by one until I give you the right answer?"

"There is no right answer."

"Spoken by the Zen master." Shaking my head, I pushed back my chair and headed to the counter. To annoy Dad, I grabbed the highest-octane box of sugary cereal, even though my body actually craved something healthy. Well, I could do junk for old times' sake. Everyone expected it, right? Just like they expected me to hang out with a supposedly bad girl like Lauren?

"I had essentially the same conversation with Cat last year." Dad held up a hand when I started to object. "Yes, you're different people. Believe me, I've been told. But it's a new year, and I want you to make good choices."

Good choices. Blah blah blah. Had they really sprung me from reform school, where I heard all about "good choices" 24/7, or just shipped me to a satellite office?

Still standing at the kitchen counter, staring at a bowl of sugary crap, I slammed the box on the counter. Bright little balls of fake food flew everywhere. "I *wasn't* hanging out with that skanky—"

Dad frowned. "With whom? Should I be expecting a call from school?"

"No." I crossed my arms. "I didn't do a damn thing."

"Language." Dad shook a finger, but he didn't actually look pissed. Instead, he went back to his vigil at the coffeemaker. After verifying for the tenth time that the coffee still wasn't ready, he glanced at me. "With Mary gone, it occurred to me that you and Cat might want separate bedrooms. Or maybe not. You must be glad to have those late-night chat sessions again."

He smiled, even though his and Mom's bedroom was next to Cat's and mine, and he'd never smiled all the times Cat and I talked so loud that he couldn't get to sleep.

But . . . I could have my own room? I swallowed hard, trying to digest a mouthful of sugary crap before Dad changed his mind. "I can talk to Cat anytime." Or never, as far as I was concerned. "I'd love my own room, Dad. Could I have Liz and Jane's? Or maybe Cat could move to Mary's?"

I'd take anything but Mary's room. It was small, smelled like Boris, and probably hadn't been cleaned since Mary was five. But Cat might not mind. If she could date a guy like Jeremy, she must not be too particular.

Besides, I'd been locked up for the last year, thanks to Dad. He owed me.

"I don't think that's—"

"Oh, come on. Cat had our room to herself last year. It's my turn." I started to bat my eyelashes before remembering that Dad never fell for crap like that. "Please?"

He sighed. "I'll have to talk to your mother. And Cat, of

course."

Excellent. Cat would ask for the same thing I wanted, just to spite me, but I was pretty sure I still had Mom in my back pocket. Everything hadn't changed, after all.

Just mostly.

♫

YAWNING, I DRIFTED into Speech Communications before the bell rang for first period, wishing I hadn't gotten up so early, or at least wishing I'd run into Mom instead of Dad. Mom wasn't the sucker anymore that she'd always been with me, but she was a marshmallow compared to Dad. Dad's Zen was laced with steel.

"Lydia?" Drew waved me to the back of the room, where a desk sat empty on either side of him. One of those desks had held Chelsea's lame ass the last two days, though, so either Chelsea was sick today or Drew was even more revved by the possibility of hooking up with me than I thought.

"Revved" wasn't exactly how I felt about Drew, who was cute but didn't have much else going on. Still, a friendly face was good.

I dropped my books on the desk to Drew's right, farthest from the door, and plunked down in the chair. Shifting in my seat, I twisted to catch Drew staring at me, stopping just short of drooling. I rolled my eyes.

Chelsea sashayed into the room in a skirt that rode up too high on her ass, both for school dress-code purposes and the sake of anyone who didn't want to gag this early in the morning. She tripped when she caught sight of me next to Drew, so I leaned across the aisle toward him, amused that I wore a low-cut top today.

I dropped my voice. "Any parties tomorrow night? Or did you wanna make your own party—like, with me?"

As I watched the Adam's apple bob on Drew's neck, Chelsea's heels staccato-stepped toward us, stopping in front of Drew. It took him a moment to drag his eyes away from my chest.

"Drew? Why is she sitting here? I sat in that desk yesterday."

"Uh, she was already—"

I grinned at Chelsea, who ran her spiky red fingernails through her lawnmower-cut hair. "I guess Drew wanted to improve the scenery." I gave Chelsea a casual up-and-down, my eyebrows lifting when my gaze stopped at her muffin top. "All things considered, I can't blame him."

Chelsea sucked in her gut. "I wasn't talking to you. I was talking to Drew."

"That makes two of us." I flashed a grin at Drew, who looked a little sick. "We were just talking about getting together."

"Uh, to work on homework. Sometime. With some other kids from English."

Liar. Still, I relished the look on Chelsea's face. It wasn't my fault Drew liked me, considering the cheap polyester miniskirts Chelsea poured herself into, and I might as well prolong her suffering.

"You didn't say she was in English with you."

The bell rang, but Chelsea stayed standing in front of Drew, even though Ms. Ciccarelli was already at the front of the room. In black slacks and a hot-pink blazer, she was one of those teachers who looked relaxed, even hip, until the moment they decided to zap you with a stun gun—or homework, as the case may be. Her toe tapping, she narrowed her gaze at Chelsea and a few other stragglers. One of the stragglers, Travis, a linebacker on the football team, grabbed the chair on the other side of Drew.

Leaving Chelsea out in the cold.

Ms. Ciccarelli rapped her knuckles on her desk. "Could everyone please take a seat? Now?"

When Chelsea tried to sit down in the desk on the other side of Drew but landed on Travis's lap, her spine went rigid.

"Chelsea?" Ms. Ciccarelli clapped her hands. "I'm sure the rest of the class is eager to get started, even though our first assignment requires you to work with a partner this weekend."

The whole class groaned.

Chelsea whirled on me. "Yeah, well, I was just standing here because this *girl*—"

I raised my hand. "Lydia."

Chelsea foamed even more. "This *girl* took my seat."

Ms. Ciccarelli frowned. "But we don't have assigned seats. I thought everyone preferred it that way."

As the rest of the class nodded and a few kids told Chelsea to get over it and go sit down, Chelsea turned bright red. It didn't exactly go with her hideous orange top, which stretched as tightly over her flabby stomach as it did over her boobs. I waved at her as she turned to go to the only open desk, right in front of Ms. Ciccarelli.

Drew leaned over to me, his breath tickling my neck. "Wanna pair up this weekend?"

I looked into his eyes, which told me what I wanted to know before I even asked. "For the homework assignment? Or were you thinking . . . otherwise?"

He just grinned.

DREW AND CHELSEA were both missing from our table at lunch, which was sort of a relief. Pretending I had even the slightest interest in Drew wore me out, and I wouldn't bother if it didn't annoy Chelsea so much.

Besides, I'd rather concentrate my efforts on Kirk Easton.

Who didn't seem to be concentrating his on me.

"Hey, Kirk." I set my tray next to his, even though someone had left her purse in that chair. I set the purse on the table, about five feet away. "We haven't really had a chance to chat since I've been back."

He glanced at the purse, then turned to look at something across the cafeteria, before shaking his head and grinning. "Lydia. Sorry. You have so many admirers, it's tough getting a word in."

"Ha ha." I punched him in the arm, acting more like my sister Liz than myself, but it'd been a while and so much had changed. I had to take things slowly, even with a guy like Kirk, if I wanted to make this work.

Whatever "this" was.

Kirk and I had been buddies since forever, close enough that we'd never hooked up, even though we were the leaders of our crowd and either one of us could go out with pretty much anyone we wanted.

Which was maybe why we never *had* hooked up.

But I'd had a lot of time in reform school to think about what I wanted—understatement—and I wanted Kirk. I mean, I think so. The last guy I'd wanted was Justin Truesdale, and the nightmare that was Justin still haunted me. That summer in the Dells, I'd lost myself for him. What did he give me? Let's just say that pole-dancing in a strip bar to get enough cash for that night's hotel room, followed by a one-way ticket to Montana, wasn't the worst of it.

Kirk wouldn't land me in reform school—at least, I don't think so—but he was the coolest guy I knew. He could control an entire room, including even the teachers. And, from what I'd heard, he made the girls he dated very happy. Well, until he dumped them.

But that wouldn't happen to me.

I smiled at him as I bit into my burger, feeling more like myself now. "So what's the party scene these days? Anything going on this weekend?"

Kirk glanced across the cafeteria, where I finally spotted Drew and Chelsea, alone at a table and having a heated argument.

"I hear you've already been scoping out the party scene." Kirk tilted his head, but his grin didn't falter the way it would with most guys. Kirk wasn't the kind of guy who'd be jealous of Drew or anyone else. "According to Drew."

I grabbed a few fries, waving them in the air before inhaling them. God, I'd missed burgers and fries at Shangri-La, where they tried to kill us with lettuce wraps and granola. I actually liked healthy food, but I drew the line at tree bark. "We have Speech together. He usually knows what's going on."

"Right now he's having a little trouble figuring out what *is* going on." Kirk's eyes twinkled. He'd always appreciated a good joke. "What's up with that?"

"We're old pals."

"Unlike, for instance, you and Chelsea?"

"I have no idea what you're talking about." I winked at Kirk. "But now that you mention it, I *do* think Drew could do better. Much better."

"Like . . . you?"

Shaking my head, I almost mentioned Cat, but something told me I shouldn't bring her up to Kirk, even though I couldn't believe her version of how everything went down last spring with Kirk and Tess. They were still nice to *me*, weren't they? So were Drew and everyone else other than Chelsea. And let's face it: she reeked.

"Lydia? That was my purse."

"Oh?" I glanced up to see Amber glaring down at me, her tray in one hand and her other hand on Kirk's shoulder. Seriously? Kirk and *Amber*? "Sorry. I didn't know whose it was." And Kirk obviously didn't stop me from moving it, so the two of them couldn't be all that. "But there are other chairs free."

"At the other end of the table." Amber set her tray down in the nonexistent space between Kirk's tray and mine, jostling everything including my mood. "I'm sitting next to Kirk."

I'd always liked Amber as far as follow-the-leader girls went, but she was starting to annoy me. Didn't she remember that I owned this crowd and had the power to kick her out of it? That I'd known Kirk since long before she'd shown her pointy little nose in town?

"Sorry. Like I said, I didn't know whose it was. But I'm sitting here now, and Kirk and I were talking, and I guess you can talk to him whenever."

Like, whenever she wasn't sucking face with him, based on the proprietary look she zapped me right now.

"I was sitting here, Lydia."

Her clenched teeth didn't do a thing for her looks, but that was Amber's problem.

"But you left." I patted her arm, which went rigid beneath my touch. "But I'm sure you can sit with Kirk tomorrow. I mean, if you get here before me."

"Which I did."

"Then maybe you should ask Kirk to save your seat next time."

I sneaked a peek at Kirk, who didn't look the least bit bothered by this whole conversation. Bored, maybe, but not bothered. Another reason why I liked him. He could give Drew a few tips on how to handle Chelsea.

He shrugged. "Sorry, Amber. We can talk later, okay? I haven't had a chance to catch up with Lydia since she's been back."

Fuming, Amber grabbed her tray off the table, banging it hard against mine, then slammed it down at the far end of the table next to Tess. Tess stared at me but didn't say a word. Not to me, but not to Amber either.

No doubt about it. All the players had changed, along with the game, and I was still at the starting line, trying to figure out the new rules.

I couldn't wait to make my first move.

LAUREN DIDN'T SHOW her face in Accounting class, but after a lifetime of hanging out with guys more than girls—except for Cat—I'd taken enough crap from girls today to last me. Besides, Ms. Frey was chill again with me, and Lauren's absence probably helped.

I caught a ride home in the Jeep with Cat, with Cat behind the wheel even after I pointed out a million times that I'd always been the one to drive. Sure, Mom told me this morning that Cat was in charge of the Jeep for now, but Mom wasn't here, so Cat should've caved.

Amazing what a boyfriend and working this past summer at a waterpark in Wisconsin Dells could do to Cat's ego.

I shrugged. I could bring her back down to earth.

"Does Jeremy still play in that band? Kirk's band?"

She gave me a cold look before returning her gaze to the road. "It's not Kirk's band."

"Yeah? That's not what I hear." Actually, I hadn't heard much of anything, but Kirk would be the leader of any band he played in. "They're still playing, right? Who else is in the band?"

Cat turned the Jeep radio to blare level.

I turned it off. "You can't ignore me. You're my sister. My twin. We live together."

"Until you go away again."

"Don't hold your breath." I leaned back against my headrest, wondering when I'd be done clawing and scratching for even the simplest conversation. It was almost worse than reform school. Almost. "So what's the big deal? Why is the band such a secret?"

Cat's hands gripped the wheel so hard, they must hurt. Finally, she blew out an exasperated breath. "It's not. It just . . . annoys me."

"Why? Because Jeremy still plays in the band that humiliated you? According to you?"

"The band didn't humiliate me. Tess did." Cat glanced at me, her eyes looking like a stranger's. "With Kirk's help."

I shrugged. "I'm sure it was just a joke. I mean, why would they want to humiliate you? You guys are still friends, right? Tess and Kirk are nice to *me*."

Tess not as much, but it wasn't as if we had any classes together. Okay, she didn't say much in the cafeteria, either, but she didn't say much to anyone. Not even Amber, and they'd always been tight the way Cat and I had been.

"You don't have a clue."

Cat's voice was so soft, I almost didn't catch her words.

"Me? Not have a clue?" I laughed.

She didn't say anything more, which was fine by me until the silence started to get annoying. I hated silence. It forced me to think too much.

"So. You don't like the band, or you don't like Jeremy playing in it. But is the band still playing? Who's in it these days?"

Cat rolled her eyes, almost as if I was a moron for asking. Or maybe for asking ten times and still expecting an answer.

"They didn't play much this summer after Jeremy and I left to work in the Dells, but they're back together again. Except for Mary, of course."

"I can't believe they let her in the band."

"She's good." Cat's eyes stayed on the road, probably so she wouldn't have to try to keep a straight face. "She picked up guitar really fast, I guess."

I couldn't help it. I snorted. "According to Jeremy? Or someone who actually plays guitar?"

"You don't have to play guitar to know if someone's good. But for your information, all the guys in the band seemed to think Mary was pretty good."

"But she's—"

Cat held up a hand. "I don't wanna hear it, okay? Been there, done that, and you don't have a clue about Mary."

I crossed my arms and scowled at her. "So I don't have a clue about Mary, and I don't have a clue about anyone in our old crowd. Pretty convenient for you, huh?"

Cat frowned. "Convenient?"

"Yeah." I nodded to myself, even though part of me felt a little sick. I mean, this was Cat. My best friend since forever. "If you can freeze me out, you slide right into my spot as head of our gang. Maybe it's why you'd go out with an outsider like Jeremy. He doesn't know you're not top dog."

When all I got was silence, I finally twisted in my seat to look at Cat. Her lips twitched a moment before she started laughing out loud.

She finally wiped her eyes with one hand. "Oh, God. You are too funny. You and Tess make quite a pair."

I frowned. "You and I used to make quite a pair, but apparently that doesn't work when you have a boyfriend."

Finally, the laughter left her eyes. "You really *don't* get it, but I guess it's not all your fault. You've been gone so long."

"Only a year." I glanced out the window. Nothing had changed in Woodbury while I'd been gone, but everyone acted like it had. "But feel free to clue me in if you really think I need it."

Cat kept driving without saying anything, but I wasn't going to beg. I stared out the window, forcing myself to appreciate the gorgeous blue sky, the shrieks of kids playing kickball in the street, even the roar of lawnmowers. Totally normal, but it felt brand-new. Almost like being a born-again virgin.

I bit my lip. Hard.

"That's actually what Tess tried last year."

My head jerked when Cat finally spoke. Tess tried to be a born-again virgin last year? Wasn't she still a virgin in the first place?

"What?"

"She tried to be you. Tried to be the new leader of our gang, the queen bee of the school."

I shook my head. "Nothing against Tess, but she doesn't have it in her. Even on her best day."

"She'd totally disagree with you." Cat turned onto our street, parked at the curb, and turned off the engine. "At least, she would've disagreed last year, but that's why she was such a bitch to me. She thought I might step into your shoes, so she did everything she could to stop me."

Cat wasn't a leader, either, but no need to point out the obvious to her. We were still sharing a room, and I didn't want to walk into our closet to find toenail clippings or Dad's shaving cream or worse in my shoes.

I opened my door to the Jeep and walked ahead of Cat to the front door. "Yeah, well, no one needs to fight over being leader anymore. I'm back."

Behind me, Cat just laughed.

Chapter 3

*At first there seemed danger of Lydia's engrossing him entirely, for
she was a most determined talker.*

— Jane Austen, *Pride and Prejudice*
Volume I, Chapter Sixteen

I DON'T EAVESDROP. I mean, why bother? Everyone has always
given me the scoop directly. For some reason, though, the usual
crowd must not know my new cell phone number, because it
wasn't ringing. So when Jeremy called Cat after school, I admit
I was curious. For news. Any news. I didn't need to hear any of
their lovey-dovey crap.

The instant Cat hung up, I pounced. "It sounds like the
band is practicing today? You're not going?"

Cat frowned. "You were listening?"

"I couldn't help it." Even when Cat went into the upstairs
hallway to take the call, she hadn't bothered to shut our bedroom
door all the way. "But don't worry. I didn't gag *too* much when
you got all mushy with the guy."

"I didn't get all—" Cat broke off, rolling her eyes.

"Whatever. Yeah, they're playing at Michael Gallagher's house at five, but I work today. Tuesdays, Thursdays, and Saturdays. Like I've told you a million times."

She acted like I didn't listen to a thing she said. Totally not true. I listened when she said something worth paying attention to, but her job at Nickelodeon Universe didn't qualify.

"I can't believe you work there. Even after you managed to escape for the summer."

I also couldn't believe Dad had let her escape to Wisconsin Dells, of all places. It hadn't done anything good for me, and it seemed to make Cat a lot snottier than she'd started out.

I leaned back against the headboard of my bed, forced to tickle Boris under his belly when he had the nerve to leap up beside me. Cat bustled around our room, then changed into a hideous Nickelodeon Universe uniform that would've mortified her a year ago. She'd changed, all right, and it wasn't an improvement. No matter how happy she pretended to be.

She finally stopped her whirlwind of activity and paused at the door. "They're nice to me. I have good hours. And it's cold, hard cash, which will come in handy next year in college."

"College?"

She rolled her eyes. "Something else you're probably too good for."

As she sailed out the door, I whipped her the bird. Not that she noticed or cared.

MICHAEL GALLAGHER. HE'D been a year ahead of us, but I barely knew him and hadn't seen him since the end of sophomore year. I remembered a tall guy with red hair cut in wild spikes, but that was it. I couldn't barge into his house uninvited.

At least, not easily.

As I pondered an excuse for stopping by the band practice, I drummed my fingers on Boris's back, which only made him purr more loudly. Stupid cat. Obviously so starved for affection, he'd take anything I gave him.

Hmmm. I could call Drew, but he was Kirk's best friend, which I'd already realized was going to cause problems. I could call Kirk, but the thought actually made me a little nervous, even though *nothing* ever made me nervous, including Kirk. Weird.

I could call Amber or Tess. After what happened at lunch today, though, Amber wouldn't cross the street to help me if I was being knifed to death. Besides, she seemed to be with Kirk— at least in her own mind—so hanging with her probably wasn't my best tactic for hooking up with Kirk.

Which left Tess. Who was impossible to predict.

Before I could talk myself out of it, I grabbed my cell phone and last year's school directory and punched in some numbers. After a few rings, I heard a surprised "hello."

"Drew?" I took a deep breath as I told myself I could do this. I was still Lydia Bennet, after all: a girl who could do anything and usually did. "I hear Kirk's band is playing this afternoon. Wanna go?"

A long pause. Too long. Followed by the answer I wasn't totally sure I wanted.

"Absolutely."

As I waited for Drew to pick me up—his idea, not mine—I wondered if I should've tried harder to think of a way to get to Michael's house without Drew. Riding with Drew limited my options, not only today but maybe indefinitely, at least when it came to Kirk. But Kirk didn't have to find out, right? More important, Cat had nabbed the Jeep to go to work.

Maybe I could catch a ride home from Kirk. He lived closer to me, after all, and he didn't have to worry about racing home to return his mom's car.

Unlike Drew.

A horn honked in front, which was actually a relief. Maybe Drew wasn't treating this like a date after all. I peeked out the tiny window in the front door. Sure enough, Drew. In his mom's silver Mercedes.

I mean, not that I could talk. It was a Mercedes, and I just shared a dinosaur of a Jeep with Cat—and from the looks of things so far, not often.

I hustled out to the curb before Drew could change his mind. "Hey, Drew, thanks. It's so great of you—"

I hauled up short at the sight of Chelsea in the back seat.

Drew motioned me inside, but he looked even more sick than the first time I had a beer.

Against my better judgment, if I had any, I climbed into the front seat. "Hey, Chelsea."

She didn't say anything, but her breathing sounded like a dragon's, and if I turned around in my seat I wouldn't be surprised to see fire coming out of her mouth.

Drew glanced at me, his mouth grim, his shoulders tense. Purely for Chelsea's benefit, I patted him on his arm. "Like I started to say, it's so great of you to give me a ride." Twisting my head enough so Chelsea could see, I batted my eyelashes at Drew. "Very sweet."

Chelsea leaned forward, breaking my light grip on Drew's arm. "Yeah, well, I guess he felt sorry for you. I mean, you don't have a car and you're sisters with Cat. Even I have to sympathize."

Drew frowned into the rearview mirror. "I never said that, and Cat's great. We've always been friends."

More than friends for a little while, but I decided not to mention it. From the pissed-off look on Chelsea's face, she already knew. Besides, I wanted to keep my options open with Drew, even though he wasn't my end goal. Okay, he wasn't even my beginning goal, but he'd been nice when no one else talked to me, and I was grateful. I also got a kick out of annoying Chelsea, and that was even before I had to smell her cloying perfume up close.

I smiled innocently at her. "I guess you don't have a car, either? Drew's sure become a humanitarian since I last saw him."

I nudged him with my elbow, and he glanced down at my boobs before giving me a sideways grin. I heard Chelsea breathing hard in the back seat, but she didn't have a comeback. No surprise.

A hostile five minutes later, we pulled up in front of a house not too far from school. Drew got out, then helped Chelsea out of the back seat from the driver's side, leaving me to fend for myself.

Lucky thing I was good at that.

Drew practically ran inside the house, obviously having figured out at some point in the car what a stupid thing he'd just done, but I was surprised when Chelsea came up next to me. And dug her nails into my arm.

"He's mine. Don't even think about it."

"I think about everything. I guess that's what happens when a girl has a brain." I pried her nails loose from my stinging arm, ran a hand over the traces of blood from the gouges she'd made, and wiped it across her cheek. "You're not in my league, so don't tell me what to do. And for the record? You reek."

Eyes wide, she sniffed the air, trying to look like she wasn't. I lasered her with an evil grin. "And I wasn't just talking about that skanky perfume you're wearing."

With that, I shot inside the house ahead of Chelsea, who was wobbling in too-high heels. On an impulse, I slammed the door and twisted the deadbolt, then sauntered in the direction of the loud music coming from downstairs, quietly shutting the door at the top of the stairs.

With any luck, no one would hear the doorbell ring.

DREW CAUGHT MY eye the instant I walked into the basement, but he didn't say anything. He also didn't exactly dash upstairs to rescue Chelsea from whatever I'd done to her. I almost thought he looked relieved.

I sat next to him on the big wraparound couch and turned to scope out the band. Kirk, in the middle front with his guitar, looked cocky and a little silly in dark sunglasses. Jeremy, in the back on drums, squinted at me as if I shouldn't be here. Too bad. I looked over at Michael, standing at the keyboard in baggy shorts and a ridiculous Hawaiian shirt, his red hair flaming as brightly as ever and looking even taller than I remembered him.

Then I spotted the last guy. Cute. Light-brown hair, tall, with mile-long, skinny legs casually crossed as he tuned up his bass guitar. I wasn't clumsy, not at all, but I'd trip and fall if I tried to stand that way while playing a guitar. He wore a tight T-shirt, cut off at the shoulders, and sported a tattoo on his bicep that I couldn't make out.

I remembered him from sophomore year—like Michael, he was a year ahead of us, so he would've graduated by now, too—but I could swear he'd been blond then. I didn't know him, though, not even his name. He'd been a quiet guy who spent a lot more time in the media center than I did, and I didn't usually notice guys like that.

As I turned to ask Drew who he was, Drew's arm came around my waist.

I sucked in a surprised breath, and he pulled me tighter.

"Uh, Drew? Won't Chelsea—"

"Don't tell me. You locked her out." He leaned close, his breath tickling my ear. It actually felt kinda good, but only because it'd been so long since any guy had tickled my ear or any other part of me. But this was Drew, not Kirk. I told myself I wasn't interested. So it made no sense, really, why I leaned into him.

Casually, of course.

His cell phone rang. His tongue touched my ear. "It's so damn hard to hear a cell phone in a basement, you know?"

I twisted in his arms, intending to give him a smart-ass answer, but my lips accidentally brushed his. Being a guy, he took advantage of it. Despite being a girl who wanted Kirk— even in his silly sunglasses, and even though he was only twenty feet away—I let it happen. I mean, just for a moment. Just to see if I still remembered what a kiss felt like.

It was . . . nice. Warm lips and arms that knew how to hold a girl, even if they'd been practicing on a pig like Chelsea. As I snuggled a little closer, I—

Ow! I shrieked as someone yanked on my hair.

Chelsea, of course.

As she jerked me to my feet, her grubby hands still in my hair, the band stopped tuning up and the whole basement went silent. Well, except for my screeching. And except for the grunt Chelsea made when I shoved her and she went down hard.

Too bad the floor was carpeted.

"You are such a bitch."

I blinked as I looked around, connecting the snotty voice I heard with Amber's face.

"Are you talking to *me?*" I jabbed a thumb in Chelsea's direction. "She started it, in case you forgot your glasses."

"I see just fine, thanks." Amber struggled to help Chelsea up off the floor. I laughed, because Chelsea had to outweigh her by twenty or thirty pounds. Needless to say, I didn't move an inch to help. "You were trying to steal Chelsea's boyfriend. Just like old times, huh?"

I rubbed a spot on my scalp where it felt like Chelsea had yanked out every hair on my head. "How would you know, Amber? Since when did you ever have a boyfriend I could steal?"

Seeing the flash of embarrassment in her eyes, I grinned, not bothering to glance at Kirk, who was talking to the rest of the band now in a loud voice about whatever song they were going to play first. I had a feeling they'd play something loud, just to drown out the catfight at the far end of the room.

Amber's mouth opened and shut, as if she was trying to come up with a response but couldn't manage a decent one. No wonder she hung out with Chelsea. They must take remedial classes together.

I rolled my eyes. "Besides, I wasn't stealing Chelsea's boyfriend. No surprise, but Drew doesn't exactly seem too hot on her." I glanced at Drew, who was leaning forward on the couch, his head in his hands, looking like he wanted to barf. "And in case you didn't notice, he was the one hitting on *me.*"

A cymbal crashed, Michael hit a jarring chord on the keyboard, and the bass guitar sounded like someone was strangling a cat.

"That's so not—"

I glanced at Drew, who was still trying to hide from the world. Or at least Chelsea.

"Drew, was I hitting on you?" Okay, that might be open to interpretation, at least from Drew's delusional perspective, but the truth was that I'd only accidentally kissed him. The fact that

I'd enjoyed it was purely incidental. "Was I making you doing anything you didn't want to do?"

I don't think a band could possibly be louder than Kirk's band was right at that moment. The cacophony of clashing instruments, seeming to play four different songs at the same moment, practically made my heart jump out of my chest. I clapped my hands over my ears.

I glanced again at Drew just as he slithered off the couch and tried to escape to the stairs. Chelsea caught him by the arm.

"Is that true, Drew? Was she hitting on you or were you hitting on her?"

Did it matter? We were locking lips, as she perfectly well saw, and her so-called boyfriend was an active participant.

"Uh . . ."

Drew had never exactly turned me on, on any number of levels, but I saw now what a complete wimp he was. He obviously liked me more than Chelsea, but he didn't have the guts to admit it. Of course, maybe she'd used her claws on him, too. Wincing, I rubbed my forearm where it still stung from her gouging me.

"Lydia, are you causing trouble?"

My head whipped around at Kirk's voice, booming out through the microphone, as I belatedly realized that the band had stopped playing. I wasn't sure this time if they'd stopped because of me or because they just needed to get on the same page. Or at least the same song. Kirk was grinning, though, and only Jeremy looked pissed. But he always seemed to look pissed when he saw me.

I stepped closer to the band and away from Chelsea and Amber. "You know me, Kirk. Always hanging out with girls who are up to no good."

I heard squeaks behind me. If Amber and Chelsea were the kind of girls Kirk and Drew actually wanted in a girlfriend, I'd been gone too long. The world really *was* coming to an end.

"Can you play guitar like your sister?"

I frowned at Kirk. "Like Cat?"

He started to laugh until a cymbal crashed in his ear. "Uh, no. I meant Mary."

"Totally." I waved a hand, knowing I could do anything my sister Mary could do, only ten times faster. Especially with a crowd watching. "But I, uh, didn't bring a guitar."

"No problem. I brought an extra." Kirk turned his back on me, and five seconds later he held up a shiny black guitar. Crap. "Wanna give it a try?"

I felt unexpected beads of sweat on the back of my neck where Chelsea had yanked my hair. God, it hurt. I'd barely even touched Drew. Ohmygod. Perfect excuse! "I'd love to, but the truth is that this—" I pointed at Chelsea, at the same time sniffing the air as if it reeked. "This *creature* went spastic and tried to pull all my hair out, no doubt because she forgot to take her meds today."

It wasn't funny, actually, since my mom had to take bipolar meds just to stay on a remotely even keel. Not that she'd ever tried to yank anyone's hair out. We usually knew something was wrong whenever she did a bunch of housework, which was why Dad always seemed a bit conflicted about making her take her meds. I wasn't sure if he loved Mom or a clean house more.

"And?" Kirk stared at me through his sunglasses as he dangled the shiny black guitar in the air.

"I don't think I can play when my head hurts like hell."

I heard someone snicker behind me. But since I'd already stolen—or at least borrowed—Chelsea's boyfriend and Amber's was next in line, I brushed it off.

Shrugging, Kirk set the guitar back on its stand. "No worries. Feel free to play another time if you want. We could use another guitar."

"Sure." After a lesson or two and maybe a beer for courage.

In the meantime, I grabbed a spot on the couch again—me at one end, Chelsea and Amber at the other end, and Drew next to Chelsea thanks to her death grip on him—and leaned back to watch Kirk play. Maybe I could learn guitar by osmosis.

Because I definitely wasn't going to run and hide.

♫

"How was the band?"

"Did they ask you to sing?"

As I slipped off my shoes in the front hall after a long but blissfully free-of-sharp-nails walk home, Dad's question sounded sincere. Cat's? Not so much.

I shrugged. "Kirk asked me to play guitar. I said I would next time."

Cat just frowned.

Dad gave me one of his clueless dad smiles. "Did you learn guitar at school last year? Mary picked it up pretty quickly, you know."

"So I heard. No, I've never played, but I figured I could pick it up even faster."

So much for Dad's smile. "She practiced for a few months before joining that band, didn't she, Cat? And of course she played piano for years before that."

"Whatever." Dying for a soda, if not some relief for my still-stinging head, I crossed through the living room and headed to the kitchen. "Not that piano has anything to do with guitar."

"Piano is the best possible foundation for—"

I tuned him out as I opened the fridge, grabbed a can of Coke from the bottom shelf, and popped the top on it. Dad was still blathering in the living room, but maybe Cat could take notes. God knows she didn't have anything better to do.

After chugging half of my soda, I headed back through the living room.

"So you're really serious about learning guitar?" Dad wasn't ready to drop it, apparently. "How do you plan to pay for lessons, let alone the guitar itself?"

I'd heard all about the ridiculously expensive guitar Dad got Mary for her eighteenth birthday last year, which she'd taken to MIT, on top of the Prius Dad bought for Jane when she went to Carleton for her first year of college. And I couldn't help noticing all the new clothes Cat had acquired since I left last year. "I thought you could maybe spring for it? As a homecoming gift?"

Rolling her eyes, Cat stormed out of the living room and thundered up the stairs to our bedroom.

Dad looked at me over the tops of his reading glasses. "And you think you deserve this because . . . ?"

"Because I do. Because you buy stuff for everyone else around here. Because you haven't had to do a damn thing for me for a year now."

"Not since I bailed you out of jail?"

"You didn't bail me out. You had them send me to reform school."

"The judge sent you to reform—er, to that school."

"At your request. I was there, Dad. You can't blow smoke up *my* ass."

We stared at each other, neither of us willing to be the first to blink. Just like always. In the old days, Mom would walk in the front door now and save me. I held my breath and waited.

Nothing happened.

Dad shook his head. "This might be a good moment to talk about your plans, both this year and after you graduate. Cat has a job and activities and is looking at colleges."

"Yeah? Am I supposed to care what Cat does?"

A door slammed upstairs.

Dad tilted his head, studying me. I crossed my arms and stared right back at him.

Finally, he sighed. "It's ultimately up to you, but plans are a good idea. And I'm pleased to see that Cat, at least, is making them."

"Yeah, well, that makes one of us."

I strode past Dad into the front hall, grabbed my shoes and the keys to the Jeep out of the cracked bowl on the front-hall chest, and headed to the door.

"Lydia, that's not a good idea."

So what else was new? I slammed the front door behind me.

Chapter 4

*"It would be such a delicious scheme, and
I dare say would hardly cost anything at all."*

— Jane Austen, *Pride and Prejudice*
Volume II, Chapter Sixteen

I HOPPED INTO the Jeep and hit the locks, but I didn't have a clue where to go or what to do.

When the front door opened, though, I cranked up the engine and pulled out from the curb with a squeal of tires. Dad expected me to do it, and I hated to disappoint.

At the corner, I stopped and drummed my fingers on the steering wheel. This was actually the first time I'd driven anything in over a year, but that wasn't the problem. Before, I'd always had plans. A destination. And, in Cat, a partner in crime.

Now, for the first time in my life—with the exception of every single moment of my stint in Milwaukee—I wondered what I was doing. My sisters all had boyfriends, not that I cared, but I'd always been the most popular with guys. Jane, Liz, and Mary were in college, and Cat was seriously looking at colleges. The concept eluded me.

I'd also wasted an entire year of my life at a reform school that could inspire a horror movie, plus the three months of my life I lost with Justin. All because I'd been too mortified to come home and admit what he'd done. What I'd done.

He'd forced me, but I could've run. Begged for help. Something. Anything.

I drove aimlessly, soon finding myself cruising Highway 494 at a million miles an hour just to blow off steam. Blinking, I finally realized I'd stopped. In front of a music store.

I didn't really want to play guitar, did I? I didn't *need* to play guitar just to hook Kirk. Picturing him and me together, I glanced in the rearview mirror. Okay, maybe I did. If I saw much more of Chelsea, my hair wasn't going to get any longer, and Kirk liked girls with long hair.

Except for Amber, who wore her dark hair in a pixie cut like a five-year-old. But maybe even Kirk went through dry spells.

Shrugging, I climbed out of the Jeep and trudged into the music store. I told myself I didn't have anything better to do.

And let's face it: I didn't.

Seeing the rows of gorgeous guitars on the wall, I sucked in my breath. Ohmygod. I didn't know a thing about guitars except that Mary played, so it must be easy, and Kirk looked good with one hanging from a strap over his shoulder.

An employee came up and offered to help, but I brushed her off. I didn't know her, but I didn't plan to embarrass myself by admitting how little I knew about guitars. I just kept gazing at them, not even touching, afraid I'd break something.

The girl kept hovering. "If you don't play yet, you might want to start with an acoustic guitar."

As I frowned, she pointed to a few dozen guitars at the far end of the store. I couldn't help picturing some old guy in overalls and a toothpick in his teeth strumming them.

"You've got to be kidding."

"That's how I started out. It's how most people start."

"My sister started on a Gibson Flying V." Or so I'd heard. Like, repeatedly. "So don't pull that beginner crap on me."

The girl laughed. "No one starts on a Flying V. I mean, you wouldn't."

"*She* did." Since Dad sprang for it even though we can't afford to replace the ratty couch in the living room, it also proved that Mom isn't the only one in the family struggling with instability. Both of my parents had it.

From the looks of things lately, so did Cat.

I turned my back on the girl, who finally gave up and went over to annoy someone else. But I didn't have a clue what to get. Glancing at a few price tags, my eyes bugged. I couldn't afford anything, either.

But Mom could help with that.

I WALKED IN the front door, hoping to catch Mom alone, because I could still talk her into almost anything. Not as easily as I once did, but a lot easier than Dad. Talking to him was like talking to concrete. Only harder.

No such luck. Mom and Dad were both waiting for me in the living room. As my stomach growled, I tossed the Jeep keys in the bowl and headed through the living room for the kitchen. I'd missed dinner, which wasn't necessarily a bad thing when no one in your family cooked. At least, not anything edible.

"Lydia." Dad. Not happy. I knew the feeling.

I kept walking. I was actually starving to death, but I also didn't need a lecture about swiping the Jeep. No one else was using it, it was long past my turn, and I hadn't totaled it or anything. Besides, old Mr. Fogarty across the street really shouldn't have a mailbox that sticks out so far like that.

"Lydia, we're talking to you."

"I'm eating." Or I would be, anyway, if I found anything in the fridge that didn't disgust me. Score! Leftover cartons of Chinese, which definitely beat all the casseroles Mom made that had the word "surprise" in them.

I pried open a carton with my chewed-off fingernail and scrunched my nose. Kung pao chicken. Stupid family. They *knew* I was allergic to nuts. Spying another carton tucked behind the first one, I opened it. Beef lo mein. Two-thirds gone, but enough to take the edge off my hunger, and I could top it off with rice and a bowl of ice cream.

So much for craving healthy food.

As I waited for the microwave to ding, Mom joined me in the kitchen. I debated whether to broach the guitar with her when Dad was only twenty feet away, but then he walked into the kitchen, too.

"We'd like to talk to you."

The microwave dinged, and I turned my back on both of them to pull my bowl out of the microwave and carry it to the kitchen table. My hands didn't tremble. They wouldn't dare.

Mom sat next to me, Dad across the table. In Mom's case, proximity might have more to do with being unable to resist cheating on Atkins than providing moral support.

I'd ask her for moral support—and a guitar—later.

They both just watched me as I dug into the beef lo mein, which didn't taste as good when vultures were circling. I also hadn't heated it long enough, but I didn't want Dad following me all the way to the microwave, let alone Mom trying to make a grab for whatever I left on the table.

I chewed in silence. But not for long.

"You took the Jeep."

No kidding. "But not to Wisconsin Dells, and I didn't paint

it black, unlike Cat last spring."

As Mom and Dad stared at me, I still couldn't believe Cat's wild week of terror late last February, when she'd skipped school and hijacked the Jeep just to spend a week living in a Motel 6 and working at a waterpark in Wisconsin Dells. I *really* couldn't believe she wound up with a summer job at that waterpark after everything she'd done. I hadn't done much worse—in my own opinion, at least—and I'd landed in reform school.

More important, I couldn't believe Cat had it in her. She usually did what *I* told her to do—although not lately—but she'd come up with that wild scheme on her own, just because Tess and Kirk made fun of her at a band practice. Kirk teased *me* today at band practice when I got into the catfight with Chelsea and Amber, but I didn't steal the Jeep and run away, did I?

When Dad finally opened his mouth to speak again, Mom grabbed the carton of kung pao chicken from the fridge and dug into it without first making a pit stop at the microwave.

Dad looked at her in disbelief before turning back to me. "I'm serious, Lydia. *We're* serious."

No, Mom was just hungry, as far as I could tell.

"You can't take the Jeep without permission."

I rolled my eyes. "Lately, I can barely go to the bathroom without permission."

Dad glared at me, not even bothering to breathe deeply or count to ten or go for another of his illusory Zen moments. "Speaking of rooms, I've given your bedroom more thought."

He could do whatever he wanted, and probably would. Thanks to bribes of Godiva chocolate, I could fix pretty much anything with Mom.

Head down, I just kept eating.

"I've decided to move you into Mary's room. At least until she comes home for winter break."

A sharp intake of breath, and it wasn't mine. "Howard? We

didn't discuss that."

Dad smiled faintly at Mom, who waved a fork in the air and sent kung pao chicken flying across the kitchen. "I thought I'd surprise you both. No offense, dear, but Lydia seems to have a knack for breaking down your defenses."

True. I wouldn't even have to work to break down Mom's defenses on this one. From the look on her face, she was already on my side.

Still, I hated to lose an opportunity to annoy Dad. He wasn't on my side, obviously, and never had been. Not that I was bitter about it or anything.

"Liz and Jane don't live here anymore, so why do I get stuck with Mary's puny room? The furniture is all for crap, and the place reeks like her stupid cat."

"I'd almost forgotten." Dad nodded, which made no sense, but that was Dad for you. "Boris is yours to take care of whenever Mary isn't at home."

I slapped my hand on the table, startling me when it stung. "She lives a thousand miles away!"

"Which is why Boris needs you."

"I can't stand Boris."

Dad tilted his head, studying me, looking way too smug. "Well, then, I hope you'll get used to him. You have no interest in activities or work or even applying to colleges, so you must have a lot of free time on your hands. When you're not busy doing your homework."

"I am *not* taking care of Boris."

"Actually, you are. Starting tonight."

"Mom!"

She patted my hand. "I'll discuss it with your father, dear. I do wish you'd find something that interests you, though."

Guys interested me—like, specifically Kirk—but I had a feeling it wouldn't help my case with Dad or even Mom.

"I'm, uh, interested in guitar." I glanced at Mom, offering her my best wheedling smile. "And I told Dad, but he seems to think Mary's the only one around here who deserves a guitar. So I guess I'm screwed, huh?"

"Please don't say—"

Dad shook his head. "I said I didn't plan to pay for it."

"Howard."

He shrugged. "Fine. We can pay for guitar lessons, but Lydia will have to come up with the guitar on her own. Mary got a guitar for her birthday, and Lydia's isn't until March."

"But Christmas—"

"—is more than three months from now. I'm happy to wait if you are."

I wasn't happy about much of anything, but I'd find a way to buy, borrow, or steal a guitar if it meant getting out of this house and Mary's stupid room and away from the ugliest cat in America.

If that didn't work, I'd ship Boris to Mary at MIT. In a UPS envelope. As an early birthday gift.

This family sucked.

♫

I GOT TO school early Friday morning, thanks to Cat wanting to hang out with Jeremy, but not early enough to beat Chelsea into Speech class. She and Drew were in the back of the room, looking nauseatingly lovey-dovey despite everything that went down at the band practice yesterday. I ignored them. I mean, not that I was jealous. The smoldering look in Drew's eyes when he caught sight of me told me more than I wanted to know, but he wasn't going to start anything with me in Speech class—or at all, unless he begged. And probably not even then.

I grabbed a desk on the far side of the room, by the window, so I could stare outside and pretend I was somewhere else.

"Mind if I sit here?"

"It's a free country."

I glanced up as I spoke, seeing a girl who'd moved to Woodbury the second half of tenth grade. Shoulder-length strawberry-blond hair, a dusting of freckles that made her look thirteen, and a sweet smile. Totally not my type.

"I don't know if you remember me, but I'm—"

"Heather MacAndrews. Yeah. I'm Lydia Bennet."

"I know." She smiled, still looking sweet, as she set down a stack of books that looked too heavy for her. They hit her desk with a thump. "I remember you from sophomore year."

I hadn't done anything to her, had I? Like, stolen her boyfriend? No, she looked too sweet to have a boyfriend I'd want, and she wouldn't act so nice to me if she were still pissed. Unless she was just collecting stories about Lydia Bennet to giggle about with her girlfriends.

Actually, she didn't seem like the type for that, either.

Ms. Ciccarelli walked in, and I didn't give Heather another thought. For one thing, she wasn't the sort of girl anyone would spend much time thinking about. For another thing, I was too busy getting nailed with homework for the weekend.

Not that I worried about that, either. After the hellish year I'd just survived at Shangri-La, weekends were for parties, not homework.

And I planned to find some.

I STUMBLED OUT of Mr. Bowman's Political Science class in a daze, loaded down with even more homework and the threat of a quiz at the end of next week. No one seemed to have mentioned to my teachers that school started only three days ago, so they didn't have to torture us this early in the term.

Head down, I slammed into someone, and my books went flying.

Annoyed, I snapped. "For God's sake, don't you—"

My breath caught at the sight of Kirk, who stooped to grab my stuff.

He grinned up at me. "Don't I what? Watch where *you're* going? I'd be happy to, but I never have a clue where you're going these days."

"Funny." I bent to pick up a couple of pens and a notebook he'd missed. "I'm going to the cafeteria. How about you?"

He was, I knew, but I wanted to play it cool. Weird. I'd never played it at *all* with Kirk, and suddenly my mind raced with strategies to catch him. Almost as if I'd been spending too much time reading *Cosmopolitan* or even *Seventeen*: how to hook the guy of your dreams in five easy steps.

But I didn't need a stupid magazine to tell me how to hook Kirk. I could do it just by being me. Lydia Bennet. Ruler—with Kirk—of this entire school.

Even if a lot of the kids in school didn't seem to recognize it anymore. But they would.

"I'm heading there, yeah." Kirk handed me the last of my books, not exactly offering to carry them for me, but that was fine. I didn't want him to turn into some pathetic doofus over me. I just wanted to go out with him. "Join me?"

I glanced sideways at him, nodding, as I wondered what the scoop was with Amber. But I'd learned a long time ago that guys were more likely to forget they had girlfriends if you didn't go out of your way to remind them.

We dropped our books at our table, then headed together through the lunch line. Amber was nowhere in sight. Excellent.

"Are you really interested in playing guitar with the band? I mean, I don't remember you playing."

I shrugged as I grabbed a slice of pepperoni pizza and a salad. "I haven't played in a while." Like, ever. "But if you give me a couple of weeks, I wouldn't mind playing with you guys."

I tried to sound like I was doing him a favor, instead of finding some pathetic excuse to hang out with him. It was as stupid as it was unnecessary, because Kirk was happy to hang out with me *without* an excuse, but I couldn't help myself. Going a year without guys had done something to me.

At Shangri-La, which was filled with more bad boys than I could handle, they'd been off-limits. It took a few months before someone told me why none of the guys tried to get close to me, when they didn't mind hitting on all the skanks in the girls' dorm: if they did, they'd get detention in the form of hard labor. The judge in Milwaukee, probably egged on by Dad, had ordered it. And no one even bothered to tell me.

Another of Dad's crimes I wouldn't forgive anytime soon.

Kirk nodded. "No problem. One or two other kids might be interested in joining the band, but I'm sure we can give you a try, too."

I bit down on my disappointment. Give me a try? Had they given Mary a *try*? From the sound of it, they'd practically worshipped at her feet.

"Whatever. I can always find a different band."

Okay, I couldn't, not easily, especially since I didn't have a guitar, let alone the first clue how to play one.

"Hey, I'd love to have you in the band. No worries." Kirk grinned at me as we headed to our table, where Amber was sitting in the chair where I'd left my books.

My books were lying in a heap on the floor. When I reached the table, Amber's books followed them there.

"Hey!"

As she scrambled to pick hers up, I grabbed her seat—or, more precisely, reclaimed mine. I could pick up my books anytime. Better yet, maybe Kirk would.

Nope. He just sat down next to me and dug into his burger and fries. With a loud huff, Amber stalked off to a different table. After a moment, I picked up my books.

"Man, I can't believe the musical chairs in this school." I poked around in my salad, searching for a cherry tomato. "It's not as civilized as I remember it."

Kirk laughed as he munched on a few fries. "It's almost exactly how I remember it. At least, sophomore year, when you were still here."

I frowned. "Are you saying I—"

"—create some excitement around this place? Yeah. I just don't know if everyone will survive it."

He glanced across the cafeteria at Drew and Chelsea, who'd been sitting alone until Amber joined them. Drew stared at me like a lost and hungry puppy. Not exactly the sort of animal I craved.

"I didn't do anything." Catching Kirk's raised eyebrows, I shrugged. "Drew doesn't seem to know what he wants, but that's not my fault. I was just being nice."

Kirk choked on something, and I don't think it was his hamburger. I almost thumped him on the back, but he was grinning. He could fend for himself.

"So you're not interested in Drew?"

"Romantically? No." Okay, his kiss *was* hotter than I would've guessed, but that could've been due to the complete *lack* of kisses in my life last year. Besides, Kirk's were probably hotter, and I wasn't stupid enough to go after Kirk's best friend, let alone when Kirk was watching.

At least, not since yesterday.

"And . . . other than romantically?"

I stalled for time as I bit into my slice of pizza. Too much cheese, not enough tomato, but the pepperoni was nice and spicy. I finally realized Kirk was staring at me, waiting for an answer. Why? Because he cared? Or because he was trying to watch out for Drew?

Drew could watch out for himself.

"Drew and I are friends. You know that." Feeling Kirk's eyes on my mouth, I wiped it with my napkin. "We've never been anything more than that."

"But he's—"

"—with Chelsea. Fine by me. I mean, I feel sorry for the guy, but it's not my issue."

I heard a gasp from farther down the table and looked up to see Tess sitting by herself, obviously listening in. She really needed to get out more.

Kirk's lips quirked, as if he shared my opinion. Being Kirk, he'd also agree it wasn't his issue.

Amber was a totally different issue, but he didn't mention her, and I sure didn't plan to.

"What's your definition of romance?"

I shrugged, even though his question hit me out of the blue, and I wondered why he was asking. Kirk always had a reason for everything, which was something I liked about him.

"Depends on the guy." Right this moment, it mostly depended on what Kirk wanted it to be. Because I wanted him like no one I'd ever wanted before, not even Justin before he turned into a monster. "What's yours?"

Leaning close, Kirk whispered in my ear. "Depends on the girl. So I guess you know what I mean."

As I felt a sudden tingling in my body that went all the way down to my toes, I nodded.

I knew *exactly* what he meant.

♫

I DIDN'T GET any calls or texts after school, from Kirk or anyone else, and Kirk didn't show up at my front door, asking me to run away with him.

For that matter, neither did Drew.

Cat disappeared when we got home from school, but without the Jeep, which probably meant Jeremy picked her up. But they couldn't be going to a party. It was way too early, and I would've heard about it from Kirk. Maybe no one at school partied anymore. Or maybe the kids in our crowd had started going to school football games on Friday night. Even though football games were the definition of lame.

Thinking about it, I lay back on my bed in Cat's and my room—since I refused to move to Mary's hellhole—and stroked Boris's rough fur until I remembered that I was in charge of Boris now. I shooed him off my bed, but he jumped up on Cat's bed and gave me a baleful look. Fine. With any luck, maybe he'd poop all over Cat's bedspread.

Finally, I heard the front door open. A moment later, Mom's screech made its way upstairs. "Cat? Lydia? Are you home?"

Boris bolted under my bed, the dumb cat. Didn't he know Mom tortured only her daughters? And her husband? And her divorce clients' exes?

Okay, maybe Boris had a point, but I wasn't sure I could squeeze under the bed. Besides, I had to get a guitar out of Mom and fix a few other problems caused by Dad.

Still, I waited until I heard her footsteps on the stairs. "I'm here, Mom. Just hanging out, waiting for you to get home."

Talk about laying it on thick. I'd have to dial it back a few notches or even Mom would see through me.

The door to my room swung open. "Oh, you're here, dear. Weren't you supposed to move to Mary's bedroom?"

I felt tears welling up in my eyes. Sure, they were totally fake, but it still annoyed me that I'd have to fix my mascara after I got done with this.

"You poor thing." Mom dropped her briefcase by the door and came over to my bed, perching on the edge of it. "Did you have a bad day? Did something happen at school?"

Sniffling, I wiped a hand across my wet cheek. "School's okay, but Cat won't talk to me, and she went out already, probably to a party." I blew my nose when an evil grin threatened. "And the only place I've *ever* felt at home was this room, especially with the wallpaper you put up for Cat and me, and now Dad wants to take even this away from me."

As I hiccupped on a final sob, I tried not to glance at the hideous pink-and-orange wallpaper filled with ballerinas that Mom had picked out and hung crookedly during one of her manic phases when Cat and I were ten. I'd wanted a lock on my bedroom door ever since. Fat chance.

"Oh, sweetie." Mom leaned forward to wrap her arms around me, smelling of her favorite floral cologne and telltale traces of chocolate. "I never knew how much it meant to you."

She was basically smothering me. I pulled back slightly just to breathe. "Of course you did. You and I have always been so close. I could tell you anything."

And I *had* told her a million things over the years, most of them whoppers. Still, it felt good that Mom always took my side, even if it told me she'd fall for anything.

"We'll fix whatever is wrong. You can count on me, dear." She gave me another squeeze, nearly sucking the life force out of me. "I don't understand why your father thinks you need to change rooms, but what else do you need?"

Kirk, spending money, and wheels. But I'd start with Kirk,

who obviously wasn't rushing to come after me.

"A guitar? I'd *so* like to learn to play guitar."

Mom nodded as she kept squeezing. "We can call it an early Christmas present, don't you think?"

Sure, but only because I knew Mom would forget all about it by Christmas, when I'd ask for something else, too.

"That would be fantastic. Thanks, Mom." I gave her a preemptive hug before she got another chokehold on me. "You have no idea how much this means to me."

"We'll sign you up for lessons, too." Mom pursed her lips, but it didn't mean she was changing her mind. Being a lawyer, she was all about logistics. "Did you look in Mary's room to see if she kept her beginning guitar books?"

I shrugged. "I was afraid if I peeked in there, Dad would shove me inside and lock me up forever."

Laughing, Mom shook her head. "Listen to you. Such a vivid imagination."

Yeah, and I planned to put it to good use. "Oh, and is it okay if I take the Jeep tonight?"

"Of course, dear."

Man, was Dad going to be pissed. Bonus.

Chapter 5

*"She has been allowed to dispose of her time
in the most idle and frivolous manner, and
to adopt any opinions that came in her sway."*

— Jane Austen, *Pride and Prejudice*
Volume III, Chapter Five

WHEN CAT DIDN'T show her face, I took off in the Jeep at seven, over Dad's protests that Mom kept shushing.

Now I just had to figure out where the parties were.

I cruised through the school parking lot, but I didn't see any cars I recognized. Of course, I'd been gone over a year. When I left town for Wisconsin Dells at the end of sophomore year, most of the kids in our class either hadn't yet passed their driver's test or didn't have wheels.

I didn't bother checking the football stadium. I hadn't set foot inside it since a really bad night during freshman year, and none of my friends had gone to football games when we'd been sophomores. I couldn't believe *everything* had changed.

I glanced at my cell phone. Still no texts or calls. I could call Drew, but my hair still hurt from doing that yesterday. I could call Kirk. No, I couldn't. I'd never actually made the first move on a guy before, and I didn't plan to start tonight.

It didn't stop me from cruising past his house. Dark, and no familiar cars were parked in front.

I cruised up and down the streets of Woodbury. Past Michael's house, in case the band was practicing. Past Tess's house. Nothing. I skipped Amber's house and didn't know where Chelsea lived, but it wouldn't matter if I did.

Finally, I drove to the Mall of America. If nothing else, I could catch a movie. Alone. Talk about pathetic.

My cell phone rang as I pulled into the parking ramp on the east side.

I answered without bothering to glance at the caller display. "Party central."

"Babe. Not the smartest way to answer your phone."

Liz. So much for getting a lead on a party. "I'll answer my phone however I want."

"I'm sure you will. Nothing's changed, I see."

"Nothing that matters." Or nothing I planned to share with any of my sisters, not even Cat. "But you must be having a pretty boring Friday night if you're wasting your time checking up on me."

"Mom said you went out but didn't seem to have any plans. I thought I'd—"

"Since when does Mom know if I have plans?" I turned off the Jeep and climbed out, then pocketed the keys and headed for the entrance. "Not that you'd have a clue, but I've never exactly shared my plans with Mom."

"No kidding. But Cat said—"

"Cat wouldn't know, either."

She didn't say anything for so long, I almost thought we got disconnected. "Does anyone know about you these days? Or are you keeping yourself a secret? That *would* be a change."

I bit off the first reply that came to mind, since it was profane even by Liz's standards, but I didn't hang up. The truth was, I didn't have any plans and wasn't completely sure any of my friends were worth my time. Not that Liz would qualify as a friend.

"Lydia? You still there?"

I sighed. "Yeah." Unfortunately.

"So what are you doing tonight? Jane and I were going to catch a movie."

"Yeah, well, I . . ." I trailed off, for the first time in my life blanking on an excuse. I must be tired. Tired of everyone in Woodbury, for starters. Tired of not knowing what I was doing, even at the Mall of America. I was at the second-floor entrance and wondered if I should head back to the Jeep.

"Join us. We were going out for Chinese first, but we could do burgers or pizza." She mumbled something to someone else, probably Jane, before getting back to me. "Jane doesn't care as long as she gets Cold Stone ice cream for dessert, even though I pointed out that Milk Duds during the movie are the only dessert a girl needs. Am I right?"

"No." As usual. "It's all about the popcorn."

"Another thing you have in common with Jane."

Wrong again. I had *nothing* in common with Jane, the world's most perfect girl, and not just from a parent's perspective. If it weren't for the fact that she never tried to bug me, unlike Liz, I might even find her annoying.

"Whatever. Hey, I'm at the Mall of America." I might as well admit it. Knowing Dad, he'd installed a GPS tracker on the Jeep. "Why don't we catch dinner and a movie here?"

More background mumbling before Liz spoke into the phone. "Meet you in twenty minutes at Chipotle?"

"No, Kokomo's. Across from Cold Stone."

"Chipotle is close to Cold Stone, too."

"Good. You can wave to Chipotle from our table at Kokomo's."

Liz actually laughed, surprising me. "I'd argue, but Kokomo's is Jane's first choice, too. Luckily for both of you, they have a wicked chocolate cake for dessert."

"I thought you planned to eat Milk Duds for dessert."

"That was before I knew we were eating at Kokomo's. I try to be flexible."

And I try to do things on Friday night that don't involve my older sisters. At least one of us was happy.

♫

I WOKE UP Saturday morning in my own bed and with a clear head. It didn't say much for my Friday night.

Actually, it'd been okay. Jane pretended to care about how things were going with me, and Liz let Jane and me choose a movie that didn't star Channing Tatum. A first.

Still, I frowned as I stretched in bed, then looked over at Cat, who was still sound asleep.

"What are you looking at? And why are you still in here? Didn't Dad say you had to move to Mary's room?"

Ahh. She'd been faking it. I'd almost forgotten I was dealing with the new Cat.

"Mom said I could stay." I tried not to grin at my all-too-easy triumph, but I didn't mind annoying Cat. "Besides, why do you care? You're hardly ever here."

She rolled over, facing the wall, and pretended to snore.

"Maybe you can fake it with Jeremy—" I snorted. No response. "But I *know* you, Cat. I've known you forever."

Something came flying across the room at me. Luckily, it wasn't Boris. I grabbed the SpongeBob pillow and tossed it right back at Cat.

"You get that from work? Nice. What does Jeremy think of it?" When she rolled her eyes, I tossed out my next question before I could pull it back. "So what did you guys do last night?"

As the silent treatment continued, I wondered why I'd asked. I didn't need to know if they'd gone somewhere to make out. *I* didn't want Jeremy. And I wasn't sure I wanted to find out that they'd gone to a party hosted by Kirk. Or Drew. Or someone else from our gang.

Or even, say, Jeremy.

"Hung out."

The words floated so softly in the air, it took me a moment to realize she'd finally spoken.

"Oh. At Jeremy's house?"

"No."

At this rate, I'd find out what Cat did last night in about five years.

"We started at the Mall of America."

This was really getting annoying. "Yeah? Where did you go then?"

For a minute I didn't think she'd answer. Throwing back the covers on my bed, I groaned to my feet. I might as well do something today. Something other than trying to talk to Cat.

"Kirk's house."

I froze in front of my dresser, then slowly whirled in Cat's direction. She didn't look a bit happier about going to a party at Kirk's house than I was about not being invited.

"You went to a party at Kirk's house without me? And you didn't tell me?"

Cat finally rolled over in my direction, completely awake and looking ready to bolt. Except that she was wearing undies and a camisole.

She sat up on the edge of her bed. "It wasn't a party—not really—so I couldn't invite you. Not that you and I have been hanging out together lately anyway."

"Whose fault is that?"

Cat held up a hand. "It is what it is. Jeremy and I ran into Kirk and Amber." Her nose curled as if she hadn't exactly been thrilled. Right. Like she had so many better options. "They were going to Kirk's house, and I would've skipped it, but Kirk said Michael and Zach were coming over."

"Zach?"

Cat frowned. "You went to that band practice, right? Zach plays bass guitar."

I'd been too busy kissing Drew and getting my hair ripped out by Chelsea to remember much else, but I nodded. "The cute, skinny guy."

"With the Cat in the Hat tattoo."

I stared at her.

"You didn't see his tattoo?" Cat grinned, something I hadn't seen her do in ages, except once last week when I caught her gazing into Jeremy's eyes and drooling. "It's the first thing I noticed about him."

"But you're dating Jeremy."

"So? I can't notice a guy's tattoo? I even drew a portrait of him from the side, just to capture it."

I almost forgot. Our artist in residence drew portraits of almost everyone she saw. I wondered when I'd show up in her rogues gallery, probably with a huge "X" over my face.

"Whatever. So Michael and Zach were there. Did the band practice or something?"

Should I have told Kirk I was ready to play guitar? No way. It'd be the last time I could show my face in front of Kirk's band—and maybe Kirk. I'd told him I could play in a couple of weeks, but I actually needed to stall as long as possible.

I finally realized Cat was back in silent mode. I looked at her, waiting, but she just stared at the floor.

"Hey, I know you're not exactly thrilled with the band, but you *are* dating Jeremy. You must have to sit in on band practices all the time."

"The band, uh, didn't practice."

"So they just got together to talk about songs?"

She kept staring at the floor, something neither of us normally did in this room, which was probably why it never got vacuumed.

"Michael and Zach didn't show up, but Drew and Chelsea did. So we just hung out."

The sudden ache in my gut had nothing to do with the fact that I was starving. If I ate anything now, I'd probably heave. "You hung out with them."

Cat drilled me with a serious look. "Kirk and Amber have been going out since last March. Drew and Chelsea since January. You can't just waltz into town and expect those guys to dump their girlfriends. A lot happened while you were gone. Besides, you don't actually want those guys, do you?"

Numb, I just stared at Cat while the wheels that were always turning in my head refused to budge. A lot had happened, all right. None of it good.

But it didn't mean I couldn't change it.

I FINALLY TOOK a shower and returned to my room ten minutes later—or a half hour, tops—to find it missing.

Okay, my *room* wasn't missing. Just all of my stuff. Clothes, books, phone, laptop. Even my bed!

"Cat? What the hell did you do with my stuff?"

Dad poked his head into my room, the benign smile on his face saying it all. "Cat went to work. You'd probably like to get a jump on your day as well." His eyebrows rose. "So I took the liberty of moving you to your new room."

"But Mom—"

"Your mother had to go into the office, but I managed as best I could. You don't have to thank me."

I stood there, in a T-shirt and shorts with my wet hair dripping onto my shirt, glaring at Dad. "Don't hold your breath."

"As we say in yoga, it's always best not to."

I felt like punching him. "Mom said I could stay here. I'll just move my stuff back."

"Your mother also promised to buy you a guitar, I understand, but I think you'll find that life isn't quite as easy as you remember it."

I went over and flopped on Cat's bed—also known as my new bed. If one of us had to leave, it wasn't me. "Thanks, but I don't remember it being easy. I remember it sucking. This is no big change."

It was, actually, but I'd never admit it to Dad. Before Wisconsin Dells and Justin and that strip bar and a jail cell in Milwaukee and reform school in Montana, my life had been pretty good. And the few times I'd run into a bump in the road, Mom had been there to fix it. Just like she would be now.

First, though, I wouldn't mind punching Dad. "Maybe you think you can tell me what to do, but Mom can let me stay here if she wants, and she can buy me a guitar, just like you bought one for Mary."

"For her birthday."

"Whatever." I glanced around the half-empty bedroom, actually liking it better this way. I also wouldn't miss Cat one bit.

"Since Mom makes the money in the family these days—" Direct hit. As I caught his flinch, I barely kept myself from pumping my fists. "I don't see you having much say."

I watched as Dad struggled to bring his breathing under control. He was all about breath and control and pretending his life was better than it was. I was all about that, too—in my own way—so you'd think we'd actually get along.

But no.

"As someone with no job and no apparent interest in college, you're not in a good position to speak. Now, get off Cat's bed and go to your new room."

So much for Dad's usual attempt at a Zen state of calm.

I scooted to the far side of Cat's bed—*my* new bed—and crossed my arms and legs, then leaned against the wall. "Nope."

The harsh breaths coming out of Dad's flared nostrils weren't even remotely calm, let alone Zen-like.

"I think you'll find you regret your decision."

"Yet another thing you'd be wrong about."

He took a step toward me, as if he planned to yank me off the bed or even spank me, which totally wasn't Dad's style. It was Liz's style, but she wasn't here.

After another step, though, he stopped. And retreated. And left the room.

Cat was so wrong. I *could* come home after a year away and take over the world, just like always. I'd beaten Dad, and he didn't fold easily. Sure, I'd have to wait until he was far enough away to toss Cat's stuff in the hall and grab mine from Mary's room, but Cat would be gone for hours and I didn't have anything going on today. I could wait.

Grinning, I curled up with Cat's SpongeBob pillow and let my eyelids drift shut.

♪

I WOKE UP with a jolt to the angry buzzing sound of a huge beehive, as if someone had just sprayed it with a hose.

Either that, or Dad was going nuts with his drill.

"What the hell?"

The drill paused. "I suggest you clean up your language. The forty-five-minute shower you took this morning apparently took care of only the surface."

"Ha ha." I tossed SpongeBob across the room, into the space where my bed once stood. It joined the fast-food wrappers, random crap, and dust bunnies that had collected under the bed. "But since when do you do home-improvement projects?"

Dad might be an engineer by training, and he'd worked as one until his midlife crisis drove him to blow most of his and Mom's life savings and open a yoga center, but he never did a thing around the house. Unless you count reading the newspaper, puffing on cigars that Mom had tried a million times to outlaw, and waving his butt in the air on his yoga mat.

Which I don't.

The drill cranked up again. "I do them when I'm inspired. And you, my dear, have inspired me."

Whenever Dad used "my dear" on Mom or any of us girls, it meant he was either pissed or on the verge of it. From the crimson color of his face, he'd already leaped off the verge. I looked more closely and finally figured out what he was doing. After years of me begging for a lock on my door, he was installing one.

Somehow, I had a feeling it wasn't for my benefit.

Still, a lock was a lock, and I'd score the key soon enough, and that would be the end of my hassles with Dad and everyone else around here. If I could just rig up some sort of escape route through my window, I'd be set.

I grinned as Dad kept working, but it annoyed me that his own grin seemed even bigger. As if he knew something I didn't.

Finally, the drilling stopped, and Dad took a step backward to admire his handiwork. Typical guy.

I rolled my eyes. "It's just a lock. You're not going to take a picture, are you?"

With the drill gripped in one hand, he glanced over at me, his lips twisted in triumph. Triumph over me? Not in this lifetime.

"No, but you might want to take a picture. This is the last view you might have of the hallway, or any other part of the house, for quite some time."

I frowned. Dad and I had always argued, but I had a bad feeling that I was going down. Even if temporarily.

When realization slowly dawned, I sprang off the bed and bolted for the door. Too late. With a slam followed by the soft click of a key turning, I was locked in.

His voice floated through the door. "When you decide to be reasonable, let me know. But you're moving to Mary's old room, and you're moving today."

Jerk. He'd pay for this when Mom got home. If not sooner.

THERE'S NOTHING LIKE knowing you're locked in for the duration to make you have to pee. Or eat something before you starve to death. Or drink something to quell the raging thirst in your throat, even if it means needing to pee even sooner.

I glanced out the open window of my room—because it was still my room, dammit—and calculated the drop to the grass below. Liz could probably do it. I'd break my neck, or at least my leg, if I tried.

My cell phone was in Mary's room, along with the rest of my stuff, and Cat must've taken hers to work, which meant I couldn't call anyone to rescue me. I wasn't even sure who I'd call. Kirk would do it, no problem, but he'd laugh when he heard what my dad pulled on me, and I didn't feel like being laughed at today. I had enough problems.

With a final wistful glance outside, I slammed the window shut. Returning to Cat's bed—*my* bed—I perched on the edge, squeezed my legs together, and tried not to think about how much I needed to pee.

And it had only been an hour since Dad locked me in.

Damn.

THE SOUND OF the phone ringing jarred me awake. I rolled over and squinted at the clock on the desk. Almost three. I'd already opened the window, punched out the screen, and peed down the side of the house, but that had been hours ago. My throat felt raw from raging thirst, and my stomach seemed to be gnawing itself to death from the inside.

Where was Mom? For that matter, where was Cat? Oh, yeah. She worked until four or five on Saturdays. But Mom never worked past noon on Saturdays. Had Dad locked her up, too? Had he finally snapped under the strain of all that yoga? Was our house turning into the setting of a Stephen King novel?

When someone knocked on my door, I jumped. With a jerk, I brought my trembling under control, but I didn't say anything.

"Lydia?"

Dad called my name as if he wasn't completely sure I'd be

inside. Good.

"Lydia, your mother wants to talk to you."

Right. She was probably bound and gagged in the basement, which was the only possible reason why she hadn't rescued me yet, and Dad just wanted me to come to the door so he could toss me out of Cat's—I mean, *my*—room. No way.

"Fine. I'll tell your mother you didn't feel like talking to her, which probably won't increase the odds of her buying you a guitar."

As Dad paused, I rolled my eyes. Mom was going to buy me a guitar and get all of my stuff back in this room as soon as Jane and Liz released her from her chains in the basement.

Dad cleared his throat, as if he'd been talking to Mom just now. Ha. He'd probably called our home phone with his own cell phone. "She said she'll talk to you when she gets home. She hopes you come to your senses by then."

That proved it. Definitely not Mom. She didn't talk that way—except maybe to her clients, who probably needed it—and would spring me the moment she got home. If she wasn't home already, of course, and locked in chains in the basement.

All things considered, it wasn't so bad being locked up in my room. Unlike Mom, at least I could pee out the window.

"Lydia, darling? Are you okay?"

That sounded more like Mom. And definitely not Dad.

I finished the paragraph I was reading of *The Catcher in the Rye* as the key rattled in the door. Mom, in her usual panic to rescue her darling daughter, couldn't seem to manage the lock. Either that, or Dad hadn't given her the right key. I'd put even odds on those two possibilities.

I finally heard a satisfying click. An instant later, the door flew open and banged against the wall.

"Lydia! Are you okay? You must be hungry. You look famished. Do you want me to make you something? What would you like, dear?"

"Something to drink? I'm ungodly thirsty." And starving to death, too, but not enough to risk Mom's cooking. "Dad locked me up and probably hoped I'd die in here."

She rushed to my side, checking my forehead for fever and peering into my eyes. The only thing my eyes would tell her was that they were brown. And pretty pissed.

She glanced around the room. "Your bed! Your father really did move it." Tsking, she glanced out the window, her brow furrowed quizzically. "And your screen! He removed the screen? Why would he do that?"

On the verge of telling her I punched it out, I bit my tongue. Let her think Dad did it. The deeper he dug his grave, the better I liked it. He was going down.

I shrugged. "No idea what's going on with Dad. He went berserk. I sure hope he can afford a shrink on the nickels and dimes he's making at his yoga center."

Mom pursed her lips and looked out the door, but Dad wasn't hovering. It actually surprised me. I mean, didn't he want to stop Mom from doing what she did best? Rescue me from Dad's punishment?

"I'll speak to him." She turned back to me, running her hand over my hair, but her wedding ring got tangled in it, and I yelped. "Oh! I'm so sorry, dear. And I'm sorry you've had such a rough day. I had to meet with clients."

"That's okay." It wasn't, but yelling at her wouldn't help. I couldn't get my day back at this point, and I needed Mom on my side. "I knew you'd come home eventually, and then you'd fix everything. Just like always."

I produced a few tears for good measure, even though the lack of liquids all day made it tough to come up with a ton of excess moisture.

"Oh, you poor sweetie." Mom frowned, running her hand through my hair again, even though I tensed as I waited for it to snag. "But, well, your father feels quite strongly—"

"Oh, Mom." The tears were still fake, but for once something felt different. Like I'd lost my protector. "You won't believe the things he said. He wished I was back in reform school."

Okay, he hadn't said that, but it *felt* like he wished I was back at Shangri-La. After all, I'd forced him to get off his yoga mat and actually wield a drill. Hard labor wasn't Dad's strong suit.

"I'm sure he didn't mean it, dear."

"He meant everything, Mom. It was unbelievable."

"Unbelievable, indeed." Dad's head poked into my room, following his words, and he still wore the snotty grin from this morning. "But your mother and I have talked, and she understands what I'm doing. What *we're* doing."

I shook my head. "You had it right the first time. It's what *you're* doing. Mom wouldn't do something like this to me. She likes me."

"I love you, dear. Your father does, too." She squeezed my hand, but the helpless look in her eye worried me. "And I still plan to buy you a guitar." She glanced nervously at Dad, who rolled his eyes. "But I'm afraid I have to let your father move you to Mary's room."

Stunned, I jerked to a sitting position. "*Why?* He's so wrong!"

She patted my hand. "It's just until you get a job or find an activity or make honor roll or some such thing. It's your choice, really, but I have every confidence in you."

The look on Dad's face told me he didn't share Mom's confidence.

Furious, I punched Cat's pillow. For once, I had to agree with Dad.

Chapter 6

"Look here, I have bought this bonnet.
I do not think it is very pretty; but
I thought I might as well buy it as not."

— Jane Austen, *Pride and Prejudice*
Volume II, Chapter Sixteen

"PARTY AT MY house this Friday."

At lunch on Monday, I eyed Kirk as I bit into my chicken wrap, forgetting the creamy-white dressing I'd drizzled on top of it a minute ago. The dressing dribbled down my V-neck shirt, a few drops scoring a direct hit on my cleavage. Drew, across the table, looked like he wanted to lick it clean for me.

"Yeah?" I scooped up a dab with my thumb and licked it myself, making Drew practically faint, but Kirk's eyebrows just danced in amusement. "Who's gonna be there?"

He held a hand to his heart. "It's not enough that I will?"

I shrugged. It was, actually, unless he was talking him, Amber, and me. Ew. The schoolwide rumors of my sexual escapades were greatly exaggerated—understatement of the century—and usually by me, but they didn't include three-ways.

Kirk touched a finger to my chin, coming away with another dab of creamy-white dressing, and licked it. This time, Drew wasn't the only one who might have heart failure.

Kirk grinned at both of us. "The usual crowd."

Which meant half of our class and, typically, dozen of kids I'd never even seen before. "Sounds good."

"The band is playing."

"Yeah?" I sucked in a breath, choking on my wrap until Kirk put his hand on my back. Not thumping it or doing the Heimlich maneuver or anything. Just holding it there. His hand was wildly hot, something I didn't want to think about any more than I wanted to think about playing on Friday with his band.

Amber shot me a glare, which meant she knew exactly what I was thinking. At least about Kirk's hot hand.

Just to annoy her, I fluttered my eyelashes at him. "Thanks."

"No prob. So, you wanna play with us?" He tilted his head, waiting for my answer. "I know you said you wanted to play in a couple of weeks, but we don't exactly get a lot of gigs, and I managed to swing this one." Grinning, he winked at me. "I had an inside track with management."

Amber started to gag, but no one held a hot hand to her back or even glanced at her.

I couldn't afford to pay attention to her, either. I was too busy trying to calm my heart palpitations. "You probably want me to play with you guys first, don't you? Like, practice the songs you're doing?"

"Hey, we're just playing in front of friends. I play lead, so you'd just be doing rhythm. That works, doesn't it?"

Only in concept. In reality, I couldn't even play a single chord, and I had a feeling I couldn't change that situation before Friday.

"It's just that—"

"You can come to the party, can't you? I mean, you don't have other plans?"

"Not exactly." Unless I counted being locked in my room for the weekend, which was always a possibility where Dad was concerned. "But I'm not sure when I can get there."

Hopefully, it'd be about ten minutes after the band stopped playing.

"We can play whenever." Kirk smiled across the table at Amber, looking way too lovey-dovey for the good of my stomach lining, before turning back to me. "But if you don't want to, that's okay. I talked to another girl who might want to play with us. You know Heather MacAndrews?"

The sugary-sweet girl in my Speech class? No way. If Kirk asked her, he must be asking everyone in the world.

"If you want her instead of me, that's cool. Like I said, I can join a different band."

The glow dimmed on Kirk's ever-present neon grin. "Hey, you're the one who acts like you don't wanna play with us. If you want to play, bring your guitar on Friday."

"Fine." I shrugged, like it was no big deal, even though I suddenly had a black hole in the pit of my stomach and might as well fling the chicken wrap out the cafeteria window. "I guess I'll give you guys a try."

But first I had to find a guitar. And someone to teach me how to play. And an excuse for why I had to skip school the rest of this week.

Because that was the only chance in hell I had of pulling this off.

♫

"SORRY I BOLTED on you last week."

No kidding. I glanced sideways at Lauren in Accounting class, even though I'd rather pretend she didn't exist.

I hadn't seen her in class since the drug-pushing fiasco, if that's what it was, but I didn't know if she'd been sick or in detention or maybe at a convention for high school kids who deal drugs.

Ignoring her, I stared at Ms. Frey, pretending to hang on every word she said, even though—let's face it—Accounting had even less meaning in my life than English or Political Science. Like, less than zero.

Lauren hissed at me, like a snake, which probably wasn't the worst analogy. "I said I was sorry."

I shrugged but kept my focus on Ms. Frey. She had her back to us as she wrote on the board, and she looked all sweet and naive in her long flowered skirt, but I wouldn't put it past her to have secret cameras installed somewhere in this room. All pointed directly at me.

Just like at Shangri-La.

"I'm *talking* to you."

Lauren obviously didn't care if there were secret cameras or snitches sitting nearby. She also must be pretty desperate for a customer—or, more likely, cash—to keep bugging me when I obviously wasn't interested.

"Lauren? Is there something you'd like to share with the class?"

Like I said. Ms. Frey must have eyes in the back of her head or amazing hearing. Or, with my luck, both.

"Uh, no."

"Lydia? Do you have an issue with Lauren?"

I had several issues with her, actually, starting with the long, pointy black fingernails she'd tapped on my desk a moment ago, which was probably why Ms. Frey was going after *me* now. Add in the goth look I'd seen too much at Shangri-La—black hair and lips and eyeshadow—and the fact that she could've gotten me busted last week by slipping drugs under my notebook? Yeah, she annoyed the shit out of me.

But I just shook my head at Ms. Frey.

Frowning, she turned back to the blackboard.

When the bell finally rang what felt like ten hours later, I grabbed my books and bolted out of my seat as fast as I could.

"Hey, wait up."

Black fingernails clutched my sleeve, but I broke loose of Lauren's grip and shot through an opening in the crush of kids at the door. I didn't need this. I wasn't a goody two-shoes, but I'd just spent a year at Shangri-La with girls who reminded me of Lauren, and let's just say it wasn't a good time.

The black fingernails grabbed me again. Unlike Chelsea's, they didn't gouge me, but that was the only good news.

I kept walking fast, shooting right past my locker, as I flicked a glance to my left. "What do you want?"

"You don't have to be so rude."

"Tell me about it. I'm not the one grabbing people."

Her brow furrowed as she glanced down at her hand, still gripping my arm. With a jerk, she let go. "Yeah, well, you were hard to catch."

"Maybe I don't like to be caught."

"That's not what I hear."

"You have no idea what you're talking about." With a sharp frown, I picked up my pace, but I couldn't exactly run in the heels I'd worn to school today. "Seriously. No idea."

She chewed gum as we walked, then blew a bubble and popped it with a touch of a fingernail. "I'm talking about parties."

So? My idea of a fun party was probably different from Lauren's. I jerked to a stop. "Hey, I've gotta get to class, and I forgot to grab my stuff from my locker."

"Maybe catch you after school?"

To sneak me drugs I didn't ask for and get me busted? No, thanks. "I'm catching a ride with my sister."

"Or at lunch tomorrow?"

Only if I didn't see her first.

"But definitely in Accounting."

I headed in the direction of my locker. "Sure. Whatever."

Lauren was turning into as big a pain as my dad, but at least Dad gave me an allowance. Lauren offered me a one-way ticket back to hell.

And I didn't plan on going.

♫

CAT DROPPED ME off at home, then peeled out before I realized she wasn't coming inside, too.

Perfect. The person I'd missed more than anyone else when I'd been locked up at Shangri-La probably didn't even glance in the rearview mirror as she zoomed down the street.

Sighing, I arrived upstairs to find my old bedroom door locked and an arrow pointing in the direction of Mary's room. Ha ha. I live with the most hilarious family.

Unfortunately.

I flopped on my bed in Mary's room. Mary's old bed, which Mom had painted neon yellow a few years ago when she thought she'd beaten her bipolar disorder and went off her meds for a week, was nowhere in sight. I wish I could say that for the rest of Mary's crap.

Her desk was still piled high with novels by writers from Germany, Russia, and Timbuktu. She'd left a few teen magazines, which surprised me. Her huge armoire was blessedly empty, but that was the only blessing about it, since it was chipped, leaning precariously to one side, and scratched all to hell.

When I shook my head, Boris leaped from the top of the armoire, landing in my arms. Man, he was trusting. Yet another thing we didn't have in common.

"Boris, you moron."

He purred in my arms, forcing me to stroke the fur on his back, even though we both knew I'd drop him in a heartbeat if anyone else showed up.

At least Boris and I understood each other. I couldn't say that about a single person in my life right now. Not Cat, definitely, and not even Kirk. If he understood me at all, he would've already kicked Amber's sorry ass to the curb and backed over her for good measure.

I looked around this tiny, disgusting room that wasn't mine, blinking back tears I refused to let fall. I'd been home over two weeks now, and no one in my family or so-called group of friends had even *asked* me about reform school, let alone the crucial question: had I actually been *guilty* of what the police claimed and Dad oh-so-blithely believed?

Not Mom, not Cat, not anyone.

These days, the only person making any attempt where I was concerned was Lauren, a girl I didn't even know, which told me exactly how low I'd fallen at Woodbury High School in the year I'd been gone.

But I could fix this. I *would* fix this. After I snagged Kirk's attention with the guitar I wheedled out of Mom tonight, everything would fall into place. It always did.

Boris twisted in my arms, looking up at me with eyes at half mast, either because he was sleepy or questioned the sanity of my plan for world domination.

He squeaked as I gently tossed him on the bed, but I had things to do. A guitar to buy and conquer.

Boris could fend for himself.

♫

I WAITED UNTIL Dad finished eating Mom's Spam surprise and headed outside to smoke a cigar on the front steps before I sprang tonight's shopping trip on Mom.

I gave her the sweetest smile I could muster. "Mom?"

"Yes, dear?" She barely glanced at me from the sink, where she was hand-washing the dinner plates and glasses even though the dishwasher was six inches from her.

I grabbed a dish towel from the drawer, knowing it'd be more helpful to her in the long run if I pointed out that we had a dishwasher that was perfectly capable of cleaning dishes.

In the short run, though, I wanted a guitar.

I picked up a glass from the drying rack, tried to ignore the fact that it was filled with soapsuds, and started wiping.

Mom glanced at me again, less distracted now. "Thank you for helping. But what did you want?"

A guitar or, better yet, an excellent excuse for why I couldn't go to Kirk's party on Friday. But Mom could help me with only one of those.

I sucked in a breath and let the words spill out of me in a torrent before I chickened out or Dad came back inside, whichever came first. "I really need a guitar. Mary's old band is playing this Friday and they want me to play guitar, but I don't have one."

A groove creased Mom's forehead. "I promised I'd get you a guitar, dear, but you don't know how to play, do you? How could you play with a band this Friday? Can't we wait until this weekend? Or look on eBay?"

I could've sworn Dad took away Mom's eBay privileges a

couple of years ago, after she went on that American Girl binge and blew a bundle on a bunch of dolls her daughters had outgrown a million years ago.

I gave her my best pleading look. Sincere, just a touch of desperation, and totally fake. Okay, not fake at all. Unless I came up with an amazing excuse for why I couldn't play on Friday night, I was toast without a guitar.

"But I really need it now. And lessons, too."

I decided not to mention how I also needed to skip school the next four days, which was my only hope of having enough time to learn a few chords and figure out how to fake the rest. They wouldn't make me play a solo, would they? No way. Only the lead guitarist had to do solos, right? Please, God?

"I just don't think—"

"Hey, I totally understand if you're too busy. You could give me your credit card, and I'll go by myself and buy it." I'd get the most expensive guitar I could find, partly because that's what Dad bought Mary and partly because it might make people not notice the fact that I didn't have a clue how to play it.

"I'm not sure . . ."

Hearing the bang of the front door, I grabbed the dishrag out of Mom's hand and tossed it in the sink. "Tell you what. Let's both go. We always had the best shopping trips, didn't we? And it's been ages since we've had one. I'll finish the dishes for you after we get home."

Better yet, Dad would be so freaked at the dishes left unwashed in the sink, he'd do them before we got home.

But I realized I needed Mom. For one thing, Cat had taken the Jeep, and Dad said I couldn't drive his or Mom's cars after old Mr. Fogarty ratted me out about clipping his mailbox. Besides, if I went shopping alone with Mom's credit card, Dad would call the credit-card company and cancel the card before I made it a block away. If dragging Mom along was the price I had to pay for a new guitar, so be it.

Maybe I could talk her into buying me some new clothes, too.

♬

I HAD A new guitar. Nothing as fancy as I'd hoped, but it was a pretty shade of turquoise, which had to count for something. Mom also sprang for a really cute top and some red boots, so I was set. If Dad was all about Zen breathing and control, Mom was all about bright colors.

But I still didn't have a clue how to play anything. I'd signed up for guitar lessons each of the next three days after school, even though the guy at the music store had warned me it'd take several months to learn how to play. He also suggested—like, five times—that I sign up for once-a-week lessons like everyone else.

I wasn't like everyone else, though. For better or worse, I did everything on the fast track.

Mom and I got home to find the dishes undone—crap— and the Jeep at the curb. I didn't feel like talking to Cat, so I trudged into the kitchen and got to work.

"You're doing dishes? By hand? What did Mom pay you?"

Cat slouched against the counter, munching on a low-carb tortilla, and eying me as if she was trying to figure out my angle. She'd been doing that ever since I got home from Shangri-La, when all she'd had to do was ask me. About anything. Apparently, she'd rather come up with her own theories.

I scrubbed and rinsed plates, then set them on the drying rack. I couldn't decide whether to let them air dry or wipe them with a towel, since Cat obviously didn't plan to help.

When she didn't leave, I shrugged. "I'm just helping out, not disappearing for hours at a time like some people I know."

I said it loud enough for Dad to hear in the living room. He snorted. Loudly.

"Whatever." Cat glanced around the kitchen as if she wanted to know what Mom had bought me, but I left my loot in the trunk of Mom's car until everyone went to bed. Dad would be apoplectic enough when he saw the guitar, but the new clothes would send him over the edge.

I couldn't wait to see Dad's face—and Cat's, too—when they saw the matching friendship bracelets Mom had insisted on buying. Thinking about it, I laughed. Mom could be a little wacked when she skipped her meds, but I got a kick out of her. Sure, she'd always bought me anything I wanted except for an early trip home from Shangri-La, but it was sweet how she insisted on taking care of me even though I could take care of myself. And always did.

"What's so funny?"

Watching me, Cat kept nibbling on her tortilla like a rabbit going after her first carrot in a month. I glanced up at the clock over the sink—just after eight—and almost asked why she hadn't eaten before now. But I didn't care.

"Nothing. Just thinking." And, as much as possible, not about her.

"You're not really gonna try to play guitar on Friday night, are you? I told you it took Mary—"

"I'm not Mary."

"No. Unlike you, Mary actually knows how to play guitar. And piano. And knowing her, maybe even drums if she had to."

I stared at her. "What's really going on, Cat? You haven't given a rat's ass about me since I got home from reform school, and suddenly you're feeling protective? Do you think they're going to try to humiliate me the way they nailed you?"

When she finally spoke, her voice wobbled. "You don't get it. You're not the queen of the school anymore, and everyone you know has changed."

"Not Kirk. And not me."

"Yeah? Has Kirk ever gone out with the same girl more than a couple of weeks in a row? He's been dating Amber for six months."

I shrugged. "Desperate, obviously. Lack of decent prospects. Luckily for him, I'm back in town."

"Funny he's not falling all over himself to get you."

It was a little weird, actually, but maybe Kirk still saw me the way I'd always seen him: as co-leader of the gang. I hadn't told him I saw him in a new way now. As soon as I did, though, he'd want to go out with me.

At least, as soon as I learned how to play my cute new electric guitar. Like, by Friday.

"You don't know Kirk as well as I do. We've been pals since forever. You guys never were."

From the pinched look on her face, Cat and Kirk still weren't. Even though she was dating a guy who played in Kirk's band, it didn't change the fundamentals.

"You might at least call Mary and ask for some pointers."

Mary? She had to be kidding. "I'm taking lessons."

"Lydia, she really knows her stuff."

"Sure, if we're talking math or science. About anything else? No, thanks."

"She could even—"

I waved a hand, cutting her off. "I'm not asking Mary for advice about guitars. Not now, not ever. Unless hell froze over and no one mentioned it to me."

Cat swallowed the last bite of her tortilla. "If you play guitar Friday night and don't get laughed out of Kirk's house, I'll be sure to mention it to you. Because if you can learn to play guitar in four days, it'll definitely mean hell has frozen solid."

With a toss of her head, she flounced out of the kitchen,

leaving me to my dishes and soapsuds and pruny hands.

Not to mention a massive dread about Friday night.

♫

GUITARS ARE STUPID, vile, disgusting things, and only a moron would want to play one.

Biting my lip so hard I figured blood would start spurting any moment, I bent my head over the instrument of torture and tried tuning it the way my teacher suggested, but nothing I did sounded like it made a bit of difference. I sucked, and my guitar sucked worse.

I couldn't even finger a stupid chord without my fingertips screaming in pain, let alone strum something that didn't make the rest of me scream. I'd also ripped off the tip of a fingernail, and the jagged edge to it was driving me crazy.

My teacher was a young woman—Jazz—and nice enough as far as that goes, but I'd been hoping for a guy. I *knew* how to tease and flirt with guys to get them to do what I wanted.

In this case, I needed someone to work a miracle and turn me into a decent guitar player by Friday night.

With another jarring twang, I gave up trying to tune the stupid guitar. Running a hand through my hair and catching my fingers on a snarl, I groaned.

"Couldn't you just tune it?" Wasn't that what I was paying her for? "Like I keep telling you, I have to play this gig on Friday, and I don't need to know how to tune my guitar. I mean, once it's tuned, it's tuned, right? So shouldn't we focus on chords and songs? There's this Green Day song I wanted to learn."

Jazz smirked and rolled her eyes.

I waited for her to say something, but she just nodded at my guitar as if she was waiting for me to tune it and didn't plan to help me one bit. I mean, except for telling me when I was doing it wrong. Like, all the time.

I frowned at her. "What? You don't like Green Day?"

"Sure. They're okay." Her lips twitched in this really unattractive way, reminding me of the smirks Liz gave me when I said pretty much anything. "But trust me. You're not ready for Green Day."

"Well, not today. Duh." Even though I'd been hoping. "It's only Tuesday, so we have plenty of time. They told you I booked lessons for tomorrow and Thursday, right?"

She sighed. "I hoped that was a typo on my schedule."

"Hey, if you can't teach me—" I gave her the kind of pointed look I got all the time from Dad, which probably wasn't the smartest idea, but I was beyond frustrated. "Someone else here probably wouldn't mind."

"Oh, I can teach you, all right. But no matter who teaches you, you won't be playing Green Day by Friday. We're maybe talking 'Twinkle, Twinkle, Little Star,' tops."

Slapping her silly was probably out of the question. "I told you I'm willing to work. I'll do whatever it takes to play decently on Friday, and it's just rhythm guitar, not lead."

"Thank God for small miracles." Jazz took another deep breath, reminding me of Dad and all the Zen breathing he did when he was around me for more than ten minutes. "No offense, but you can't learn guitar in a few days, at least not more than a few chords."

Then why did Kirk act like it was so easy? "But the band already has someone who plays bass guitar."

Jazz choked on something. "Bass isn't easy, either. Not at all."

"Hey, I've watched guys play bass. Four strings and they just seem to pluck at them? How much easier—"

Jazz held up a hand, cutting me off. "Do you want to learn

guitar or not? You keep telling me about this gig on Friday." She rolled her eyes, the jerk. "But all you're doing is talking, when you're supposed to be learning to tune a guitar. I swear we're spending half of your lesson talking."

"You say that like it's my fault. I *asked* you to cut the boring stuff and just tune my guitar for me. Then we can get to the music already."

"Mistake." Shaking her head, she grabbed my guitar and tuned it in about thirty seconds. "But you're paying for this. We'll try doing it your way and see how that goes."

"Thanks. So let's get started, okay?"

Another eye roll. "Whatever you want, Princess."

I knew I should've insisted on having a guy teach me. For starters, when a guy called me "Princess," it meant something entirely different.

Chapter 7

*[E]ven Lydia was too much fatigued to utter more than
the occasional exclamation of "Lord, how tired I am!"
accompanied by a violent yawn.*

— Jane Austen, *Pride and Prejudice*
Volume I, Chapter Eighteen

AT LUNCH ON Wednesday, I dragged my feet over to Cat's new
table, which was as far from my usual table as you could get
without sitting outside. I glanced out the windows to the sunlit
courtyard and wished I'd kept walking.

I cut straight over here from Political Science, with a slight
detour to grab a Coke out of the vending machine, after taking
one look at the lunch line and feeling the remains of breakfast
gurgle in my stomach.

Right now, I couldn't face anything: food, Kirk, or anyone
else who might say anything. I figured I'd be safe with Cat. To
the extent humanly possible, she didn't speak to me.

I glanced at Jeremy and her, eating off each other's trays. A
few other strays sat at their table, a couple of art-freak girls and
three guys who played in band or orchestra but didn't do much

else.

"Okay if I sit with you guys?"

The girl next to Cat, a tiny wisp of a thing who seemed too engrossed in her sketchpad to have noticed me, looked up and smiled brightly, then frowned when she saw it was me. She glanced at Cat, who seemed oblivious to everyone but Jeremy.

Or she was pretending to be, anyway.

I set my tray down but didn't ask again and didn't plan to. For this kind of treatment, I might as well sit by Amber or Chelsea. When Cat still didn't look up, the art-freak girl finally nudged Cat. Hard.

Cat would've slugged me if I'd done it.

"Lydia?" Cat acted as if she hadn't seen me standing here. Right. "What, uh, brings you here?"

I wasn't actually sure. The fact that Kirk would probably bug me again about playing on Friday? Or maybe it was even simpler than that: I'd stayed up half the night practicing guitar in the basement, fueling myself on stale Doritos and a six-pack of Coke. I'd woken up feeling like hell. My eyes burned, my stomach felt like someone had whacked it with a machete, and it hadn't even been worth it.

I finally understood what Jazz meant: all the lessons and practicing in the world wouldn't teach me crap about guitar in time for Friday night.

Shrugging, I ignored everyone else at Cat's table and sat down. "I just felt like it. Amber and Chelsea are both a pain in the ass."

Especially when they were convinced I was trying to steal their boyfriends, even though it wasn't true. I was trying to steal only one of their boyfriends. Chelsea could keep hers, although she probably had to use all ten of her fingernails on a daily basis to manage it.

"No kidding."

The wispy-looking girl, who'd probably blow away and splatter against the wall if a strong breeze blew through the cafeteria, said it. Cat just looked at Jeremy, who hadn't even glanced in my direction. As if I didn't exist.

Weird.

I popped the top on my Coke as I glanced at everyone else's lunch trays. Cat had a quesadilla, her usual default choice. Jeremy had barely touched his cheeseburger, but that was what happened when a guy got so stupid over a girl. The two art waifs grazed on salads. Ready to barf, I didn't let myself look at the guys at the far end of the table.

I should've gone outside.

Why hadn't I? Cat had made it crystal clear what she thought of me coming home: not much. I didn't know anyone else at this table, but that was why I *had* come over here. I didn't want anyone to bug me about Friday night. I didn't even want a guy like Drew drooling over me, which had to be the definition of a lousy mood.

Jeremy finally caught my eye for an instant before his gaze skittered away from me and back to Cat. "Kirk says you're playing with us? On Friday night?"

"Are you asking Cat or me? I hear Cat already went that route, but it didn't go so well."

Jeremy glared at me, his right fist clenching under Cat's hand. "She didn't—"

Cat rubbed his hand. "She's just trying to get a reaction, Jeremy. Forget it."

Was that what I was trying to do? But why did a girl *have* to work so hard to get a reaction out of her own twin sister?

"Hey, Jeremy's the one who mentioned playing with the band, not me." I tapped a hand on my chest as my empty stomach finally rumbled. "I'm an innocent bystander."

"Right." Cat sounded snotty, so much like Amber or

Chelsea, I wondered why she didn't hang out with them. I mean, seriously. "You're totally innocent."

I stared at the rim of my Coke can, trying not to let her words dig a hole inside of me. I was invincible, wasn't I? The leader of the gang? Even if my so-called gang was sitting on the other side of the cafeteria and didn't seem to notice I was missing?

Grabbing my Coke, I lurched to my feet. "Well, it's been real. Catch you later, Cat. At home? Sometime this year?"

She didn't even look up when I headed outside, and neither did Jeremy or any of their geektoid friends. But I didn't give a rat's ass. I'd show them all on Friday night. Somehow, I'd figure out how to play my guitar, because I was going to be the star of Woodbury High School again.

Or at least, please God, not a freaking embarrassment.

"LYDIA, IT'S AFTER midmight. Go to bed. You have school tomorrow."

Not if I cut class, which was the only hope I had at this point of making Friday night work for me. Unless, of course, I could get one of the guys in Green Day to sit in for me.

I glanced at Mom, standing at the bottom of the basement stairs, and tried not to roll my eyes at her paint-stained bathrobe and the ratty nightgown she wore underneath it. She'd driven me to school in that outfit too many times to count, which was probably why Dad finally bought the Jeep: to keep Mom inside the house until she put on something decent for work.

"I'll head upstairs in a little bit, Mom." Like, in two or three hours, which was how long it'd take me to finally nail this C chord. If I was lucky. "Promise."

She nodded, smiling at me, but winced when I mangled the chord again and it sounded like Boris when I tossed him off my bed and he flew through the air.

"I'm glad you're enjoying guitar so much, dear, but sleep is important, too."

So was a well-balanced diet, but no one who lived in this house got one.

I gingerly touched my sore fingertips with my thumb, wishing someone would invent a painless method of playing guitar. Jazz kept telling me everyone went through this. I wouldn't put it past her to lie to me.

"Honest. I'll go to bed as soon as I get the hang of this chord." I strummed it again, trying not to flinch.

Mom actually looked like she didn't believe me. Or maybe like she wanted to either return the guitar to the store or burn it. "You may want to go to bed and try again after school tomorrow. Everything always seems fresher in the morning. Or, well, afternoon. It's already quite late, and I—"

"I'll be upstairs right behind you. Really."

Depending on one's definition, of course. My own definition was usually pretty flexible.

"But I think you should—"

I held up a hand. "Mom, seriously. I'm seventeen. I know when I need to go to bed."

Now, probably. I covered a yawn with my hand, but not fast enough to escape Mom's sharp gaze.

Tsking, she walked across the basement to where I sat hunched over my guitar, eased it from my grasp, and set it on the stand. A moment later she turned off my amp and tugged me to my feet. Next thing I knew, I was leaning back on my bed, propped against the wall. Fine. I'd humor Mom, then sneak back down to the basement in ten minutes and shut the doors at the top *and* bottom of the basement stairs so I could practice all night without anyone hearing me.

The only problem?

I woke up, tucked in bed with my covers pulled up to my chin, a half hour before school started the next morning.

Argh!

♫

I WASTED TEN whole minutes trying to talk Mom into letting me cut school today—just this once!—and then had to shower, dress, and eat in record time. Cat nabbed the Jeep and left for school before I finished getting ready. Sure, it was only four minutes before school started, but you could make it in two minutes if you didn't obsess about stop signs and took the corners on two wheels.

Mom didn't drive like that—at least, not when she was on her meds—so the final bell rang just as I leaped out of Mom's dented gray Saab and slammed the door.

I flew up the steps of school, ran past my locker on my way to Speech Communications, and skidded to a stop in the doorway.

"Welcome to class, Lydia. Glad you could join us."

I heard a few snickers as Ms. Ciccarelli met me at the door, her gaze landing on my backpack.

She frowned. "You remember, don't you, that students can't bring backpacks into class?"

I'd remembered it every step of my sprint down the hall. A new school rule they adopted last year just because some jerk called in a fake bomb threat. "Yeah, but I was running late."

She sighed. "Leave it by my desk, please, and then find a seat."

"Nice going, loser. Forget anything else today?"

Chelsea's whiny voice carried all the way from the back of the room.

As I opened my mouth to slam her, Ms. Ciccarelli touched my arm and gave me a tiny head shake. She actually looked sympathetic, which surprised me. I couldn't remember the last time a teacher had been genuinely nice to me after the first ten minutes of the first day of class each year.

Ms. Ciccarelli pointed to an open seat by the window—right behind that annoying Heather MacAndrews—before striding to the back of the room.

"Chelsea, I realize this is Speech class, but your form of communication isn't what I'm trying to develop in my students." This time the snickers weren't aimed at me, and Chelsea's face flamed a really unattractive shade of brick red. "Unless you'd like a trip to Mr. Paymar's office, I assume we won't be hearing from you again until I actually call on you."

"Ms. Ciccarelli, she's just so—"

Ms. Ciccarelli whirled on Chelsea, whose words broke off. She then rat-a-tat-tatted back to her desk at the front of the room, where she jotted something on a sheet of paper. The grim set to her mouth was softened by the vase of pink roses at her elbow, but not much.

"Chelsea?" Picking up the sheet on which she'd just written, Ms. Ciccarelli motioned my favorite pal to the front of the room. "Please give this to Mr. Paymar. I've also requested that the nurse administer a hearing test, since you seem to be having difficulty with that this morning."

As Chelsea tried to argue again, the idiot, a roar of laughter broke out in the room. I glanced around, trying not to grin too much in case Ms. Ciccarelli busted me for it, but I didn't see Drew laughing or even smiling.

Instead, he was totally scoping me out, one eyebrow raised in an unspoken question.

We both knew his question wasn't if I planned to play with the band tomorrow night.

♫

I STOMPED MY foot as the sound of my putrid E chord reverberated around the small practice room at the music store. "I can't do this!"

Jazz looked up from her own guitar, still strumming the same chord, which sounded a lot different coming out of her guitar. Maybe if I'd gotten a more expensive guitar . . .

"You're actually doing okay, you know." She blew a bubble with her gum, an annoying habit she'd started in the middle of my first lesson after first pulling a pack of cigarettes out of her guitar case and then blinking when she realized she couldn't light up in here. "Be patient. It's coming."

I shook my head. "It's not coming fast enough."

"To play a gig tomorrow night?" She laughed, not even pretending she empathized with my perfectly understandable problem. "Hey, I told you that on Tuesday."

"You told me you could teach me."

"Teach you? Yeah. Teach you by Friday? Princess, *no* one could teach you enough to play a gig by Friday, which is exactly what I told you at your first lesson."

I huffed out an exasperated breath. Exasperated with this stupid guitar, with Jazz, even with myself. It had to be a first.

"Yeah, well, I'm still gonna play."

And it would turn out okay, somehow, even if I had to fake the chords I didn't know, which was pretty much all of them. Kirk was going to fall all over himself to dump Amber and hook up with me.

"Good luck with that." Jazz was chewing her gum again, but

she stopped blowing bubbles near my face. She also sounded different somehow, the snottiness gone from her voice. "I mean it. Everyone has to play their first gig, and most people blow it, but at least you're getting the experience out of the way early."

I gritted my teeth. "I'm not going to blow it."

"Hey, I'll drink to that." She grinned, as if the thought amused her. "The minute I get off work tonight."

I wished I could join her.

♫

I TRIED EATING a burger for lunch on Friday, despite my panicking stomach, and I tried sitting at my old table again, next to Kirk.

Neither idea worked out too well.

So much for hoping no one would bug me about tonight's gig. Kids kept stopping by our table, wishing me luck. Sincerely, but as if I needed it, which made no sense. No one at school except Cat knew I'd never touched a guitar before Monday night, so why did everyone think I needed all this luck?

Cat wouldn't have blabbed, would she? My own twin sister? My former partner in too many crimes to count?

No way.

For one thing, I'd kill her.

When another girl I didn't know left our table after wishing me "all the luck in the world," Kirk turned to me and grinned. "All set for tonight? Or would you rather bag out on it? Like I told you, Heather said she'd be happy to play."

I'd also kill Heather, then toss Chelsea and Amber onto the funeral pyre for good measure.

I grinned back at Kirk, even though my teeth hurt and my stomach clenched. "No problem. I'm all over it."

His eyebrows went up. "Hey, did Cat give you our song list? I told Jeremy to make a copy for her to give you."

When Kirk could've given me a copy any day this week? Or driven over to my house? Was he too tempted by me to trust himself?

I shook my head. Yet another reason to kill Cat.

"Weird. But no prob." He reached into his backpack, which kids weren't supposed to have in the cafeteria, either, but rules like that never applied to Kirk. In the old days, they hadn't applied to me, either. "I have an extra copy right here."

I bit my lip as I scanned the sheet. Sure, I recognized most of the songs, but I didn't know how to *play* anything. Jazz had taught me to play exactly five chords, and not well, and we'd started working on "Knockin' on Heaven's Door" last night. She hadn't taught me anything remotely useful, though. Like, how to skip town and never be found again.

"Does it look okay?" Kirk's brow furrowed as he studied me, and it probably mirrored the look on my own face.

"Sure. Fine." I set the song list down on the corner of my tray before my hands started shaking. Every other part of me was already shaking, and Kirk didn't usually miss much.

"So you're good to play?"

"I, uh—" My brain scrambled for an excuse, but I'd spent all week trying to come up with one, with no luck. Epic brain failure. "Yeah, I think so. But like I said before—" Only a million times. "It'd be better if we practiced first."

Kirk shrugged. "That's why the band is getting together early to practice. Six o'clock. Didn't Cat mention that to you, either?" After another long look at me, and a glance across the cafeteria in the direction of the table where Cat and Jeremy sat, Kirk swiveled his head as if he was looking for someone. After a moment, he whistled as Heather MacAndrews came into the cafeteria from outside. "Yo, Heather!"

After waving to Kirk, she dropped her books at Cat's table, then joined us. Tall and willowy, and almost gorgeous if you liked strawberry blondes with freckles, she didn't seem to realize how good she looked. Well, from some guys' perspectives.

Kirk wasn't that kind of guy, but a grin lit his face. "Heather, you know Lydia, right? Can you still play tonight? I mean, if Lydia can't? Or maybe you two could even alternate songs."

I frowned. I didn't share a stage—or the spotlight—with any other girl, and I didn't plan to change that tonight.

"Like I said, Kirk, if Heather's already in your band, no problem. I'll find another one." Like, in about five years, when I eventually learned how to play chords without making everyone around me wince.

Heather shook her head. "I don't need to play tonight, Lydia. Kirk asked you first. I can do it some other time. Or, like you said, with some other band."

She even looked sweet as she said it. Genuinely.

I glanced across the cafeteria as if I had better things to do. Unfortunately, except for running as far away from this school as quickly as possible, I didn't. "It doesn't matter to me which of us plays."

Part of me would be relieved if Heather played, but I'd never backed down from a challenge in my life. Torn between wanting to impress Kirk and wanting to avoid the distinct possibility of school-wide humiliation, I finally realized I was clenching my fists.

Kirk looked at both of us, then across the table at Amber, who didn't exactly look thrilled at the prospect of *either* Heather or me playing.

Finally, he looked up at Heather. "Sorry, but you're right. I did ask Lydia first."

"No problem! I'll come watch you guys tonight if that's okay." Still smiling, Heather headed back to Cat's table. Cat and

Jeremy both greeted her like a long-lost friend, even though they treated me like dirt. Not that this bothered me or, for instance, made me want to rip Cat's hair out.

Watching the three of them, I sighed. Technically, I'd won this battle, but I was going to go down in flames. Knowing my friends, someone would bring marshmallows to roast.

♫

HEAD DOWN TO avoid the constant stream of kids wishing me luck—and were they really wishing me luck, or hoping I fell flat on my face?—I plodded into fourth-period Accounting and took my seat. Goth-chick Lauren was already there, filing and buffing her sharp claws as she pointedly didn't look at me. A bottle of black nail polish sat on the corner of her desk.

I took a slow breath, relieved that at least Lauren didn't seem to give a rat's ass about my gig.

"Playing guitar tonight, huh?"

So much for staying off the radar of the one girl in school who didn't hang out with anyone I knew.

I shrugged. "Yeah. I guess."

"Do you even play? I heard—"

I held up a hand to cut her off as I kept an eye peeled for Ms. Frey. "I play. But I've never practiced with Kirk's band before, so I'm not sure how it'll go down."

"Yeah? Your sister Cat is telling everyone that you don't know how to play. She said you just got a guitar this week, and you've been staying up all night trying to learn it, and you're just jealous because your sister Mary was so good." Lauren shook the bottle of nail polish, then unscrewed the top and started in on her left hand. "Man, I'm glad I just have a baby brother. It must suck to have so many sisters to compete with."

"I don't compete with anyone." I wasn't sure if I said that out loud or in my head, but at least in my head it came out in a dull monotone.

But my stomach started churning wildly the moment Lauren told me what a total shit Cat had turned into. We'd always been best friends. What had I ever done to her? Be more popular? Get more guys? Talk Mom and Dad into sending me to Wisconsin Dells that summer?

I couldn't help any of that, could I? Wasn't I just born this way? On top of the world?

"Hey, are you okay?"

I blinked as the bell rang. Ms. Frey closed the door with a bang, and Lauren's voice made its way through the haze suddenly clouding my brain.

But . . . Cat told everyone? Kirk and the rest of the band? And they were all laughing at me now the way everyone laughed at Cat when she sang with the band last spring?

"Lydia? Are you there?"

"Of course she's here, Lauren. The weekend homework assignment is on the board. You might want to consider writing it down and perhaps even doing it this weekend."

Somewhere in my brain I registered Ms. Frey's soft-soled shoes coming down the aisle in my direction, but my head was spinning—Cat?—and I could barely remember how to breathe.

Cat did that to me?

The footsteps stopped at my desk, but no one said a word, not even Ms. Frey. It was as if twenty-five kids and one teacher were collectively holding their breath. Was *I* even breathing?

Ms. Frey's hand was on my desk now, but not touching me. In some remote corner of my brain I registered neatly trimmed nails, no polish, not even a ring. Words were coming out of her mouth, but the roar inside my own head drowned them out.

Cat did this to ME?

"Lydia? Lydia." The hand on my desk suddenly slapped the top of it, and I blinked.

"Uh, yeah?"

"Should I send someone with you to the school nurse?" Ms. Frey glanced around the room, looking for volunteers. To my left, Lauren raised her hand. "Someone other than Lauren?"

I blinked again, a few times, and the haze started to clear. No one was laughing, but I felt like an idiot. "No. I mean, I'm okay. Fine."

"You're sure?"

I sucked a deep gulp of air into my lungs, so deep I coughed hard. "Totally."

After a last long look, she frowned and headed back to the front of the room, and I started scribbling her mind-boggling homework assignment into my notebook.

I finally realized Lauren was leaning in my direction when her scratchy voice hit my ears. "Your sister is just being a bitch, and you'll do fine. Besides, you get an excuse to hang with Zach Lashinski. He's hot."

Frowning, I glanced at Ms. Frey before whispering back at Lauren. "Zach? The bass player? You think he's hot?"

"Totally. But I'm not really his type, and I'm pretty sure you wouldn't be, either."

Apparently, I wasn't the only screwed-up person in this room. Lauren was so out of touch, she didn't know I could get any guy I wanted. Not that I wanted a guy with a Cat in the Hat tattoo.

I wanted Kirk. And he'd soon be mine.

But why I needed to play a stupid guitar to make it happen, I have no idea.

Chapter 8

It was not to be supposed that time
would give Lydia that embarrassment from which
she had been so wholly free at first.

— Jane Austen, *Pride and Prejudice*
Volume III, Chapter Nine

FOR THE FIRST time since Dad exiled me to Mary's skanky, Boris-filled room last weekend, I was actually glad I didn't have to share my old bedroom with Cat. I didn't need her to see me hyperventilating as I tried to find something to wear tonight. Preferably, something that made me look invisible.

So far, no luck.

Hands on my hips, I chewed on my lip as I glanced again at the outfit I'd laid out on my bed. Black skinny jeans. Check. But my new red boots and cute top suddenly looked . . . wrong. As in, the opposite of invisible, which meant they'd call even more attention to my inept fingers. For the first time in my life, I didn't want attention.

Why had I done this? Amber obviously hadn't played guitar to hook Kirk. Amber would have trouble playing solitaire, let alone a musical instrument.

"Knock knock." Actually, no one knocked on my door, which suddenly swung open under the power of Liz's rude hand. "How's the family's newest musician?"

As Liz and Jane walked into my room, followed by a sullen Cat, I kicked my red boots under the bed. Hissing, Boris went after them. "I don't remember inviting anyone in."

"That's why we had to take the initiative. Even though I'm usually pretty respectful of a person's privacy."

Even Jane raised her eyebrows at Liz.

"Good." I grabbed my jeans and top off the bed, rolled them into a ball I'd probably regret later, and tossed them in the closet. "Because I like to be alone."

Okay, being alone was actually new to me, and something I'd *never* craved, but I'd take it over hanging out with sanctimonious sisters, not to mention a snake like Cat. I couldn't even look at her. I might poke her eyes out if I did.

No one said anything. Finally, Jane went over to my closet, stooped down to retrieve my outfit, and shook it out. "New top? It's cute. I like how it goes with the boots under your bed."

So much for hiding anything from Jane, at least.

Her gaze swept the room, landing on my guitar. "And it'll look good with your guitar. I see Mom took you shopping."

I whirled on her. "What's *that* supposed to mean? That my clothes suck?"

Liz took a step toward me, as if she actually had to defend Jane from me, but Jane waved her off. She glanced at the door, nodded to Cat to shut it, then took a step closer. My outfit dangled from her fingers.

"Mom may not be perfect—"

She frowned at Liz, who snorted.

"—but we all know she's the consummate shopper. She bought you a guitar, and her eye probably twitched until you let her buy you a rock-star outfit. Am I right?"

Close. It took only two seconds of twitching to get me to agree to the outfit.

I shrugged. "I pick out my own clothes."

Jane lifted one eyebrow. "You don't let Mom pay for them? I would."

"And often have." Liz nudged Jane with her elbow, and they both laughed.

Cat was the only one not saying anything. She stood by the closed door, sneaking furtive glances at it as if she'd rather escape the first chance she got.

Smart girl. I hadn't yet ruled out killing her.

"So." Liz stepped toward me again, but this time not looking quite as menacing. At least, not overtly. "You've got a gig tonight at Kirk's house. What time? Eight?"

"We're supposed to practice at six. Just the band." I hoped.

I resisted the urge to look at the clock on Mary's desk, even though the ticking sounded like a time bomb. I had less than half an hour to get there on time, not that it mattered. Without a crowd around, the band would *really* hear how badly I played. I could strum my A and G chords competently. On a good day, and with some luck, maybe E. D and C, no way. And I hadn't even tried anything else. My fingertips ached from practicing, and my ego was about to hurt even worse.

"So get dressed. We'll all go."

My gaze flew to Liz's face. She wasn't smirking, which only meant she might be getting better at hiding it.

Although I doubted it.

"You're not coming. The practice is just for the band." Please, God, let it be true. "And you and Jane don't go to high-school parties."

Cat looked like she'd rather claw her way through the closed door than stay in this room another second. Fine by me.

Liz grinned, which meant that my evening was about to go

from bad to disastrous. "Jane and I have gone to a lot of high-school parties. We love high-school parties."

Jane rolled her eyes.

"In fact, we went to a great party at Kirk's house last spring. Didn't we have fun, Jane?"

Cat rolled her eyes this time, but Jane actually nodded. "We had more fun than Kirk and Tess, definitely."

Something flickered in Cat's eyes—a cross between cocky and horrified—and I realized she hadn't told me about it. I couldn't imagine what Jane might've done. I mean, she never did anything wrong. Liz? I could imagine a lot.

Jane handed me my outfit. "Really, Lydia. We're going. We should've gone last year when Cat sang with the band, and I'd rather not make that mistake again."

"It wasn't your mistake, it was Cat's." I glared at her. "But Cat makes a lot of mistakes."

"We all do." Jane backed toward the door, towing Liz along with her. "But I try never to make the same mistake twice."

I threw my outfit against the wall. "Thanks, but I don't need your help."

"True." Liz opened the door, shooing Cat and Jane out before turning back to me. "You need Mary's help. But Mary isn't here."

"Thank God for small favors."

"Yeah, and thank your sisters for bigger ones. Babe, you're going to appreciate this."

I crossed the room in three strides and slammed the door on Liz's smug face.

"Don't hold your breath."

"GET IN THE Jeep already."

My guitar case slung over one shoulder, I shook my head at Liz. I'd already told her I wasn't climbing into any car driven by Cat—not ever again—and Cat was behind the wheel of the Jeep.

Leave it to Cat *not* to ride with Jeremy the one time I wish she'd disappear with him, preferably forever. But I couldn't tell Liz or even Jane what Cat had done to me—what she'd told everyone in school—because I wouldn't put it past Liz to laugh.

"You're going to be late."

"Whatever. I'm not driving with Cat."

Liz rolled her eyes, then started talking slowly, enunciating each word as if she was talking to a toddler. "We're all driving there together."

"Not if Cat's behind the wheel. And I told you the party doesn't start until eight. The guys in the band are the only ones showing up at six."

God, I hoped that was true. I didn't need Amber to see this. It was bad enough that *I* had to be there.

Liz and Jane looked at each other, sharing some sort of secret language that only the two of them understood. It'd always been like that with them, which was why I still didn't understand what they were up to. Did they just want to witness my destruction? Hadn't the YouTube videos from the strip bar in Milwaukee been enough for them?

With an exasperated huff, Liz climbed into the passenger seat of the Jeep. I stayed on the sidewalk, not budging.

"Come on." Jane motioned to me, then dug into her purse and extracted a key ring. When I still didn't move, she headed to her Prius, parked at the curb right behind the Jeep. "We'll go in the Prius."

I glanced at the Jeep and back again at Jane. When I opened my mouth to ask what was going on, the Jeep's engine revved up and Cat peeled away from the curb.

Leaving me with Jane.

A lightbulb went off in my brain. As an English major, Jane knew all about fiction. Maybe she could come up with a fictional reason why I couldn't go tonight.

"Hey, could we—"

Jane shook her head. "We're going to the party, Lydia. Kirk's a friend of yours, right?" Her nose scrunched, letting me know exactly what she thought without saying the words. "If he's any friend, he'll understand when you tell him you don't want to play guitar."

"You mean that I *can't* play guitar. Cat already told the whole school."

"She didn't."

"She did."

I followed Jane to the Prius, stowing my guitar in the back seat before I got in, but I wondered if I should just put my guitar back in the house. Let's face it: one way or another, I wasn't going to be playing anything tonight. I had no idea why I'd insisted on playing with Kirk's band. Like Kirk said, Heather could play with them instead.

Which of course was why I said I'd play.

"We can leave your guitar in the car if you want. You don't have to bring it inside."

"You don't understand—" I bit off the rest of what I almost said, remembering that I was talking to Jane. Always perfect, totally loved by everyone even without trying.

"I do understand." She opened the driver's door but didn't climb in, probably wondering if I'd bolt the moment she did. Unlike Liz, she wouldn't be able to catch me. But running from Jane wouldn't solve my problems. Shrugging, I climbed into the passenger seat.

Ready to face my doom.

♪

"YOU MADE IT." Kirk waved at me from the far end of the cavernous living room, where the rest of the band was already assembled and busy tuning their instruments. His grin faltered when he saw I didn't have a guitar. "Aren't you playing? Where's your guitar?"

"It's—" In the Prius, I almost said. But didn't.

Behind me, Jane nudged me in the back, but I had no idea what she wanted me to do. She and I hadn't exactly worked out nonverbal communication yet. At this point, we weren't even too good with verbal.

"It's where? Are you playing?" As Kirk spoke to me, he kept looking over my shoulder at Jane. But not with the dopey look most guys had on their face when they looked at Jane.

"Lydia? What's going on?"

I blinked, realizing Kirk was staring at *me* now. I'd spent the last week trying to come up with a decent answer to his question, and I'd never been so stymied in my life.

"I'd like to—"

"What Lydia means to say is—" Jane brushed past me, moving toward him, and it shocked me when he backed up a step. Almost as if he was afraid of her. Weird! "She can't stay. She was just stopping by to let you know."

I couldn't stay? Did Jane know something I didn't? As she twisted sideways to give me a smile Kirk couldn't see, I frowned at her. I couldn't walk out on Kirk's band, let alone Kirk, without the best excuse of my life. I *wanted* Kirk. Blowing him off was no way to get him.

Was it?

Based on the storm cloud racing across his face, no.

When Jane grabbed my arm, I shrugged her off. Maybe if I could catch Kirk alone, I could explain the guitar problem. Actually, maybe we didn't even have to talk about guitars. We could talk about the two of us.

"Lydia?" Kirk sidestepped Jane, as if she was covered in poison ivy. "Is this about you not playing guitar? I heard—"

Behind me, Liz's voice broke in. "You heard about Lydia and Mary teaming up tonight to perform a special early gift for our parents' twenty-fifth anniversary? How would you? Mary flew in from college as a surprise this afternoon, and even Lydia didn't know about it until we got Mary's call from the airport."

Jane nodded. "That's why Lydia can't play at your party. She's been playing guitar a lot longer than Mary, but Mary thought it'd be sweet if they both played for our parents."

"Lydia, is that true? I heard you don't even play guitar. Or you just started playing this week." Kirk's voice sounded strangled, and I glanced at the guys in the band, who looked confused as hell. Especially Jeremy. With Liz and Jane on either side of me now, I sneaked a quick glance behind me. No Cat. No surprise.

Since she was the one who'd busted me with Kirk and everyone else who mattered, she couldn't exactly hang around while Liz and Jane served up major whoppers just to save my ass. Why they cared enough to do it, I had no idea.

And weren't Mom and Dad coming up on their twenty-*third* anniversary?

In any case, I obviously couldn't grab a moment alone with Kirk. I'd begged the Universe for an excuse to get out of playing tonight, and Jane and Liz had come through. I had to go with it, even if it only postponed my doom.

I shrugged. "Kirk, I'm really sorry. Like they said, it was a huge surprise to me, but I guess that's what sisters do. At least my sisters."

Liz punched my arm as Jane wrapped an arm around my shoulder and squeezed a little too hard.

She gave Kirk a bright smile. "We really have to run. Sorry! Jeremy, Cat asked me to let you know that she can't make it tonight, either."

I shuffled alongside Jane and Liz as we headed out of the living room and through the long front hall to the front door. Cat, who was waiting by the Jeep, didn't look happy about this weird twist of events orchestrated by Jane and Liz.

I knew the feeling.

♫

"WHAT THE FUCK?"

I hauled up short at the Prius, refusing to go anywhere near Cat or the Jeep, which was parked three cars away. Jane and Liz were already at the driver's door of the Prius, their heads bent together, whispering, even though they seemed to have the telepathic thing down cold. Even before I left for Wisconsin Dells—and Milwaukee and Shangri-La—Cat and I had never been like that.

I stepped between them. "Is Mary really in town? Or was that some lame excuse to get me out of playing tonight?"

"It worked, didn't it?" Liz gave Jane a high-five, totally ignoring how I felt about it. "Don't tell me you wanted to play guitar tonight."

"I didn't ask you to—" I swallowed hard as a million emotions swirled through me. Embarrassment at hiding behind my sisters. Relief at not playing, even though the relief would last only until the next time Kirk's band played. Crushing anger at all three of my sisters who'd done this to me, but especially Cat. She hadn't even been in the room with us when it all went down tonight, but it was her fault that everyone knew I didn't play guitar, and she'd pay.

"Babe, if you want to play, you can still grab your guitar and go right back inside." Liz shook her head. "No one's stopping you."

It was more complicated than that, and Liz knew it.

She gave me a strange look. "You don't know how to play guitar, do you?"

Besides the A, G, and E chords, and not even those all that well? Not exactly. "I'm taking lessons."

"That's great." Jane smiled at me, but since she'd smiled the same way at Kirk five minutes ago, it didn't exactly comfort me. "But Cat told us—and so did Mom—that you just got a guitar on Monday night. You know it took Mary at least three months, right? And I have the impression that was pretty fast."

I rolled my eyes. "Why does everyone keep comparing me with Mary? But is it true? Is she in town this weekend?"

Jane shook her head. "I couldn't think of a better excuse. Sorry. And the anniversary—"

"It's not for two more years. Yeah, I did the math."

I glanced down the street as a car cruised toward us. It was too early for the party, but I wouldn't put it past Amber or Chelsea to show up now. To keep an eye on me or just to laugh hysterically the moment I mangled my first chord.

"You guys didn't do me any favors. I still have to play guitar sometime, and now I'll be teased mercilessly in school on Monday for having my sisters protect me. Thanks a lot."

"You're welcome." Liz must've spotted the car coming down the street, too, and headed for the Jeep as Jane unlocked the Prius. "We went through this with Kirk once before, you know. He won't give you any grief on Monday."

"Right."

Liz opened the passenger door to the Jeep but glanced back

at me. "Ask Cat. We did it for her last year, which is probably why she came up with the idea to do it tonight for you."

"Well, no wonder." I shot another glare at Cat, the little shit. "I'll be sure to thank her personally."

The first chance I got.

♫

I SPENT THE rest of the weekend—when I wasn't wrestling my Accounting homework into submission—plotting my revenge.

Against Cat.

It wasn't Jane's or Liz's fault, after all. They were just dupes for my twin sister. It wasn't Kirk's fault, either, or anyone else's in the band. They'd all just jumped on Cat's nasty gossip the way a starving dog lunged after a bone.

No, this was all on Cat. If I happened to nail anyone else— like, say, Chelsea or Amber—that was just a bonus.

I leaped out of bed and got the first jump on the shower Monday morning, then caught an early ride to school with Mom, who kept asking if I wouldn't rather ride in the Jeep with Cat. Not in this lifetime, but I just shook my head and claimed I needed to find something in the school media center.

I got to Speech class twenty minutes before the bell rang, which was fifteen minutes before anyone else would show up, but I didn't want to blow this. My plan involved taking Cat down, but it took a village to take down a sister, and I had to start somewhere. Chelsea would be excellent practice. Okay, I also wanted to avoid all the kids who'd see me in the hall and ask if I'd bailed on Kirk's party because I couldn't play guitar.

Striding to the back of the room, I grabbed the desk Chelsea had sat in all of last week. She'd just sit on the other side of Drew, but it would bug her, and that would be satisfying enough. For now.

Sure enough, Drew and several other kids arrived five minutes before the bell rang. I'd already noticed that Drew and Chelsea didn't usually walk in together, which probably meant they weren't driving to school together, which surprised me. I mean, Chelsea didn't seem bright enough to pass a driver's test. No wonder Drew liked her. No challenge.

A grin lit Drew's face as he headed to the back of the room and sat in the desk next to me.

He glanced to the front of the room, probably keeping an eye out for Chelsea, before leaning in my direction. "Missed you on Friday night. At Kirk's house."

"Yeah. Couldn't make it, thanks to my stupid family." I lifted one shoulder, trying to look bummed. "Good party?"

Drew glanced again at the door. "Not as good without you."

"Which means . . . what?" I turned sideways, trying not to roll my eyes when he looked down my shirt, mostly just wishing Chelsea were here to see this.

He finally met my eyes, but not before scoping me out intensely enough to make me shiver. "Meaning . . . I'd still like to get together."

"Yeah?" That made one of us. "What about Chelsea?"

Speak of the devil. She scooted into the room as the bell rang, giggling with some other girl—Heather, I was startled to realize—and only belatedly glancing to the back of the room. By now all the seats around us had filled, and the snarl on her face told me she realized it.

Perfect.

As I grinned at her, I noticed that Ms. Ciccarelli hadn't shown up yet, which was probably why Chelsea stormed to the back of the room. She slammed her hand on top of my desk, making my pens fly.

"Not cool, Chelsea." I glanced around the room, seeing a

half dozen faces laughing at Chelsea, not me. At least, I hoped so. "What's your problem today?"

"Same as every day. You. You know I sit here. I thought you got over that."

Out of the corner of my eye I noticed Ms. Ciccarelli walk into the room and softly close the door, all the while zeroing in on Chelsea. Pasting an angelic look on my face, I bent down to pick my pens up off the floor.

Pens retrieved, I sat up straight again and arranged them in a line. Slowly, neatly, just to drive Chelsea nuts.

She knocked them off my desk with a sweep of her hand. "I *said*, I thought you got over that."

"And *I* thought, Chelsea, you'd learned not to create disturbances in my class." Ms. Ciccarelli was right behind Chelsea, who jumped at the sound of her voice. "Luckily for you, we're starting extemporaneous speeches today. I don't want you to miss it, so I can't send you to Mr. Paymar's office. I'll let you speak first, though."

From the look on Chelsea's face, she'd rather go to Mr. Paymar's office. Which was weird, really. What was the big deal? Extemporaneous meant no preparation. In other words, no homework. It didn't get any better than that.

Chelsea shot me a glare oozing with hatred, then one at Drew that wasn't much nicer. How did she manage to keep the guy?

She finally looked at Ms. Ciccarelli, having saved all her saccharine for her. "I'm sorry, really. It's just that I had all my stuff on that desk, but when I had to go to the bathroom, Lydia threw all my books on the floor and stole my desk."

I blinked as Ms. Ciccarelli's gaze narrowed on me. Chelsea had to be smarter than I thought to come up with a whopper like that. Of course, a mealworm had to be smarter than I'd given Chelsea credit for.

"Lydia? Is that true?"

I rolled my eyes. "Not even remotely. I was the first one here today, and Chelsea showed up ten seconds before you did. I could be wrong, but I think that was just Chelsea's first attempt at extemporaneous speech."

Several kids laughed, but Drew had a pained look on his face and Chelsea clenched her long, hot-pink nails into her fists.

"She's lying, Ms. Ciccarelli, like she always does. It's probably why she got sent to *reform* school." Chelsea smirked at me before giving Drew a disgustingly lewd look that probably promised a blowjob if he played this right. "Drew, it's like I said, right? Lydia stole my seat?"

Drew glanced from Chelsea to me, then finally up at Ms. Ciccarelli, looking like he wanted to barf. He also looked like he was about to rat me out in exchange for sexual favors from Chelsea. Talk about making a mistake. I'd crush him like a bug if he did.

I twisted sideways, catching his eye before straightening my shoulders for maximum cleavage. The bead of sweat on his upper lip hadn't been there a minute ago. I touched the tip of my tongue to the corner of my mouth. Casually.

Drew finally dragged his gaze away from me and looked at Ms. Ciccarelli, who was rolling her eyes. "I—"

Ms. Ciccarelli held up a hand. "Chelsea, find a different seat. Class, although we're focusing this week on extemporaneous speech, I think Chelsea and Lydia have just given us excellent examples of how to use body language in a debate to sway the judges."

She muttered something else under her breath as she headed to the front of the room. With a final look of disgust at both Drew and me, Chelsea stomped behind Ms. Ciccarelli to a desk at the front of the room. Everyone else just laughed.

So I'd won the battle, but was Drew the spoils of war?

Heaven help me.

Chapter 9

*Poor Lydia's situation must, at best, be bad enough;
but that it was no worse, she had need to be thankful.*

— Jane Austen, *Pride and Prejudice*
Volume III, Chapter Seven

BY THE END of third-period Political Science, I was almost ready to admit that Jane and Liz had been right: no one was giving me shit about Friday night.

Just to be safe, though, I cruised into the cafeteria and through the lunch line in record time. Kirk and Tess were already at my usual table, at opposite ends, but I beat everyone else. Hauling up short, I debated whether I should've taken more time getting here.

"Lydia." Kirk waved at me, maybe because he'd spotted the pinched look on Tess's face. "C'mon over. Hey, how was that thing for your parents?"

"Totally lame." I rolled my eyes as I set down my tray and took the seat next to Kirk. "My sisters like to spring things on unsuspecting victims."

"You don't have to tell me." Kirk glanced at Tess, who was

studiously avoiding both of us. "But it's cool. Heather played with us and turned out fine. She's really—"

"Hey, that's great." I didn't want to hear what Heather was, including way better than me at guitar. So was everyone. "Like I said, I was sorry I couldn't make it."

"Do you still want to play with us?"

"I'm, uh, not sure." My stomach churned, and I hadn't even touched a bite of my beef-and-bean burrito. I wanted to talk to Kirk alone. Like, seriously alone. Tess already made that impossible, and I spotted Amber heading to our table. "If Heather is playing with you guys, I don't need to."

"You still get first shot at it. Hey, I'm sorry I said you didn't play guitar. I don't know why Jer— I mean, why someone would've said it."

I sat up straight the moment he started to say "Jer." Jeremy said it? And Kirk couldn't connect the dots and realize that Jeremy heard it directly from Cat?

"Weird, huh?" I shrugged. "Yeah, I started playing years ago." At age four, on a toy guitar Mom bought for Cat and me in Mexico. "It's probably why Mary started playing."

So much for a serious chat with Kirk. I was lying my ass off, and Cat could bust me so easily. Oh, wait. She already had.

"So do you wanna practice with us? We're getting together on Thursday."

Thursday. Not exactly the six months from now I'd been hoping for. "Seriously, it's cool if Heather plays with you. I mean, she already did. It's not her fault I couldn't make it on Friday night."

"But she—"

"She's probably halfway decent at guitar, and the truth is that I've started thinking about getting back into—" I glanced around the cafeteria, trying to look casual, as my brain scrambled for an excuse. I sent up frantic prayers for anything.

Kirk's voice interrupted my frantic search. "Into what?"

Finally, it hit me. My excuse had to be the definition of "anything," which meant I had to work on my prayers. "Gymnastics. That's what I used to do."

Not on Woodbury High's team, but for a couple of months before I left for Wisconsin Dells, and for a few days after I arrived—before I got canned just because Bunny Fletcher's husband didn't believe my boobs weren't assisted by padded bras, and I decided to show him.

Stupid move, but gymnastics had been fun.

"Gymnastics? Are you joking? Aren't those girls—"

Kirk glanced at my chest, and probably at the slight gut I'd acquired at Shangri-La. But at least he looked. I'd started to wonder if he even noticed my body. Or me. Or anything other than Amber.

"I'm pretty good at gymnastics. The equipment, at least." The floor exercises, not so much, but I hadn't needed to be good at them for the circus.

Kirk kept staring at my boobs, as if he was lost in thought and the thought was focused exclusively on them. For some reason, it annoyed me. I touched his chin, returning his eyes to mine.

"But I wouldn't mind catching your band practice, if that's okay. Even if I don't play guitar with you."

Kirk hesitated a moment, then grinned—until Amber slammed her tray on the table across from him. "Absolutely. We're always glad to have you."

"We are?" Amber practically spit on the table.

"Yeah." Kirk aimed the same grin at Amber he'd just shared with me. "Lydia has always been part of the gang."

I glanced down at my untouched burrito. I'd always been the *leader* of the gang, along with Kirk, but I'd left for a year. Nothing good had happened while I'd been gone.

Looking up again, I caught Amber batting her eyelashes at Kirk as if I wasn't even there.

So this was going to take a little work. But I worked at what mattered to me in life, and Kirk mattered. Because he was supposed to be mine.

♫

THANKS TO THE spare key I'd made years ago, not long after Dad bought the Jeep but refused to let me drive just because I didn't have a permit, I nabbed the Jeep after school and took off without Cat.

She'd probably get a ride home from Jeremy, and I might get grounded for a week, but it felt good. Besides, I could still talk Mom out of just about anything. Just not *quite* everything, as I realized when Dad moved me into Mary's old room.

I drove straight home, then waited ten minutes and called Mom to say I'd looked everywhere for Cat and couldn't find her after school, so I'd finally taken the Jeep. She was in the middle of preparing for a divorce trial tomorrow, so she just murmured the right things.

"Don't worry, dear. I'm sure she's all right."

She didn't think to ask where I'd found a key to the Jeep.

When Cat got home fifteen minutes later, accompanied by a slamming front door, her screams were deafening.

"Lydia, you are so busted! You know you can't drive the Jeep. *I* get to drive it."

Grinning, I stroked Boris's mangy fur and felt like purring as loudly as he was. I barely even blinked when the door to my room crashed open and banged against the wall.

I smiled sweetly at Cat. "Was there something you wanted?"

Her glare could start a bonfire. "You stole the Jeep."

"Like I told Mom, I couldn't find you. What's the big deal? Couldn't you get a ride home with Jeremy?"

Her eyes turned into slits, reminding me even more of a snake. "I'm sure you know perfectly well I couldn't."

I did? What was she talking about?

"Why? He didn't have band practice today." Unless Kirk was hiding stuff from me, which was always a possibility. "The next one is on Thursday."

"And you know this because—?"

"Because he *told* me. Duh." Kirk had definitely said Thursday. Why did Cat look so shocked?

"He didn't tell *me*."

I shrugged. "Last time I checked, he didn't talk to you much. You guys aren't too cozy, are you? Not since—"

I broke off when I saw the pained look on Cat's face. But how was this news? Cat herself had told me how Kirk and Tess talked her into singing with the band, then got a ton of kids to laugh at her. It didn't sound like Kirk, but Cat's voice *was* a little flat.

"You don't know anything about it."

I frowned, not having a clue what she meant. She'd told me all about it in half a dozen emails, hadn't she? What didn't I know?

"So if you didn't get a ride home from Jeremy, how'd you get home? Don't tell me you walked."

She looked flustered and pissed but not sweaty. Besides, her feet would be dead if she tried to walk more than a block or two in those heels.

"Kirk gave me a ride."

Kirk?

My hands clenched, but I didn't realize until Boris screeched and leaped off my bed that I might be strangling him. Partly to avoid meeting Cat's gaze, I leaned over the side of my bed to find

Boris cowering beneath it. I held out a hand, but he didn't budge. "Sorry, dude."

His bright-green eyes glared at me, even after I gave him a little finger wave.

"You actually like that cat?"

My head jerked up, and my body followed. I leaned back against the wall. Casually. "Boris? You must be kidding."

Cat glared at me, her own green eyes not nearly as bright as Boris's but her claws just as sharp.

I crossed my arms, trying to look relaxed. "So. Kirk gave you a ride home. That was nice of him, considering how much you hate him. Did you mention that to Kirk when you told him I don't know how to play guitar?"

Cat's jaw dropped.

"Oh, wait. I forgot. *Jeremy* told him I don't know how to play guitar." I put a finger on my chin. "Let's see. I wonder how Jeremy, not to mention every kid in school, would've known that. Huh. Can't imagine."

"You don't know anything about it."

"Funny. You keep saying that, and yet I seem to know quite a bit." More than Kirk had meant to share, but I usually found out everything anyway. "I know him a lot better than you do. He *likes* me. He must've been taking pity on you."

"He didn't—" Cat broke off, looking as if she'd swallowed her own tongue.

"Sorry, babe." God, I sounded like Liz, but Cat was obviously pissed at me, and all I'd done to her so far was swipe the Jeep. Big whoop. "Face it. I'll always be tighter with him than you are. Like, by a mile."

"He told me—" She clapped a hand over her mouth, shot a final glare at me, and stormed out of my room.

Easing off my bed, I walked over and shut the door with a soft click. Operation Crucify Cat was rolling. I just wasn't sure how I'd done it.

♫

IN SPEECH CLASS Tuesday morning, I nabbed the desk next to Drew and was busy ignoring—but enjoying—the poisonous looks Chelsea kept darting at me. The final bell to start classes hadn't rung yet, and Ms. Ciccarelli was nowhere in sight.

"Thanks. That was really sweet of you."

Sweet? Of me? At the sound of the soft voice, I didn't check to see who'd spoken, sure the words weren't meant for me.

"Seriously."

I finally glanced up, but the look aimed at me from in front of my desk wasn't a bit poisonous. It was almost syrupy sweet.

"Heather? Were you talking to me?"

She nodded shyly. "We hardly even know each other, so it was really cool of you to let me play with the band."

"I didn't—"

She held up a hand. Long, gracefully tapered fingers. No wonder she could play guitar. My own fingers were too short and stubby to form chords, even if Jazz claimed they weren't.

Since I'd given up on playing with Kirk's band, I should cancel this week's lesson with Jazz.

"I know. Kirk said you couldn't play last Friday because you had to hang with your family, but he also said—"

I shook my head. I didn't need Chelsea or even Drew hearing that I'd chickened out on playing with the band.

Heather glanced at them before dropping her voice. "Anyway. Thanks. I worked really hard on guitar all summer, but this was the first time I've played with an actual band. I didn't really know anyone."

"No worries." She seemed so sweet, I was practically having

a diabetic reaction just listening to her. "I'm too busy these days to play. Or, well, I'm going to be."

"Yeah, Kirk said you—"

I waved a hand to stop her, even though there wasn't much point. If Kirk had told Heather that I planned to try out for gymnastics—was *nothing* a secret around here?—he'd probably tell Amber and Drew, which meant Chelsea would know, too. If she didn't already. Still, I didn't want to talk about it, and definitely not in front of Chelsea or even Drew. I couldn't even fit into a leotard right now without looking like a stuffed sausage, and that wasn't how I wanted to look. Especially in front of Kirk.

The bell rang, and Heather gave me another smile before returning to her seat by the far window. Heather was too sweet, too nice. Maybe even more than Jane.

If that was possible.

♫

DAD SOMEHOW FOUND my spare key to the Jeep and busted me from driving it until the end of time—or whenever Mom talked him into changing his mind. But I wasn't grounded, and I also wasn't going anywhere with Cat. I walked home from school on Tuesday, glad it was September and not January. By January, or even November or December, I needed to get some wheels. Wheels not driven by Cat.

As I sauntered along the sidewalk, enjoying the fresh air and blue sky in a way I'd never appreciated when it was crammed down my throat in Montana, I tried to figure out what I could do next to Cat. I mean, not that I'd really done anything yet, even if she acted like I had.

She and Jeremy hadn't sat together at lunch—he actually sat next to Kirk at my table, and she hung out with the art geeks, pointedly *not* looking at him—and they both looked miserable. And pissed. Excellent.

Walking in the front door, I caught Cat heading out, dressed in her dorky Nickelodeon Universe clothes.

"Have fun at work. If that's possible."

She barely even glanced at me as she brushed past.

"How's Jeremy? I see you guys aren't hanging out at lunch. Trouble in paradise?"

Halfway across the lawn, she whipped around. "Like you don't know. Thanks a *lot*."

Turning, she headed for the Jeep.

"Happy to help." And I was, if it meant Cat was miserable, even though I hadn't even begun to do anything rotten. A thought crossed my mind, then lit up like a neon billboard. "Hey, if you're tired of Jeremy, do you want me to keep him company? As a favor to both of you?"

She slammed her palm against the Jeep, yelping as she did. She clenched her teeth. "You wouldn't dare."

"Yeah? Watch me."

♫

AS THE NEXT two days crawled by, Thursday night's band practice was the only thing on my horizon. I'd gotten out of playing guitar. But since Kirk would be playing, and Amber would undoubtedly be hanging out, too, it really didn't offer much of an opportunity. For anything.

I walked to Michael's house, and not only because Cat had the Jeep. If I didn't have wheels, I could maybe catch a ride home from Kirk. He even gave *Cat* a ride the other day, and they didn't like each other.

If I worked it right, maybe I could shove Amber out of the

car as we went around a corner.

No one answered the door, which was ajar, so I walked inside and down the stairs to the basement. Once there, I blinked at the darkness. The band was already here—including Heather, who looked nervous—but no one else. No Amber, not even Chelsea and Drew. This would be easier than I thought.

"Hey, Lydia." Kirk shaded his eyes with one hand to look out at me and wave from the brightly-lit far end of the room. "Glad you made it."

Heather waved, too, and Michael nodded. Jeremy didn't look up from his drums. Zach glanced back and forth from me to his bass guitar as he tuned it, but I couldn't read his reaction. Not that I cared. He wasn't Kirk.

I leaned back on the wraparound couch, on the end closest to the band, and watched Kirk and Heather on their guitars. Heather looked terrified, but her fingers worked the chords in a way I definitely couldn't. She had a scratched guitar and wore preppy clothes—a pink polo shirt and khaki bermudas with Birkenstock sandals—and didn't look at all like a musician. I pictured my own gleaming turquoise guitar and rock-star outfit and wished I could combine Heather's skills with my fashion sense.

Okay, I was a little jealous. Every guy in this room would choose the skills over the clothes. It didn't mean they'd want to *date* a girl like Heather. They just liked her playing in their band. Same thing with my sister Mary.

Not that I was annoyed or anything.

The band started their first song, no one singing. Oh, yeah. Maybe Cat had been right that no one in the band could sing. After a minute, though, Kirk nodded at Heather, who started singing, her voice tentative as she looked down to play her chords.

By the end of the chorus, her voice wasn't so tentative. In

fact, she sounded good. Soft but sure. Not surprisingly, sweet.

"Hey."

Hunched forward on the edge of the couch, my eyes glued to Heather and almost forgetting Kirk and everyone else, I jerked at the sound of a voice at my ear. Practically *in* my ear. My head slammed into Drew's mouth. Crunch.

Flustered, I reached out for him to make sure he was all right. Not my smartest move, since he tugged on my right hand, drawing it around his waist as he sat down next to me.

"Drew? What are you doing?"

Nibbling on my earlobe, apparently.

His breath tickled my ear, making me squirm, as a husky whisper floated into my ear. "I said I wanted to get together, and Kirk said you'd be here."

As his octopus tentacles went around me, I tried pulling away. Glancing wildly at the band, even though I didn't *want* to catch their attention—especially not Kirk's—I saw Jeremy's half-closed eyelids, which didn't mean he wasn't looking, and Zach's full-on stare. No one else seemed to notice what Drew was trying to do to me. With me.

Thank God.

Drew's lips traced a path around my ear and down my neck. I'd wanted to feel this again—this heat, this passion—but from Drew? Especially when it meant I'd probably feel something far more painful from Chelsea in a matter of seconds?

"Drew." I turned my head slightly, even though a tiny part of me actually liked the kisses, despite the fact that they were from Drew. "We can't—"

His lips landed on mine, tasting sweet, I guess, as he eased me back against the couch. The more I struggled to stop him, the more tangled I got in his arms. And now his legs, which intertwined with mine.

I finally pulled away. Slightly. As much as I could without

slugging him. "Uh, Drew? Chelsea?"

He drew a ragged breath as his dark-as-coal eyes sucked me in. God, he was good at this. I had no idea. "I want you, Lydia. Always have."

"Always?" Even when he and Cat had been an item? Or at least Cat's dream of an item? Ew.

Wait. I was pissed at Cat, wasn't I? Willing to do anything to make her feel as lousy as possible?

"Always." He started nibbling again just as someone said something into the mic.

As the sound registered, I jerked away from him. My gaze shot to the band, and everyone was looking at Drew and me. It didn't help when I yanked up the neckline of my shirt, where Drew's hands had tried a not-so-subtle grope. I crossed my legs, knocking Drew's left leg away from my shin.

When Kirk grinned, I realized he'd been the one talking into the mic. "Hey, you guys. Are we missing something?"

As I felt every inch of my body flush, Drew laughed. Like he wanted everyone to know. Like he'd take out an ad in the school newspaper tomorrow.

I scooted a few inches away but didn't say anything, and the band started playing another song. With Heather singing again, this time in a duet with Kirk.

Great. Heather got Kirk—at least in a duet—and I got Drew. Not my plan. Not my choice. Sure, I hadn't exactly fought him off, but I also didn't want him.

A few minutes later, when Heather started singing "You don't always get what you want," I almost threw up.

DREW LEFT FIFTEEN minutes after our mini makeout session,

finally, when he realized I wasn't going to resume it.

No one else showed up, which surprised me, because Cat had said last year that a lot of kids used to come to listen to the band play in Michael's basement.

So I sat alone, looking like the definition of pathetic.

Perfect.

When Kirk strummed the last chord of the last song, I stood up, trying not to look hopeful. Or eager. Or, heaven help me, like sloppy seconds.

Kirk packed up his guitar and amp in a hurry, then walked right past me toward the stairs. Looking annoyed.

"Kirk?" I scrambled but didn't catch him until he was halfway up the stairs. Which was probably better, come to think of it. No witnesses. "I was wondering if—"

He turned his back on me, which stung. "Sorry. I've gotta go."

As he took off again, I followed, even though I'd never felt so stupid in my life. Not even in that strip bar in Milwaukee, which said something.

"Was it something—" I cut myself off on the brink of sounding weaker than I ever had in my life. I wanted Kirk, but not enough to beg. "I mean, any chance I can catch a ride home with you? Cat had to take the Jeep to work."

He whirled on me at the front door, but he still wore his silly sunglasses, and I had no idea what was going on in his eyes. From the grim slash of his mouth, I had a feeling it wasn't anything good.

"What are you doing with Drew? *Playing?* He has a girlfriend, you know."

I glared at Kirk, even though it wasn't my most attractive look. "I didn't come here with Drew, and I'm not hooking up with him, and he left when he figured it out. But he said *you* told him I'd be here today."

Kirk gave me a look I couldn't decipher, then started toward his car, but more slowly, as if he didn't mind me tagging along. So I tagged along.

"I didn't tell him to make out with you."

"Maybe not, but I bet you knew he wanted to."

"You knew it, too. He told me you guys were planning to hook up."

"One of us was." I shrugged, but my nerves jangled. I had one shot at fixing things with Kirk, and the odds weren't good. "I told you I wasn't interested in him."

"You don't seem to mind kissing him, though. Or totally making out with him."

Was he jealous? "It was an accident."

Kirk lifted his sunglasses long enough to give me an incredulous stare with his gorgeous blue eyes. Eyes like that really shouldn't ever be covered by sunglasses.

I touched his arm, even though I knew I was risking the strong possibility of him brushing me off.

"Honestly. I don't know where Drew was coming from." Okay, I did the moment his tongue landed in my ear. "He took me by surprise, and I didn't want to make a big scene or slug him or whatever. But he left. You saw him leave."

We'd reached Kirk's midnight-blue Mustang and both stopped at the passenger door. A speck of hope fluttered inside me when he didn't open the trunk to shove me inside head first. Let's just say my expectations were pretty minimal.

Kirk dropped his sunglasses back down. "Have you ever slugged a guy who tried to kiss you?"

Quite a few. Ever since I lost my virginity the hard way in ninth grade to Blake, the senior football player who laughed as tears rolled down my face, I'd slugged a lot of jerks. Most of them had told the world that I *hadn't* slugged them, that I'd done everything they'd wanted in every position imaginable.

And everyone in school believed it. Including Kirk, obviously. Why wouldn't he? I was pretty sure my own sisters believed it. Even Cat, who knew better.

I felt a stupid, traitorous tear in the corner of my eye, and I turned away to brush it off before Kirk saw it. I wanted him, but not his pity. I also didn't want someone who believed everything he'd ever heard about me.

I turned back to him, my smile shaky. "Not that it matters, but yeah. I've had to slug a lot of guys in my life. Being a guy, though, you probably wouldn't understand."

"You wouldn't have to slug me."

"Why? Because I'd be so thrilled to have Kirk Easton in my arms?"

He gave me a crooked smile that told me everything but promised zip. "Something like that."

"Funny." Even though it wasn't. At all. "I could've sworn you were the one lecturing me a few minutes ago about making out with a guy who had a girlfriend. What's Amber?"

He hesitated a moment too long. "Amber is—"

I held up a hand. "Your girlfriend. Thanks, but I don't need to steal guys from their girlfriends." At least, not right this moment. "And I don't hook up with guys who have no intention of breaking up with their girlfriends."

I wasn't sure *what* Kirk wanted, but I wasn't waiting around to find out. He knew where to find me. I decided to let him. Turning, I started to walk away. Headed home. Alone. Without the guy I wanted more than anything.

"Don't you want a ride?"

I glanced over my shoulder at Kirk, the bittersweet smile on my face not even fake. "Yeah, but I'm willing to wait."

Just not forever.

Chapter 10

*"I will answer for it, he never cared three straws about her.
Who could about such a nasty little freckled thing?"*

— Jane Austen, *Pride and Prejudice,*
Volume II, Chapter Sixteen

I TRUDGED ALONG the sidewalk, heading home, scuffing the toes of my black Converse as I kicked every stone I found in my path. A car drove by and honked, but I didn't look up.

Another car slowed and then stopped.

"Hey. Lydia?"

I glanced sideways at the orange VW Beetle, not recognizing it, not caring. And kept walking.

The Beetle inched along next to me, then zoomed ahead a few houses before stopping. The driver—tall and skinny with light-brown hair—got out and stood by his door, watching me.

Zach Lashinski. The bass player with the Cat in the Hat tattoo. Also known as a possible ride home.

I kept shuffling along the sidewalk, but headed slightly in his direction, and finally stopped when I drew parallel with his glow-in-the-dark orange car.

We'd never spoken, so I wasn't sure how he knew my name, but maybe he made a point of finding out the names of all the girls who made out with random guys at his band practices.

I stepped onto the boulevard and looked at Zach over the top of the sea of bright orange.

"Hey. You're Zach, huh? Nice job on bass."

Not that I'd really noticed. When I hadn't been fending off Drew, I'd been focused on Kirk and Heather. Yeah, part of me wanted to burn my guitar in a raging bonfire, but the rest of me wanted to know how they played so well.

"Thanks." His mouth quirked, as if he somehow knew I hadn't been paying a bit of attention to him, but it only meant he had a brain. "You need a ride?"

I didn't know him, but he played in Kirk's band and seemed safe. Not that anyone I knew would think Lydia Bennet would worry about pesky little things like safety.

Shrugging, I reached for the door handle. "If you don't mind? I live—"

"I know." He grinned, making me wonder if he'd been checking me out. Until he spoke again. "I've given your sister Mary a ride home a few times. How's she doing?"

I rolled my eyes. "Probably studying. That's all she does, last time I checked."

He got into his Beetle, reached across the front seat, and unlocked my door, then waited for me to climb in, too. "Guess you haven't checked in a while, huh? She spends a lot of time with her guitar. Probably why she's so good."

As he started the engine and pulled away from the curb, I sighed, calculating in my head the number of blocks until home, the number of minutes I had to listen to another person drone on about Mary. Had *everything* changed while I'd been gone? Even Mary?

I didn't know Zach, so I decided not to share my opinion on Mary. It didn't leave me with much to say. I almost asked if he used to have blond hair and why he changed it, but the light brown looked good. Soft, shiny, and just barely in his eyes. "So you like bright orange, huh?"

His car looked like something an eight-year-old kid would want. It might explain his Cat in the Hat tattoo.

He stared straight ahead at the road. "My mom bought it for my sixteenth birthday. She thought it looked perky. What can I say?"

I rolled my eyes. "Don't say anything. Just save up for a new paint job."

Frowning, he kept driving.

After a minute of silence, I started to get annoyed.

"Hey, no biggie. You like bright orange, and you've got wheels, which is more than I can say."

He flicked a glance at me. "I hate bright orange."

"So you've got wheels but can't afford a paint job. Dude, I know the feeling."

He sucked in a breath, almost as if something annoyed him, even though I was the only other person in the car.

"I can afford the paint. I just don't want to hurt my mom's feelings."

Wasn't that what teenagers did on a daily basis? Bug the crap out of their parents?

"That's nice." Not to mention lame and mildly pathetic. If his mom wasn't driving the car, why would she care what color it was? Wouldn't she want her kid to be happy? "Did you get the Cat in the Hat tattoo for her, too?"

The glance he shot me this time wasn't nice. He just drove in silence, not bothering to speak or even turn on the radio. I turned it on for him, flinching when classical music started playing. When I reached out to change the station, he touched my wrist, stopping me.

"Don't." He didn't look at me. "Please."

A minute later, he pulled up in front of my house. When I thanked him for the ride, he just nodded and stared out through the windshield.

Without another word, I climbed out and walked up to my house, hearing the gravel crunch under his wheels as he slowly pulled out from the curb.

Weird guy. My life was filled with them.

♬

WHEN I WALKED into Speech class on Friday morning, I wasn't surprised to see Drew and Chelsea sitting in the back of the room but at opposite corners. Even though the only people at the band practice yesterday were the guys in the band, Drew, and me, word tended to get around.

Was Drew the type to cheat—or at least make a valiant effort to cheat—and then confess? Or had Heather spilled the beans to Chelsea? She seemed too quiet, too sweet, to gossip. But Chelsea was sitting on Heather's side of the room, two desks back, and I'd seen them talking together at lunch.

I glanced around, wondering where to sit. Not by Chelsea. I was allergic to jellyfish.

I headed to the back of the room and grabbed the empty desk next to Drew. I wasn't hitting on him, and I didn't want him to hit on *me*, but there was no reason to kill a friendship with a guy just because of a mistaken and aborted makeout session.

"Hey." I set my books on my desk, noticing out of the corner of my eye that Chelsea had quit trying to pretend she wasn't watching me. Turning my back on her, I smiled at Drew, who had a pained expression on his face. "How's it going?"

He looked as if he were being tortured to death. "It's been better."

"At least you got your extemp speech done yesterday. You can sit back and relax."

Following my own advice, I lined up my pens next to my books and notebook, then leaned back in my chair. Ms. Ciccarelli had made extemporaneous speeches sound so easy, but she made up for it in her tough comments afterward. I'd done mine, though, and life was too short to worry about Ms. Ciccarelli or whether Drew and I should've sucked face in Michael's basement yesterday.

I had much bigger regrets in my life, and I didn't even spend my time worrying about those.

I felt Drew leaning over toward me a moment before I heard his soft voice. "Are you okay? I mean, are you pissed? Or, I don't know, interested?"

"Pissed? Interested?" I dropped my voice as I glanced at Drew, who for once in his life didn't try to sneak a peek down my shirt. "Are there any choices in between?"

He glanced over my shoulder, probably at Chelsea, but I didn't turn to confirm it. Too many girls, including Chelsea, had tried to yank out my hair, and it was short enough already.

Finally, Drew looked back at me. Okay, this time he glanced down my shirt. "Sorry. I thought you— Well, I thought it'd be cool."

I waved a hand. "Everything's cool between us, right? We've always been pals."

It probably wasn't the right moment to tell him I liked his best friend, not him. *Never* was probably the right moment for that.

Drew shrugged, and I thought I heard a little sigh. He was actually a decent guy, just too easily led—or maybe too easily distracted. Chelsea was right up his alley, but he'd been a fool to pick Chelsea over Cat.

At least, the Cat I used to know.

"You're right." Drew finally grinned and punched me in the arm, something guys did to my sister Liz but never me. I wasn't sure what I thought of it, but I'd choose it over him kissing me again. I think. "We've always been pals."

Whew. That'd been easy. Unlike the rest of my life lately.

"But, uh, Lydia?"

I looked at him, lifting my eyebrows, as Ms. Ciccarelli stepped into the room and the bell rang.

"You're not going out with Kirk now, are you?"

"Not last time I checked."

"Because he's dating Amber, you know."

I just rolled my eyes. Guys.

♫

I GRABBED A spot at my usual lunch table, a couple of seats down from Kirk. Close enough to show I wasn't embarrassed about yesterday, far enough away so Kirk wouldn't think I was begging for action.

I wasn't sure I'd made the right decision, though, when Heather took the open seat between Kirk and me. She immediately turned her back on me and started chatting up Kirk.

I leaned forward to catch Kirk's eye. "Hey, the band sounded good yesterday."

"Did you even—" Heather bit off what she was going to say, but I had a good guess it wasn't nice. Maybe she *was* hanging out with Chelsea. Her face flushed, though. "I mean, thanks again for letting me play with the guys."

I waved a hand, feeling as I did my still-sore fingertips from getting up at dawn this morning to practice guitar. I had no idea why I was still trying—I mean, I'd escaped the noose of the band gig and wasn't exactly a glutton for humiliation—unless it was to wake up Cat. "No biggie. Life's a crunch right now, and it's easier this way."

Easier, less humiliating, you name it. Besides, it wasn't as if Heather was some hot chick who'd make a play for Kirk. She might be sitting next to him right now, but only because I hadn't. She also wasn't hot. Girls with freckles were physically incapable of it.

She shrugged. "Well, I owe you."

I blinked but didn't say anything, even when Kirk caught my eye and his mouth quirked slightly.

His eyebrows went up. "You planning on coming to more practices? You're always welcome, you know."

"Thanks." I just wasn't sure what "welcome" meant when it came to Kirk. I'm guessing Amber didn't completely know, either, based on the scorching look she zinged me as she dropped her tray with a clatter across the table from Kirk.

"Totally welcome. Especially when I'm not there."

Ignoring her, I munched on the tip of a carrot. I'd brought my own lunch today so I wouldn't die of food poisoning accidentally inflicted by Mom. Carrots, pea pods, an orange, a low-carb tortilla. In other words, not much. I didn't have a clue if I'd actually try out for gymnastics, but I liked to keep my options open. If I kept eating the burgers and fries in the school cafeteria, the only thing I'd be able to leave open would be the top button on my jeans.

Finally, I glanced at Amber. "Sorry you couldn't make it last night. Should I let you know when I'll be there? I'd be happy to."

"No doubt." She glared at Kirk, looking so fierce I wondered why she'd even bothered sitting here today. Lack of options? "But I can always ask Kirk. Even though he doesn't seem to go out of his way to warn me."

"You can always ask me anything." Kirk grinned at her, making me gag, but a moment later he turned back to Heather and started talking about guitar riffs or something equally beyond me, as if Amber and I weren't even there.

I polished off my veggies and tortilla, grabbed my orange for the road, and stood up. Bright sunshine poured in through the cafeteria windows, and I heard a patch of grass in the courtyard calling my name.

Nothing else seemed to be calling my name these days, and I didn't plan to beg.

♫

I GLANCED UP when a shadow crossed the grass in front of me. Lauren, goth chick, pain in the ass, and reputed druggie. Come to think of it, I had a sketchy reputation, too, according to the people in this school, and I knew how accurate *that* was.

"Mind if I join you?"

Yeah. But I shrugged anyway.

She dropped onto the grass, landing cross-legged, almost as athletic and graceful as Liz. Spying her lunch—an apple and a bag of Skittles—I grinned. Also like Liz.

People were hard to figure, and even harder to pigeonhole. At least accurately.

Lauren munched on her apple as she pulled open her Accounting textbook. I hoped she didn't plan to turn this little get-together into an impromptu study session.

I peeled my orange. When the juice squirted all over my hands, I wished I'd packed a napkin. Or maybe a fire hose.

Glancing up from her book, Lauren tossed a paper towel in my direction without saying a word.

"Thanks. Guess I forgot what a mess these are."

She nodded, absorbed again in her Accounting book, and I wondered why she'd bothered to sit here. Had everyone else turned her down?

"We're not having a quiz today, are we?" I glanced at the chapter she was reading. "I don't remember Ms. Frey saying anything about it."

"She didn't. But Zach told me she used to spring pop quizzes on his Accounting class on random Fridays last year."

"Yeah?" Zach? The guy who gave me a ride home last night but brushed me off the whole way? "You know him pretty well, huh?"

One shoulder rose and fell a fraction of an inch, as if she'd expended as much effort on the subject as she planned to.

"He gave me a ride home last night."

Why had I said such a stupid thing to a chick who'd basically told me she had the hots for Zach?

"Yeah?" Lauren's gaze didn't lift from the page, but I could've sworn she went a little tense. "How did that work out for you?"

I frowned. Lauren sounded so casual, almost disinterested, which actually made me feel even more stupid.

I popped an orange section into my mouth, savoring the tang. "It saved me from walking."

"Oh?" Lauren finally looked up at me, her eyes studying me the way Jane's often did. "Why didn't you get a ride from Drew Mitchell? I heard—"

I held up a hand to cut her off. "It's not true."

"But Zach said—"

"Zach?" The latest orange section suddenly tasted sour in my mouth, and I swallowed hard against the bitterness. "When did you talk to him? How well *do* you know him?"

She grinned, startling me. "Pretty well. We used to hang out

138

practically naked together."

My jaw dropped.

"In a wading pool. When we were in pre-school. Zach and his mom live next door to us." Lauren wrapped her half-eaten apple in another paper towel, then ripped open her bag of Skittles, scattering half of them. "So you're interested? I told you he was hot."

"He's not—" I broke off, realizing I wasn't sure *what* Zach was. Not hot, not exactly. Cute. Sure of himself. A mama's boy, though, based on the orange VW. He also had a Cat in the Hat tattoo, loved classical music, and didn't even try to hit on me. I mean, not that I wanted him to. Guys just did.

Except for Kirk. And apparently Zach.

"Maybe he's not conventionally hot, but he's hot, trust me. I've seen him practically naked." She winked, and we both laughed. "At least, when he was four."

THE TWENTY MINUTES I spent in the courtyard at lunchtime and the afternoon sun pouring through the west-facing windows in sixth-period English class left me warm and sleepy, which wouldn't be so bad if Mr. Skamser weren't known for being unpredictable. Especially on Friday afternoons when half of the kids had droopy eyelids and the other half were focused on making weekend plans.

I'd read *The Catcher in the Rye* twice, for lack of better things to do, and decided that Holden Caulfield had to be the most fucked-up guy ever. It didn't say much for J.D. Salinger, who must've identified so much with the loser that he never published another novel. Even a girl as stupid as Chelsea, or a guy as indecisive as Drew, wouldn't have gotten into the messes that

Holden slid into on a daily basis.

The only good thing about the book, really, was that Holden made me feel better about myself.

"Lydia? Are you following the discussion?"

My gaze shot to the front of the room. Mr. Skamser had caught me daydreaming, which stunned me. I mean, yeah, of course I'd been daydreaming. But he'd *nailed* me on it. I thought I'd long since perfected the art of looking engaged and alert while thinking about my next party or my next shopping spree with Mom and her credit cards. Apparently, getting up at six a.m. to practice guitar, after staying up past midnight to reread this stupid book, had taken its toll.

I nodded at Mr. Skamser. "I'm all over it."

"She's all over *something*."

My head jerked to my left at the sound of Amber's so-called whisper to the girl next to her, which was loud enough to carry to the whole class. Bitch.

Mr. Skamser, perched on the front edge of his desk with his skeleton-thin body twisted up in its usual pretzel form, looked in Amber's direction, too. "Amber? Did you want to add something to the discussion? I think you passed on the opportunity yesterday, didn't you? Have you found a chance to finish chapter ten yet?"

We were just supposed to read through chapter *ten?* And Amber hadn't even managed that? No wonder she hung out with Chelsea. But how weird that a guy as smart as Kirk would hook up with a girl who was obviously brain dead.

She shot me a nasty look, as if *I'd* sicced Mr. Skamser on her, even though she'd done it to herself. I almost gave her a snotty little finger wave, just to taunt her, but I'd rather keep Mr. Skamser's focus on her and not deflect back to me.

"I, uh—" Amber actually stuttered. Bonus. "I pretty much read it."

"Pretty much?" Mr. Skamser gave a long-suffering sigh, something he bestowed on two-thirds of the class on a regular basis. But his standards were higher than some of the teachers here, who'd obviously conceded defeat years ago. "Since I'd like everyone to use precise language in this class, would you care to tell us whether 'pretty much' means that you've read the first ten chapters of the book?"

Amber's face was crimson and heading toward purple. It wasn't the first time Mr. Skamser had nailed her, and this was only the third week of class.

"It means—" Totally floundering, Amber looked frantically around the room, probably hoping someone would throw her a lifeline. Her gaze finally landed on me, and her lip curled. "It means I've read more than Lydia Bennet."

Startled, I sucked in a breath as half of the class started chattering, the girl next to Amber gave her a high-five, and the guy behind me couldn't stop laughing.

Mr. Skamser quelled the outburst with a single sweep of the room. "Amber, I don't think Lydia is your concern. I asked whether you'd finished reading the first ten chapters. May I assume that you still haven't?"

He reached for his grading book and red pen, the color he used when someone pissed him off. Craning my neck from my seat in the second row, I could see that the current page was filled with red ink.

"I, uh, I mean, I—" Amber started stuttering so badly, she finally erupted in a coughing fit.

Mr. Skamser uncapped his red pen and wrote something in the grading book. I was still grinning when he looked up from his book, his lips pursed. "While I'm at it, Lydia, I suppose I should ask you the same question."

I answered right away. "Whether I've read the first ten chapters? Or how to define 'pretty much'?"

Surprisingly, only a few kids laughed, even though I was at least as funny as Amber and not nearly as pathetic. Mr. Skamser smiled, which was even more of a surprise.

"For now, I'll leave the definition of 'pretty much' to the dictionary." Mr. Skamser's red pen hovered over the grading book. "Have you read the first ten chapters?"

I paused a moment, hating to sound like a suck-up but wanting to crush Amber like a bug. Crushing her like a bug won. "I've actually read the whole book. Twice."

As Amber coughed the word "bullshit" into her hand, most of the class turned in my direction. And stared.

"No way. She totally didn't."

I just smiled at Amber. Sweetly.

Even Mr. Skamser had a look of disbelief on his face, which was a little weird considering the brain trust I had for my three older sisters. Jane was majoring in English in college, and Liz and Mary were off the charts in every academic subject. What was so strange about me reading a stupid book? It's what people did in my family.

"You read the whole book?"

I nodded at Mr. Skamser, daring him to call me a liar.

His head tilted as he studied me a moment, but he finally gave me a clipped nod.

"What's your opinion of Holden Caulfield?"

I shrugged. "Not much."

"See? I *said* she didn't read it."

Another loud whisper from Amber, who seemed to be cruising for detention. Knowing her parents and the kick they got out of grounding her, it was a bad move on a Friday afternoon. She wouldn't be able to party this weekend.

Or, for instance, hang out with Kirk.

I raised my hand as I decided to do the unthinkable. At least, unthinkable for me. "Mr. Skamser?"

He lifted his eyebrows but didn't say anything. Close enough.

I knew the school policy manual inside and out, since it'd been used against me so often. Still, I'd never used it against anyone else, not even a snot like Amber. "I'm feeling a bit uncomfortable with the bullying situation that seems to be going on with—" I glanced in Amber's direction, smothering a smile when realization hit her eyes. I looked back at Mr. Skamser. "Well, I think it's obvious. And I don't understand it."

"Like hell she doesn't."

She really did try to whisper it this time, again to the girl next to her, but the room had gone deadly silent and everyone heard it. Including Mr. Skamser.

"Amber?" Mr. Skamser waited until she met his eye, then sighed. "Lydia is right. You've been trying to provoke her since the bell rang. I have to ask you to pay a visit to Mr. Paymar, although you can wait until the end of class to do so. I'm sure you don't want to miss a moment of our discussion of Holden Caulfield."

"But I can't. I have to—" Amber's hands were making wild circles in the air. She finally shot me another glare. "I mean, all I was saying is that Lydia obviously lied about reading the book, and you can't seem to see it."

Mr. Skamser held up a hand as he untangled himself from pretzel form, hopped off his desk onto the floor, and stretched to his full string-bean height. "The moment the bell rings, yes, you need to see Mr. Paymar. In fact, I'll be happy to escort you to his office." Turning back to me, he frowned. "Lydia, may I ask you to elaborate on your opinion of Holden Caulfield? In what sense is it not much? You don't *think* much of him or don't *know* much about him?"

I glanced at the beat-up paperback on my desk. "Oh, I know him, all right. I know his type. The guy keeps making one stupid decision after another, half the time because he's too embarrassed to tell people to stick it. He calls everyone else a phony, but he's totally one. No offense, but I'm guessing that *women* who teach English are a lot less likely to waste everyone's time making the class read about a loser like Holden Caulfield. I mean, he totally fell apart for no good reason."

I heard a little nervous laughter. Mr. Skamser's face was blank, which didn't tell me anything. Still, I could handle detention if it came right down to it. I didn't have any plans this weekend anyway.

"Lydia, I have to ask." Mr. Skamser paused, almost as if he hated the thought of giving me detention less than two minutes after he'd given it to Amber.

I shrugged, waiting for it.

"How is it possible for me to hear that particular opinion of poor Holden Caulfield only twice in my teaching career, and both times from a member of your family?"

He laughed, slapping his bony leg as he did, which stunned the crap out of me.

"Yeah?" I looked up at Mr. Skamser, who seemed to actually expect an answer. "Who was the other one?"

He tilted his head, studying my face, as if he still wondered whether I'd actually read the book or was just getting my opinions from one of my sisters. "Liz. Three years ago in this very room."

I blinked, but it made sense. Liz didn't take shit from anyone. Including, apparently, Holden Caulfield.

"Have you discussed the book with her?"

I rolled my eyes. "I didn't even know she ever read it."

I mean, except for the fact that Liz read everything, in every genre, you name it, when she wasn't playing sports or listening to some rock band.

"It's just that—" Mr. Skamser's gaze swept the room as if he were deciding whether to pursue this in front of thirty kids. "You and Liz don't seem, at first impression, to be particularly similar." He tilted his head. "Perhaps it comes from being sisters."

When he started to move on to another victim, I raised my hand.

"Yes, Lydia?"

"What's weird is that Liz and I are the only two students who've *said* this to you. I bet most kids are afraid to tell you what a loser Holden is. I mean, you obviously think the book is important, because it's the first one you asked us to read. They don't want to piss you off this early in the term."

Mr. Skamser gave me a quirky little smile that looked like it made his face hurt. "Actually, I used to assign this closer to the end of the term, but your theory is interesting. Class?" He glanced around the room. "Who else shares Lydia's opinion on Holden Caulfield?" When no one's hand went up, his eyebrows rose. "Perhaps I should ask only those of you who've actually read at least ten chapters."

Dead silence. If I didn't know already that I'd lost my power in this school, I'd know now. Amber, that sniveling little shit, seemed to have all the power in this room. Besides Mr. Skamser, of course.

She raised her hand now. "I think you had it right the first time. Lydia is just pretending she read the book by telling you the same crap her sister told you."

"Really?" Mr. Skamser pursed his lips. "So you think Lydia's—and Liz Bennet's—opinion is crap, Amber? Even though you haven't read the book yet?"

"Neither has Lydia."

"She said she did, and I choose to accept that. What I'm more interested in learning is whether anyone else shares Lydia's opinion of Holden Caulfield."

Everyone seemed to be watching Amber, waiting for her

reaction. When she shook her head, the girl next to her and a half dozen other kids shook theirs, too. Drew, in the back of the room, looked mildly terrified. I rolled my eyes.

"Fascinating." Mr. Skamser nodded at Amber before turning back to me. "What may be even more fascinating is that I share Lydia's opinion. Both as to Holden Caulfield and Lydia's belief that students don't want to piss me off, as Lydia would say." He gave me another smile, actually looking amused. "It's why I decided to assign it first."

Amber's jaw dropped so low, I could've shoved a large rock in her mouth. Believe me, I was tempted. The guy behind me laughed, but not at me this time, since he also slapped me hard on the back. Everyone else in class just stared at me.

Right this moment, that was good enough for me.

Chapter 11

Lydia was bid by her two eldest sisters to hold her tongue.

— Jane Austen, *Pride and Prejudice*,
Volume I, Chapter Fourteen

I WALKED HOME after school, enjoying the sunshine, fresh air, and even the exercise more than I'd ever admit to Cat, who thought she was winning some stupid battle with me every time I refused to catch a ride with her in the Jeep.

When I reached our block, I saw old Mr. Fogarty across the street, mowing his lawn for the fourteenth time this week. I rolled my eyes. The guy had to be ninety, minimum, and his scrawny back was stooped more than Quasimodo's, but he spent every waking moment in his yard. In the winter, he shoveled his driveway and sidewalk every day, whether or not it snowed.

I guess that's what happens when you live alone and all of your friends are gone. Great. Something for me to look forward to.

I waved at him. "Hey, Mr. Fogarty."

He glanced up, staring a moment before offering me a hesitant smile. He probably still hadn't forgotten the time I blew up his mailbox with firecrackers. And, okay, I nailed it with the Jeep two weeks ago. But that was an accident!

Head down, I kicked a stone with the toe of my shoe. No one ever forgot a thing you did wrong, let alone forgave you.

No one I knew, at least.

"Lydia?" Mr. Fogarty's voice had gotten a lot more feeble in the year I'd been gone. "Is that you?"

"Yeah. Nice to see you."

He turned off the lawnmower and waved me over to his yard. After a moment's hesitation, I crossed the street. Mr. Fogarty couldn't punish me more than my family or friends already had, and God knows I didn't have anything better to do.

As I approached, Mr. Fogarty pulled a handkerchief out of the back pocket of his baggy old khakis and wiped it across his brow. I wondered if he should be out here in the yard all day, working like a dog. His wife had died years ago, but didn't he have any kids or grandkids to take care of his yard? And why didn't I know if he did?

"Hey." I waved, trying to be friendly. "You wanted to see me?"

He took his sweet time folding his handkerchief into a perfect square and tucking it back in his pocket. Finally, he looked at me—and his smile reached all the way up to his crinkly blue eyes.

"It's nice to have you home again. We missed you."

Was he mistaking me for Cat? Sure, I *had* been gone, but Liz and Jane and now Mary were basically gone, too. Had he forgotten all the pranks I'd pulled over the years? Were we talking Alzheimer's or dementia?

"I—" I had no idea what to say. At a minimum, he'd lost his memory, but he couldn't help that. "Thanks. That's very nice."

"Were they good to you at that school?"

I blinked. "Which school?"

The old guy actually snorted. It sounded a bit like the Jeep when it started up on a cold morning. "Reform school. Howard never did say where you were, but I've always made it a point to keep tabs on you girls. Almost like you were my own daughters."

More like granddaughters, but I tended to leave the finer details to people like Liz or Mary. "You did? Then I guess you probably *did*, uh, know about—"

"The firecrackers?" He barked a laugh that sounded like it kicked up more than a little phlegm. "Used to do that myself. Besides, your parents bought me a new mailbox."

And again two weeks ago. "Sorry about that."

A few years too late on the firecrackers, but at least I'd squeezed in my apology before Mr. Fogarty bit the dust. From the looks of his way-too-flushed cheeks, I might've made it just in time.

"The hose in the window well took longer to clean up." He coughed, and I didn't know whether to slap him on the back or call 9-1-1. "But girls will be girls."

My eyebrows shot skyward. "They will?"

He nodded. "Liz was quite a bit like you when she was younger, before she channeled all that energy into sports. You just needed a place to channel it, I always told Howard."

Howard—a/k/a Dad—had never mentioned it to me. In fact, I'd always avoided Mr. Fogarty after Dad put the fear of God in me about Mr. Fogarty and his temper. Had he mellowed with old age, or had Dad been pulling one over on me?

I wasn't putting my money with Dad.

"The important thing is that you're home now. Howard says you need a job? Something to occupy you?"

"He said that?" I tried not to glare, since this wasn't Mr. Fogarty's fault. I knew exactly whose it was. "I mean, yeah, maybe he *said* it, but he and I don't agree on much."

The crinkly blue eyes looked amused. "You're a teenager. Of course you don't. Even Liz had her battles with Howard. You two have quite a bit in common."

"Liz and me?" He couldn't be more wrong. Right now, the only person in my family with whom I had anything in common these days was Mom, and that was mostly limited to shopping. "You must have me confused with—" I broke off, horrified when I realized I'd admitted out loud that Mr. Fogarty must've lost a few bricks from the patio of his brain. "What I mean is—"

Chuckling, he waved a hand. "Forgive the ramblings of an old man. I always forget that you girls don't like to be compared. Not even Jane and Liz, who've always been so close, or you and your twin."

"We're not identical twins. Not even close."

He smiled. "Right again. Well. If Howard is wrong about you wanting a job, forgive me. I was hoping to talk you into mowing my lawn. And perhaps doing other jobs around this run-down old place."

He frowned up at his house as he said it, even though he'd never allow a single inch of it to be less than perfect. My family's house didn't look half as good. But, then, Dad got his kicks on a yoga mat, not working in the yard like Mr. Fogarty, and Mom couldn't be trusted with power tools. Even when she *was* on her meds.

"Isn't there someone else . . ." I trailed off, not wanting to mention his kids or grandkids, partly because I didn't know if they existed and partly because I was afraid they did. If they did, they were total losers.

"You're just the girl to do it." He started to smile just as a wracking cough shook his body.

Suddenly, every excuse in my arsenal for why I couldn't do it went up in smoke. Not because I needed the money, even if I did, but because Mr. Fogarty needed me. Or at least he thought so. And because he smiled at me.

Other than Mr. Skamser today, and the guys my age who wanted something, no one had smiled at me in too long.

If that made me desperate, too damn bad.

♫

TWO HOURS LATER, I walked in the front door of our house, dripping sweat all over the ripped T-shirt and hot-pink gym shorts I'd found in a skanky pile of Liz's workout clothes. Dying of thirst. Every muscle in my body screaming at me.

"Nice work on Mr. Fogarty's lawn. Are you finally paying him back for all the crap you've pulled on him over the years? Or is this some community service thing for ex-cons?"

I barely glanced at Cat, curled up on one end of the ratty old couch at the far end of the living room, as I shot past her on my way to the kitchen. Two tall glasses of water later, I ignored her when I went back through the living room, headed for a long, hot shower.

"I said, you're finally paying him back? Or—"

I stopped in the front hall but kept my back to her. I didn't have to look at Cat to know she'd have a smug, snotty look on her face. It was the only look I'd seen on her since the moment I got home from Shangri-La.

But *had* I been paying Mr. Fogarty back? If so, why was he paying *me*? Should I pay *him*? And was I certifiably crazy even for *considering* paying him?

I'd pondered a million questions like that the whole time I'd trudged up, down, and across Mr. Fogarty's lawn, then clipped and weeded and stood there while Mr. Fogarty rattled off a long list of back-breaking projects. But I refused to discuss my questions or pangs of guilt with Cat. It'd be like talking to

Chelsea or Amber.

"He paid me." I gritted my teeth, but Cat didn't have to see that. "I guess he was relieved to find out that *someone* in this family was capable of hard work."

When Cat cursed, I tore up the stairs, my quads and hamstrings screaming in agonizing harmony.

Half an hour later, still aching but showered and dressed for something more fun than lawn work, I headed downstairs. Cat and the Jeep were nowhere in sight, and Mom and Dad weren't home from work yet, but Liz and Jane were holed up at the kitchen table, their heads bent together.

Not needing more crap from any of my sisters, I tiptoed through the back hallway on my way to the basement.

"Hey." Liz, of course, never missed anything. "Looks like you're going out?"

Only if my luck changed. I hadn't heard about any parties tonight, let alone been invited to one. Not that I planned to share that with Liz or Jane.

If I added Cat to the list, and I did, it meant I didn't have a single person to share anything with.

I poked my head into the kitchen. "No plans."

The moment the words came out of my mouth, I wanted to erase them—or run screaming from the house. But Cat had obviously commandeered the Jeep for the evening, and the muscles in my legs were fried beyond recognition.

Hmm. Maybe Dad had actually plotted with Mr. Fogarty to destroy my escape options. Yep, I was definitely keeping all the dough he paid me.

"Wanna hang with us?" Liz glanced at Jane, not me, as she said it, as if she had to get permission from Jane to wreck their plans for the evening.

Thinking I heard a noise, I glanced sideways but didn't see anyone at the front door.

"What? You're trying to check out your options? Cat—"

"—is long gone." I shrugged. "Yeah, I noticed."

Jane shook her head. "She's picking up takeout Chinese. We didn't know what you were doing tonight, but I told her to add seafood delight to the list, just in case."

My eyebrows went up. "Why?"

"Because I remember that it's your favorite, silly."

Liz snorted. "The fact that it's one of *Jane's* favorites had nothing to do with it, I'm sure."

Jane whapped Liz in the arm, and they both laughed.

I sighed. I hadn't had seafood delight—a medley of shrimp, crab, and scallops that taught me everything I needed to know about the quality of Mom's putrid fish sticks at a young age—in a year and a half, minimum.

"I guess I don't have much going on." Seeing Jane's hopeful smile, I tossed in an escape hatch. "Right now, I mean. I might be headed to a party later."

"Really?" Liz gave me a lazy glance, like a leopard before it pounces on its prey. "Cat didn't know about any parties tonight."

"Yeah, well, Cat doesn't know much. Period."

"You're wrong about—"

Jane put a hand on Liz's forearm, stopping her. "What Liz means to say is that you've been gone a year. Cat is different now. You're different. Everyone's different."

Liz shook off Jane's hand with a flick of her wrist. "I *meant* she was wrong about Cat. Just like you and I were wrong, in case you forgot."

I rolled my eyes. "I'm not wrong, and you two haven't changed a bit. Except Liz maybe dresses a little better."

"And you still say whatever you think." Instead of jumping to her feet and clobbering me, though, Liz grinned. "But you're around more often to say it."

"Lucky me."

Leaving them, I headed to the basement. Maybe I could catch a movie by myself on the big-screen TV downstairs. Maybe my sisters would deliver my seafood delight on a silver platter. Maybe pigs would fly.

"Don't go too far, babe." Liz's voice reached me before I could slam the door to the basement behind me. "We're looking forward to a wild evening of sisterly love."

I *did* slam the basement door. Hard.

I'D BARELY MANAGED to pick out a movie—*Animal House*, which reminded me of my own home, only without the great parties—when Liz yelled downstairs that the Chinese food had arrived and was waiting for me.

In the kitchen.

So much for praying for deliverance from my sisters, not to mention the whole silver-platter scenario.

After a last look at the TV, I clicked it off and headed for the stairs. Seafood delight had better be worth it.

"She joined us. Will wonders never cease?" Cat flicked a glance over me, head to toe, as if there was something wrong with me. I'd showered, hadn't I? And I hadn't even stolen a single item of my outfit from her or anyone else.

I gave Cat a snotty look right back. "Hey, the bigger shock is that you broke loose from Jeremy long enough to go slumming with your sisters. Or did he wise up and find someone else?"

"Like you don't know."

Jane paused in the middle of a bite of seafood delight. "That's enough. What happened? I know you've been gone a while, Lydia, but you guys were always so close. Just like—"

She broke off, as if she didn't want to brag about how tight she and Liz had always been, leaving Cat and me to compete with them, and leaving Mary shut out.

Nowadays, *I* was the one shut out.

Liz poked Jane. "Did you mean like *us*? That's why we're living together? I knew there had to be a reason."

I rolled my eyes. "You guys even had to pick boyfriends who are best friends. How convenient."

"What can I say?" Liz grinned at Jane, who looked like she wished she'd never brought up the subject. "The Book ordained it."

"*Pride and Prejudice* didn't ordain a single thing." Cat smirked at me. "After all, Lydia just went to reform school. She didn't *marry* Justin or anything."

"You little bitch."

Leaping to my feet, I picked up my plate of seafood delight and sent the contents flying at Cat's face.

"Lydia!" Jane frowned at me as she leaped to her feet to help Cat, who was lucky I'd just sent the food flying, not the plate with it. "I can't believe you did that."

Liz didn't move an inch. In fact, she kept chewing on kung pao chicken while Jane hurried to the sink for paper towels to help wipe off Cat, but then she grinned. "No kidding. Not only did you throw away your favorite food, but you forgot that Cat is vegetarian. Seafood delight is totally wasted on her."

Jane threw a wet paper towel at Liz. "Can't you ever be serious?"

Liz calmly plucked the paper towel off her shoulder and zinged it back at Jane. "If the situation calls for it. But I think Lydia responds better to humor."

"She should. She's a total joke. Just ask anyone."

Everyone whirled in Cat's direction. She was covered in seafood and sticky rice and halfway soaked from the wet paper towels Jane kept dabbing on her. Grabbing the latest one out of Jane's hand, she flung it across the kitchen. It clung to the fridge for a moment before dropping to the floor.

Jane shook a finger at Cat and me. "I don't understand what's up with you two."

I held up a hand. "Don't ask me. Cat turned into this totally different person while I was gone. Maybe it's because she has a *boyfriend*." I sneered in her direction, happy to see her flinch. "But boyfriends don't seem to have changed either of you guys."

"Thanks to you, I don't *have* a—"

Breaking off, Cat clapped a hand over her mouth. Jane and Liz looked as shocked as I was, and I couldn't even come up with something sarcastic to say.

But Cat and Jeremy couldn't have broken up. Kirk and Amber were still together, and even Drew and Chelsea, and both of those couples made even less sense than Jeremy and Cat. Besides, despite my threats, I hadn't even made a fake play for Jeremy. Who could he have dumped Cat for?

Uh, oh. Heather? She *had* just joined the band.

I felt the tiniest flicker of pity for Cat. She didn't deserve my pity, but she was way more cool than a goody two-shoes like Heather. Even if she'd been a total jerk lately.

I shook my head, almost sorry I'd thrown the seafood delight at her. And not just because my stomach was rumbling. "I can't believe he'd pick someone like Heather over you."

Jane frowned. "Who's Heather?"

Cat frowned, too, but she looked confused. "Heather?"

She didn't even know. The situation was worse than I thought.

I shrugged. "Anyway. I'm sorry."

"You should be. You were the one—"

"Stop." I might harbor the slightest scrap of pity for Cat, but I wasn't taking the fall. "Before you make me stop you."

I'd already taken way too much crap in my life, and even spent a year locked up in Shangri-La, for things that weren't my fault. But enough about Justin.

Cat was glaring at me, though, as if the problems in her love life *were* my fault. I glanced at Liz and Jane, who both seemed to be stunned into silence. For Liz, at least, it had to be a first.

Finally, Jane looked sideways at Cat, who clenched her fists so tightly, she had to be hurting.

"Cat? You and Jeremy broke up?"

She kept glaring at me. "Because of *her*."

Her finger shook as it pointed at me, but I just rolled my eyes. "Right. Blame it on me when the guy probably just got disgusted when you told the *whole school* that I didn't know how to play guitar. Or maybe he found someone else. Like Heather. Who just joined the band."

"He's *not* with Heather."

"The ex-girlfriend is always the last to know."

"Actually, she's often the *first* to know." Liz held up her hands when everyone stared at her. "I'm not saying that Jeremy has a new girlfriend." She offered Cat a less-than-confident smile. "I'm sure he doesn't. This is probably just a timeout, right? Like, maybe you guys had a fight, and he'll be back. Every couple has fights, right?"

Her fork halfway to her mouth, Jane blushed.

"Fine. Everyone except Jane and Charlie. But it's not like Alex and I never fight."

I snorted. "Probably over which one of you gets to drive his Lamborghini."

Grinning, Liz slapped a hand on the table. "Perfectly good example of something worth fighting over."

Only in Liz's opinion. I rolled my eyes. "I don't think Cat will ever fight Jeremy for that broken-down piece of scrap metal he drives."

"See?" Cat jabbed a finger at me. "She knows what Jeremy drives. She's been in his car."

When Jane and Liz looked at me, a question in their eyes, I pushed back from the table. "Hey, it's been great. No, really. But we seem to be out of seafood delight." I smirked at the globs of rice still clinging to Cat's shirt. "And now all three of you seem to be cruising down that slippery slope into dementia, so I'm outta here."

I made it three feet before a hand clamped down on my shoulder, holding me in place.

Liz's, of course. "What's going on with you and Jeremy?"

"Other than the fact that I've apparently stolen him from Cat and get a charge out of cruising around town with him in a butt-ugly, beat-up brown Hyundai?"

"He drives a Toyota. A Toyota Corolla."

"So I was right on butt-ugly, beat-up, and brown?"

Liz didn't say anything, but her lips twitched.

I rolled my eyes. "I've never been in his car. I have better taste in both cars *and* guys."

When a chair slammed against the floor, I glanced past Liz to see Cat rounding the end of the kitchen table, headed for me, murder in her eyes.

"You little—"

Liz whirled in Cat's direction, her hands releasing my shoulders in time to give me a quick escape. I didn't hesitate. Flying out of the kitchen in the direction of the front door, I grabbed the keys to the Jeep. A minute later, the Jeep rumbled to life, and I was gone.

But where I was headed, I didn't have a clue.

WHEN I SLIPPED back in the front door, four hours and one-and-a-half movies later, every light in the house was blazing, along with Dad's eyes.

Mom, next to Dad at the front door, didn't look pissed. I could deal with, or even ignore, pissed. She looked hurt, which was somehow worse.

"You took the Jeep."

What was his first clue?

Dad crossed his arms. "And you threw an entire plate of food at Cat."

"That wasn't smart, Lydia." Mom shook her head. "Seafood delight is the most expensive item on the menu."

Dad rolled his eyes. "What Lydia did wasn't *nice*. We don't need to discuss whether it was smart."

"But it wasn't, Howard, and Lydia has always been very smart about money."

My money, sure. Someone else's money? Not so much.

"Not that you guys would believe me, but Cat started it. Then she came after me like some wild-ass thug, and I barely had time to run out the door before she ripped me to shreds."

Not that I seriously thought Cat could rip me to shreds. She'd never worked out, and going out with Jeremy hadn't helped her muscle tone. I could take her in a heartbeat.

But I'd rather take the Jeep. Even if it meant driving aimlessly around Woodbury until finally heading to the theater in Oakdale, where I wouldn't run into anyone I knew.

I glanced from Dad to Mom, not eager to meet Dad's livid gaze for more than a split second.

"Cat? Rip you to shreds?" Dad made a tsking sound, as if he expected more of me even in my fibs. "Are you sure you're not mistaking her for Liz?"

"No mistake. Liz and Jane were there, and they saw the whole thing."

"They did see it, and neither one seemed to think you were in great danger of being ripped to shreds."

"Of course not. Liz knew she could handle Cat, and Jane can't believe poor Cat would ever do anything wrong. She doesn't know Cat the way I do."

Mom nodded until Dad shook his head at her. But I had Mom on my side, or at least willing to listen to my side, and I counted on it.

Dad pointed to the chair next to his in the living room, as if he actually expected me to listen to a stupid lecture after already having an incredibly sucky Friday night.

I yawned. "Hey, I had a long day, and I'm tired, and you can ask Liz if you don't believe me." I took a step toward the stairs. "Jane has a sweet but skewed perception of reality, and Cat is just plain delusional."

"She's not *delusional*, dear."

Dad looked at Mom and groaned. "Let's focus on Lydia, shall we?" He turned to me. "Your own perception of reality might require some adjustment. We'll work on that first thing tomorrow."

"Bring it. I can hardly wait."

Chapter 12

Lydia stood her ground, determined to hear all she could.

— Jane Austen, *Pride and Prejudice*
Volume I, Chapter Twenty

"**FIRST THING TOMORROW**" came earlier for me than anyone else in the house, based on the utter silence when I made stealth tracks downstairs at six a.m. Dad was good with threats, but his follow-through didn't worry me. I'd already survived far worse than Dad in the last year, hadn't I?

After grabbing a hard-boiled egg and a banana, I headed to the basement, closing the door at the top of the basement stairs with a soft click. Even if Dad carried out his vague threats, I could chill first by getting in some time on my guitar.

At six a.m.? I shook my head, wondering if I'd had a lobotomy but hadn't happened to notice.

I ran through my usual warm-up drill of chords and notes before opening my rock-and- roll songbook. I still couldn't nail my D chord to save my life, but I now had a dozen chords down cold, even my C chord. I also knew some notes, which were easier and didn't kill my swollen fingertips so much. At this point, though, the callouses on my fingertips almost made me feel like I knew a thing or two about guitar.

Even if my teacher, Jazz, didn't seem to agree.

"Lydia?"

When Dad suddenly materialized in front of me, I jumped so high, I almost dropped my guitar.

"Dad! Geez!"

He didn't apologize—being not only a guy but my dad, the word "sorry" didn't seem to be in his vocabulary—but he sat down on the beanbag chair near me, nodding his head as if I should keep playing.

Right. I hadn't played my guitar in front of anyone except Jazz, and I didn't feel like playing for a guy who was about to lower the boom on me. With my luck, he'd increase the punishment when he heard my D chord.

Wearing his rattiest yoga pants and a stained T-shirt, Dad crossed his legs in the beanbag chair, looking both like a yoga nut and way too comfortable for a guy on the run toward fifty. "You sounded pretty good when I was coming downstairs. Before I startled you into silence, apparently."

I frowned. "You don't have to act so shocked."

"I'm not shocked, just observing." Dad tilted his head, studying me. "Mary used to practice in the living room, so I was in the habit of hearing her. I haven't heard you play."

"She played in the living room?" Weird, even by Mary's standards. "Not even in her bedroom?"

Dad nodded. "I always suspected it was her way of needling your mother on a daily basis that she'd given up piano for guitar." He offered me a faint smile. "Since your mother started spending longer hours at her law office, the person most affected by it was me."

Good.

Dad gave me this weird look, as if he could read my mind. If he could, he never would've sent me to reform school. He would've asked for *my* side of the story and maybe even given me a hug. I'd never needed one more than during those nightmarish days in Milwaukee.

I set my guitar back on its stand.

"You don't want to play anymore? Didn't you just start?"

I glanced up at him, then quickly back at my guitar when I felt a stupid teardrop threaten. Dad could punish me all he wanted, but he'd never see me cry. Not in this lifetime.

"You said you wanted to punish me first thing today." My voice sounded a little funny, but I just talked faster. "I'm sure you don't want to waste your day waiting."

When Dad didn't say anything, I finally looked at him.

"Lydia, it doesn't have to be this way." Dad leaned forward, his elbows on his knees.

I fiddled with my amp, even though I'd already turned it off. "But it *is* like this. You take everyone's word over mine, and you get your kicks by punishing me. So bring it. I don't give a flying fuck in space."

"You shouldn't—" Dad shook his head, but he had to realize it was too late to change my language. "I don't get my kicks, as you say, from punishing you or any of your sisters."

"Yeah? Could've fooled me."

"Cat and I struggled through a few things last year."

"Well, raise the flag."

He kept going as if I hadn't said a word. Or, as usual, he just didn't listen to a word I said. "It's normal. I struggled against my parents, too."

I just stared at him. Dad thought *any* part of his life was comparable to mine? The thought was so ludicrous, the last trace of tears vanished in a heartbeat.

"No kidding. Did *your* dad ship you off to reform school

without even asking for your side of the story? Must've been a major drag. I bet you're still recovering, huh?"

Dad gave me one of his long-suffering looks. "It was the only choice I had."

Right. "Is that what you told your shrink? Did your *shrink* believe it?"

He does actually go to a shrink. Mom likes to claim it's part of his spiritual journey as a yoga master, but she might not want to think about the fact that he first saw the shrink after Mom went off her bipolar meds for a few days and played bumper cars in the parking ramp at the Mall of America.

Right now, he flinched as if I'd slugged him with a baseball bat—something I'd wanted to do since the day he told the judge in Milwaukee that, yes, he and Mom agreed that reform school was the best thing for me. He hadn't even *told* Mom about Shangri-La; he lied to the judge. But adults lie all they want, no problem. Teenage girls who commit the heinous crime of trusting a guy get shipped to reform school. In my life, anyway.

He didn't say anything, just stood up and walked to the stairs, head down, as if I'd totally slaughtered him.

Served him right.

So when I heard the door softly shutting at the top of the stairs, I don't have a clue why I started to cry.

I DIDN'T TOUCH my guitar again, but I stayed downstairs watching *Animal House*, so busy wondering when Dad would summon me upstairs for my punishment that even John Belushi couldn't make me laugh.

At least, not much.

"Lydia?" Mom, not Dad. With any luck, coming to ask if I

wanted to go shopping. "You hurt your father's feelings, dear."

"Yeah?" My gaze didn't leave the TV screen, but it's possible that I smiled. "He has feelings? Who knew?"

"I don't understand this. You've always been such a good girl."

Only in Mom's opinion. Not even in mine. And definitely not in Dad's.

"And you're home now and, well, safe. Safe from all those nasty creatures they send to reform school."

Blinking, I finally darted a glance at Mom. "Nasty? You mean, like me?"

She waved a hand, but she seemed more nervous than her meds usually allowed. "Of course I don't mean you. That was a mistake. You never should've been sent there."

I glanced back at the movie. "Have you mentioned that to Dad? He's the one who sent me."

"The judge insisted on it. Your father told me so."

I snorted. "My *father* lied to you. I was right there in the courtroom, Mom. The judge gave Dad a few options. Dad picked the most convenient one. For him."

"He did not— He wouldn't." Mom sputtered, but the wild look in her eyes had nothing to do with bipolar disorder and everything to do with finally realizing that Dad really was an asshole.

I nailed his coffin shut. "He totally did. He also told the judge not to mention the other options in his court order, since he figured you'd eventually see it."

A few tears gathered in my eyes, but they were pure crocodile. I'd already cried enough real tears over what Dad had done to fill a bathtub.

But never in front of anyone.

"He didn't." The look in Mom's eyes, almost deadly, was what made her a good courtroom lawyer. It terrified the crap out of *me*, even though Dad was the one who should start running. And packing his bags.

Without another word, Mom marched toward the stairs. As she hit the bottom step, she looked back at me.

"Don't worry about being punished, dear, but I hope you'll get out in the sun. It's a nice day. At least, it was."

When the shrieking started a minute later, I knew it wouldn't be a nice day for Dad.

Excellent.

♫

I HESITATED AS I passed my old bedroom on my way to my new one. Cat was flopped on her bed, *The Catcher in the Rye* in her hands, but it looked like she'd barely made a dent in it.

I shook my head.

"Like *you've* read it."

"I have." Twice, I could've said, but the dark circles under Cat's eyes told me that more torture would just be overkill.

"Right. I heard what happened in English. Now you've got Skamser wrapped around your finger? How'd you do that?"

I rolled my eyes. "I slept with him. Satisfied?"

"Ew." Cat looked like she wanted to puke. "Only you would do something like that."

Unbelievable. I shot her a nasty look, then stomped down the hall to my room. Reaching the door to it, I whirled and headed back to Cat's room. Crossing to her bed in three pissed strides, I grabbed *The Catcher in the Rye* out of her hands and flung it through the still-punched-out window screen.

Cat leaped to her feet, following me to the window. A squirrel was already rubbing its tiny paws over the book like it was an overgrown nut.

"Where the hell do you get off? You're buying me a new one, and I'm telling Dad."

"Dad won't be much help to you." I jabbed my thumb in the direction of the shrieks still coming from downstairs. Dad was toast. "But you didn't used to be a squealer. Yet another ugly change you've made in the last year."

"And you didn't used to—" She broke off, glaring, as if she wished she had the guts to finish her sentence.

I crossed my arms. "I didn't used to what?"

"You didn't used to—" She took a deep breath, her nostrils flaring. "Sleep with every guy you met."

My eyebrows went up, but my stomach lurched.

She made a face. "I mean, you always *acted* like it, but I thought you were just toying with people."

"Yeah? The way you claim Tess toyed with you?"

Cat nodded, her lips quivering, even though it'd been six months since the band fiasco went down, and she'd wound up with the drummer in the band.

Oh, wait. Not lately.

"What *is* up with you and Jeremy? Did you guys really break up?"

As I asked the question, I knew she wouldn't answer. Cat hated me now, even though I didn't have a clue why.

Her lips were still quivering. "You know we did. And you know why."

"Wrong on both counts." I met her hostile gaze. "Unless I was right about the Heather scenario."

"This has nothing to do with Heather!"

I held up a hand. "Whatever. It also has nothing to do with me. No matter what you say."

"Kirk said—"

I frowned. "I thought you didn't talk to Kirk. Or Amber or Tess or any of them."

"I don't unless I have to." Unable to look at me, Cat glanced out the window, where a bunch of squirrels were having a raucous party on *The Catcher in the Rye*. Even if they didn't eat the pages, at this point the only thing in that book's future was a pair of rubber gloves and a one-way trip to the garbage can. "But Kirk still talks to *me*. At least, if it affects his stupid band."

"Jeremy's in that stupid band, you know."

"No kidding." Cat flicked a glance in my direction, but she seemed to be a million miles away. "Kirk told me Jeremy was quitting the band if you joined it. That's when I told them you didn't even play guitar."

I sucked in a breath, unable to process it. Jeremy would quit if I joined the band? What would be so horrible about *me* joining the band? They put up with Mary! Worse, even though I knew Cat had been the one who ratted me out, hearing it directly from her quivering mouth still hit me between the eyes.

Which was exactly where I wanted to hit her.

Visualizing it, I punched my right fist into the palm of my left hand. "You little shit."

"But you don't play. I mean, you just started."

"You *squealed*, Cat. You didn't used to be the sort of little shit who squealed."

Her shoulder lifted in the tiniest shrug imaginable.

I backed away from her. "And I didn't do anything to make Jeremy dump you, but I can't blame him."

She looked up at me when I reached the door, but all of the accusation in her eyes a few minutes ago was gone. An apology was also missing in action.

I shook my head. "You suck."

168

I PULLED ANOTHER afternoon of hard labor for Mr. Fogarty, grateful for the sunshine and the cash and not much else. Okay, being outside also gave me a reprieve from Mom's tirade against Dad, which showed no signs of letting up by dinnertime. She served an amazingly decent burger to me and a veggie burger to Cat, then dropped a minuscule charred hockey puck on Dad's plate.

He deserved it, and more, but I didn't need to watch.

By Sunday, I was ready for anything that didn't involve hedge clippers, paintbrushes, or Mom's screaming, so I gave Drew a call. He said we were still friends, right?

Once he got past the stuttering, probably because Chelsea was three inches away from him and breathing fire, he admitted that the band was practicing at two o'clock at Michael's house.

But he didn't offer me a ride.

Fine by me. I was getting used to walking everywhere, and catching rides with Drew sometimes came with drawbacks. Like getting my hair yanked out by Chelsea.

I ran a hand through my hair as I hung up, wondering if it would ever grow out. Wondering if I wanted it to. No one in the world mistook me for Cat anymore, and seeing how she'd turned out made me grateful for that.

At two o'clock, I took off for Michael's house in a miniskirt and without breathing a word to Cat. She hated the band, didn't she? And hated me more? I didn't even need to get to the fact that the drummer in the band had dumped her.

Reaching Michael's house, I walked inside without bothering to ring the bell. Once again, his parents were nowhere in sight. I wish I could say the same for mine, who'd now been fighting at the top of Mom's lungs for over twenty-four hours straight.

I went down to the basement, feeling almost unsure of myself. Definitely a new experience. Because of Kirk? I liked him, but I'd known him forever. Drew and Chelsea? No way. Drew finally knew the score—I'd flirted, maybe too much, but wasn't interested—and Chelsea wasn't worth my time. Jeremy? He hated me enough to threaten to leave the band, but he wasn't the first person I'd ever met who hated me. Just the first guy.

Squaring my shoulders as I reached the bottom step, I strutted into the basement as if I owned it.

I blinked when the first person I saw was Cat.

Her jaw dropped when she saw me, but I don't know why. I'd come to a couple of band practices, hadn't I? Unlike her?

I glanced at the wraparound couch, which held Cat, Amber, Drew, Chelsea, and two other girls, leaving a space big enough for maybe half of me on the end closest to the band. Right next to Chelsea.

Swallowing my disappointment, I sashayed over to the couch and plunked down next to Chelsea, then wiggled my butt until she scooched a few inches closer to Drew.

Drew stared at my bare legs, and his Adam's apple bobbed in time to the music, but that was Chelsea's problem. If I exacerbated her problem by not tugging my skirt down, that was just a bonus.

The band finished a Green Day song I loved with an unexpected flourish by Heather on her guitar, something I couldn't have pulled off if they paid me a million bucks. As I stared at her, envious, Kirk shaded his eyes against the glare of the band lights and called out to me through his mic—as if I weren't sitting fifteen feet away from the guy.

"Lydia, is that you? Thanks for coming out."

Chelsea snorted, but it only made her resemble a pig even more, and that worked for me.

I waved at Kirk. "Hey. You're sounding good."

He looked good, too, except for his stupid rock-star sunglasses. Tight jeans, a black T-shirt with the sleeves cut off, and arms that were both tan and ripped. Okay, Kirk was hot. But his girlfriend, Amber, was five feet away from me, and Kirk hadn't exactly called, let alone asked me out, and I didn't feel like begging. I was as good as he was, and I was *way* better than Amber.

I just wish I could stop biting my lip.

The band started its next song, Lady Gaga's "Paparazzi," with Heather singing in her soft, sweet soprano. The guys in the band watched her as she sang, all of them except Jeremy acting like they had a crush on her. Jeremy always looked like his eyes were closed when he played drums, and now his closed eyes seemed to be facing the wraparound couch—aimed at Cat—but still. Definitely no worship of Heather.

It was the only thing I liked about Jeremy.

An hour and a half later, when the band finished its last song, I wondered why I'd just wasted a gorgeous September afternoon in a dark basement, sitting with people I couldn't stand, listening to a band that had replaced me. Easily.

And that was before Kirk walked right past me to Amber, pulled her to her feet, and wrapped her in the biggest hug I'd ever seen him give a girl.

As my shoulders slumped, Chelsea's hips sent me flying off the end of the couch.

"Hey! You bitch."

"Sorry." Not according to her nasty grin. "I guess I forgot you were there. It's just that you're so—"

"Skinny? Unlike you?"

Her glare made her look even less attractive, if that was possible. "Easy to forget. You're just so easy to forget."

Next to her, Drew had gone rigid, but no one else seemed to notice. Kirk was whispering something to Amber, Jeremy and Cat eyed each other warily, and the two girls who'd been sitting next to Amber took off for the stairs.

I gave Chelsea an amused up-and-down. "Talk about easy to forget. You could've invented the concept of amnesia."

I heard someone laugh—Cat, shocking me—a moment before someone else grabbed my arm. Zach. Shocking me even more.

"Need a ride? I was heading in that direction, if you're ready to go now."

I frowned at him. Zach? Who hated me the last time he gave me a ride and didn't bother to hide it? Who probably *did* find me easy to forget?

"I don't—"

"Great." He didn't let go of my arm, just tugged me to the stairs. Part of me was too surprised to fight him. Part of me—okay, my legs, from all that weeding yesterday—was grateful I wouldn't have to walk.

As I followed him upstairs, I heard dead silence behind me. Apparently, I wasn't the only one Zach had shocked, but I was the one leaving with him in a butt-ugly orange VW Beetle.

Why he'd asked, I had no idea.

"GOOD FRIENDS WITH Chelsea, huh?"

I blinked as I fastened my seatbelt, wondering if he was serious or actually had a sense of humor. Oh, wait. He must. He wore a Cat in the Hat tattoo and drove a bright-orange car just because his mom liked it. "She's a real trip."

Zach pulled out from the curb. "You don't want to mess with her."

I shrugged. "She shouldn't mess with *me*, but she's not my issue. I just feel sorry for Drew."

"Yeah. Real sorry."

He switched on the radio. Vomit-inducing classical music poured out, just like the last time. Unlike the last time, I didn't try to change the station.

I was too busy being annoyed with Zach.

"Of course I feel sorry for Drew." My jaw clenched, maybe because I didn't feel a bit sorry. Drew was an idiot and a wimp. He deserved Chelsea. "He could've dated my—"

I broke off, not sure I should mention Drew's past history with Cat, such as it was, since Cat was now with Jeremy—or at least had been, and might be again.

"Your what?" Zach flicked a glance at me before returning his gaze to the road. "He could've been lucky enough to date *you?*"

I bristled at the way he said it, as if I had a disease. Did every guy in the band hate me? Even the ones—like Zach—I didn't know?

"Not that it's any of your business, but he's not my type. Like, at all."

"So you were just giving him artificial resuscitation the last two times I saw you as a humanitarian gesture?"

"Ha ha ha." Pissed, I crossed my arms and wondered if I should leap out of the car the next time he slowed for a corner. But I was still wearing the miniskirt—which he didn't seem to notice, by the way—and something about his hostility made my lips twitch. I mean, seriously. The guy was too funny. I slid him a glance even though his own gaze was locked on the road. Mr. Driver's Ed. "I guess we have that in common, huh?"

When he finally looked over at me, his light-brown hair—soft and shiny enough for me to covet—almost covered his eyes. Hazel eyes, I decided after a moment. Probably the first thought I'd had about Zach that didn't involve his tattoo, his car, or his overprotective attitude.

I nodded in answer to the question in his stupid hazel eyes.

"We're both into humanitarian gestures. Me with Drew, you with me."

Frowning, he glanced at my lips and—just for an instant—at the tops of my thighs. Maybe he wasn't *completely* impervious to miniskirts or the terror known as Lydia Bennet.

His gaze went back to the road, but his knuckles were white on the steering wheel, and I don't think it was because I'd pissed him off. At least, not today.

"I didn't give you a ride to kiss you."

Kiss me? He'd even *thought* about kissing me?

Grinning, I twisted in my seat, even though it made my miniskirt ride up a little. Or maybe *because* it did. He didn't glance down at my legs again, though. His jaw clenched, and his knuckles were nearly popping through his skin, but he must've already looked at me as much as he could handle.

"So why *did* you give me a ride? I walked to Michael's house, and I could've walked home. You really *do* get off on humanitarian gestures? Like a Boy Scout?"

The corner of his mouth twisted. "Only on Sundays."

I laughed. He was funny when he relaxed around me, which wasn't often. Leaning back against my headrest, I tugged my skirt down—another humanitarian gesture—and wished we could hang out together. But we were just a few blocks from my house, and Zach didn't look like the kind of guy who did joyrides. It didn't fit with the classical music.

We rode in silence until we reached the corner closest to my house, when he cleared his throat. "You're okay, Lydia."

I blinked. "Yeah?"

"I gave you a ride to get you away from Chelsea."

"Thanks, but I can—"

"And Drew, who can't handle you. And Kirk and Amber."

It was too late to fling myself out of his car, unfortunately, but I contemplated slugging the guy. Hard.

"You forgot Cat and Jeremy. What's the matter? You think they can somehow handle me?"

He tilted his head. "Doubtful. But whatever is going on with them isn't about you. They might think so, but it isn't."

"And you know this because—?"

He pulled up in front of my house. Shocking the hell out of me, he turned off the engine and half turned toward me. "I hear everything, and I pay attention."

I rolled my eyes. "You must've heard enough about me, then, to make you faint. No wonder you're into humanitarian gestures. Maybe you think you can reform me?"

"I wouldn't even try." He glanced at my hair, but I couldn't tell if he wanted to run his hands through it or shave it all off and ship me to a convent for wayward girls. "I hear everything, but I didn't say I believed it all."

"Imagine my relief."

I grabbed the door handle and started to open it—jumping when he reached across to stop me.

I couldn't help it. I slapped his hand. "Don't do me any favors, okay? You gave me a ride I didn't need and saved me from Chelsea, which I also didn't need. You don't need to believe me or *not* believe what other people say about me. So go bug someone else. Like maybe Heather."

I turned to reach for the door handle again, partly because I wanted to get out of this stupid car and partly because I was two seconds from crying. I refused to cry in front of Zach any more than I would in front of my dad.

He didn't stop me this time, but he spoke again, so softly I barely heard it. "You're not as bad as you claim to be, Lydia. It's just that you're—"

"—not your type. Too wild. Too whatever."

I couldn't believe I'd filled in the blank for him, but I'd heard this speech too many times in my life.

Shoving the door open and climbing out, I didn't even bother to yank my skirt down. Zach didn't give a rat's ass. He probably *did* like a goody-goody like Heather, just like the other guys. And I wasn't into guys who played classical music and drove butt-ugly cars just to make their mom happy.

With any luck, I wouldn't see Zach again. As I heard his car slowly pull away from the curb, I hoped I got my wish.

Chapter 13

"Her character will be fixed, and she will,
at sixteen, be the most determined flirt
that ever made herself and her family ridiculous."

— Jane Austen, *Pride and Prejudice*
Volume II, Chapter Eighteen

I KEPT MY head down the next couple of weeks—at school, at home, you name it—and focused on homework, guitar, Mr. Fogarty's never-ending list of jobs, and a few ugly trips to the school gym to reacquaint myself with the uneven parallel bars.

I hadn't shaved my head, but I might as well have entered a convent. A convent of one.

Cat and I did our best to avoid each other. I didn't see her with Jeremy. In fact, except for random passes in the hall, I didn't see either of them, period.

I was so used to my new cloistered life that I barely looked up when Lauren tapped my arm in Accounting class.

"The band is playing a gig this weekend. Eight o'clock Friday night at the pizza joint next to Cold Stone Creamery off

Valley Creek Road. Russo's?"

I glanced at her. "The band?"

The only band I could think of was Kirk's, but Goth Chick didn't exactly strike me as the type to hang out with anyone from school. At least, if the rumors were true, not anyone who wasn't doing drugs.

She nodded. "I promised Zach I'd come. You know, for old times' sake."

I frowned. "Because you used to get naked in wading pools together?"

I still couldn't picture it. Okay, I could picture Lauren doing it—she looked like she was up for pretty much anything—but Zach? No way. He'd probably been the only four-year-old in town who never ran around naked or did a damn thing his mom didn't want him to do.

Ms. Frey walked in then, so Lauren just gave me a cryptic smile and pretended to flip through her textbook. She didn't ask me to come watch the band with her. She probably thought I'd get in the way of her making a date with Zach to get naked afterward, in a wading pool or otherwise. But why would I have the slightest interest in Zach? I still wanted Kirk. More important, I *didn't* want Zach.

Last time I checked, hell hadn't frozen over.

FRIDAY NIGHT, I had no idea why I had a sudden craving for Cold Stone ice cream. Or maybe a slice of pizza.

I really had no idea why Dad let me take the Jeep.

Cat had been hiding out in her room when I got home from my guitar lesson, where Jazz had finally let me move on to a new song: Coldplay's "Yellow." I was in such a good mood, I almost knocked on Cat's door and asked if she wanted to go out—for Cold Stone or pizza, not necessarily to hear the band—but my hand hesitated. Finally, I shook my head and headed downstairs.

As I walked out to the Jeep, my good mood gone, I still couldn't believe she'd blabbed about my guitar prowess or lack thereof. Sure, the band would've figured out I couldn't play guitar in five seconds *without* her help, but the Cat I used to know would never have done it.

Ten stomach-churning minutes later, I walked in the door of Russo's. Kirk and the rest of the band were setting up in the corner at the far end, framed by floor-to-ceiling windows on two sides. Seeing Kirk in his usual rock-star sunglasses, I grinned and let out the breath I'd been holding.

Some things didn't change.

My grin faded when I spied the table closest to the band. Drew, Chelsea, Amber, and Tess. No chair for me. Not that I wanted to sit with any of them except maybe Drew, and even Drew created too many complications in my life.

Just like everyone else I knew.

As I stood by the door, debating where to sit or whether to leave, it took me several moments to realize that someone was calling my name. It wasn't anyone in the band, and it definitely wasn't anyone at Drew's table.

Out of the corner of my eye, I spied Lauren. Sitting at the bar.

My mind flickered to a memory I thought I'd long since buried: that judge in Milwaukee, who'd droned on about all the things I couldn't do if I ever got out of reform school. I'm pretty sure sitting at a bar was on the list. A bar in a family pizza parlor? It wasn't a chance I planned to take.

Pretending I hadn't heard Lauren, I strolled over to Drew's table. Casually. Feeling everyone's eyes on me.

But not like in the old days, when I ruled.

Not at all like the old days.

"Hey, Drew." I ruffled his hair as I walked by, unable to resist annoying Chelsea and totally forgetting for a moment that Kirk might be watching. "Good to see you."

Drew blinked several times, probably trying to find his tongue or his brain. Ignoring Chelsea and Amber, I gave Tess a friendly wave. She sat so straight, I could've sworn she had a pole up her ass. In fact, it was how she'd looked all semester: unhappy but stoic. No wonder. She was forced to hang out with Amber and Chelsea.

I nodded at her as I grabbed the nearest empty table. "Hey, martyrdom is so last year." In my case, literally. "Join me? It's been ages since we've really talked."

Not since I'd been back, definitely. Before that? In truth, Tess had always been closer to Cat than to me. I'd had Cat and, for better or worse, a million guys. I hadn't needed or wanted girlfriends, but some of the girls had worshipped me.

Girls like Tess.

She gave me a quick head shake, her gaze darting everywhere but at me or anyone at her table. Finally, she put her straw to her mouth and sipped.

And proceeded to choke.

She kept choking, totally hunched over and bug-eyed. When no one at her table did anything, I leaped to my feet to pound her on the back or try the Heimlich maneuver or maybe just slap her. With Tess lately, I couldn't decide.

Lauren beat me to it.

"Ow!" With a final cough, Tess sat up straight again, even as Lauren gave her another whack between the shoulder blades. Based on the grim set to Lauren's jaw, I'm pretty sure the last one was unnecessary. "Stop! I mean, uh, thanks. Lauren. I'm good now."

She sneered as she said Lauren's name, looking as if Lauren

had delivered live cockroaches to their table rather than helped her out when her so-called friends didn't.

It was pretty much how I'd treated Lauren ever since she tried to slip drugs to me in Accounting class.

Seeing Tess deliver the sting, and Lauren wince, I shook my head and waved Lauren over to my table.

The look she gave me mirrored the one Tess had given her. Without a word, she walked back to the bar.

Wow.

"Even Lydia Bennet has to admit she's shit when a skank like Lauren Kjelstad disses her. Is it too late to send her back to reform school? Maybe we can send them both." Chelsea flipped her hand through her lawnmower-cut hair to emphasize her words, which she'd already emphasized loudly enough for everyone in Woodbury, Minnesota, to hear.

Including, for instance, Zach. I watched as he calmly, methodically, set his bass guitar on its stand, stepped down from the makeshift stage, and walked over to Chelsea's table. But he didn't look at Chelsea.

Instead, slapping both his hands on the table, he got in Drew's face. "Hate to say it, but it's hard to believe you chose this one over Lydia or, for that matter, Cat Bennet. You might want to rethink your taste."

Oh. My. God.

Wait. How did Zach know about Drew and Cat? The guy *must* pay attention.

"How dare you?" Chelsea leaped to her feet, even though Drew fumbled to grab her hand and tug her back down. "Who *are* you? Besides a total loser, obviously."

She laughed, loudly and totally fake, but she also shot a wide-eyed pleading look at Amber and Tess. Amber offered her usual pinched smirk, which could mean anything, including gastric issues. Tess glanced at me, looking terrified, as if she was holding her breath.

Amber didn't surprise me, but what had happened to Tess? Depending on her mood, the Tess I knew would've either fed Chelsea to the sharks or given Zach a good, hard shove. She hadn't been afraid of anyone.

Except maybe, appropriately, me.

"Hey, we need to finish setting up." Kirk, sunglasses in place, came up and put his hand on Zach's shoulder.

Zach didn't budge. He kept glaring down at Drew, whose Adam's apple bobbed like crazy.

"Zach. Dude."

Zach glanced over his shoulder at Kirk. "I can't help it if your girlfriend is pals with her." He flicked a cold glance at Chelsea. "She apologizes and shuts the fuck up, or I leave."

Everyone stared at Chelsea. Okay, everyone but Drew, who kept swallowing convulsively. He seemed way too young for a heart attack, but you never know.

But seriously? Drew really needed to grow a spine. Cat was so much better off without him.

Even if she didn't have Jeremy these days, either.

"We don't need this crap, do we?" Chelsea, still standing, wobbled on her heels. Her voice wobbled, too. "Guys? Is it our fault if Russo's lets *anyone* in?"

She cut me a scathing glance. Grinning, I gave her a little finger wave.

No one at her table said a word. Drew touched her hand, but he was avoiding Zach's stare.

"Guys? Seriously. This place reeks."

Probably not the smartest thing to say in front of Russo's manager, Antonio Russo, son of the owners and an old boyfriend of Jane's. He strolled over from behind the bar, casually.

"Miss? I'm afraid you're disturbing our other guests. I'll have to ask you to leave."

I nodded my thanks to Antonio, even though he probably didn't remember me. I'd been a zit-prone and hair-challenged seventh grader when he and Jane had gone out their whole junior year of high school.

Antonio's eyebrows danced a moment before he turned back to Chelsea with a serious face.

Arms crossed, she glanced from him to me. "Now I get it. Lydia's probably slept with this guy, too."

I blinked.

Zach, Kirk, and Drew all looked at me. Amber smirked. Tess looked everywhere but at me. Avoiding all of them, I glanced at the bar. Lauren had disappeared.

Antonio pasted a polite smile on his face. "Miss, please leave. Your friends may want to leave, too."

Tess's mouth formed a perfect "O," her first real reaction to anything tonight except when she nearly choked to death. Amber wiped the smirk off her face and glared at Kirk.

Kirk sighed. "Hey, Antonio, totally understand. But okay if my girlfriend and her friend Tess stay? They promise not to create an uproar."

He grinned over the tops of his sunglasses at Amber, who didn't grin back.

"Amber? Tess?" Chelsea waved a hand wildly at them, even more wildly when they studiously avoided her gaze. She frowned at Kirk. "Kirk? We were all gonna listen to you guys tonight."

Sunglasses back in place, Kirk gave her a brief smile before turning to Drew. "Sorry, dude. Catch you soon?"

After a long moment, Drew nodded. "No prob. See you."

Pushing back from the table, Drew stood up and pulled a couple of bills from his wallet while Chelsea tugged on his sleeve and screeched in his ear.

Everyone else, including Antonio, remained frozen.

Finally, Drew and Chelsea left, Chelsea still screeching. An instant later, a waiter appeared at my table with a Coke—not a Diet Coke, unlike every other girl I knew—and an order of shrimp cocktail. Since I hadn't ordered anything yet, I shook my head. The waiter shrugged and pointed at Antonio.

Maybe Antonio *did* remember Jane's bratty little sister, even though we hadn't eaten here since before Shangri-La. Since before Milwaukee. Since forever.

Antonio nodded before returning to the bar, at the same time Kirk and Zach walked back to the stage.

"Chelsea sure got *that* right. The poor guy must be another Lydia conquest."

Unlike Chelsea, Amber said it only loudly enough for Tess and me to hear.

Forcing myself to grin, I stabbed a shrimp in the cocktail sauce. "You didn't used to be so gutless, Amber. What's the matter? Trying so hard to keep your sharp claws in Kirk makes you a little nervous?" When she sputtered, I took a bite of the shrimp. Yum. "Can't blame you."

When her nose flared, reminding me of a gorilla, I can't say it was a good look for her.

I also can't believe I used to hang with Tess and Amber. And Drew. And even maybe Kirk? In the year I'd been gone, the girls had become whiny, bitchy, and pathetic. Even without regard to his lousy taste in girlfriends, Drew couldn't seem to form an opinion. And what *was* it with Kirk and his stupid sunglasses?

Had everyone, along with Cat, always been like this?

Worse: had I?

Pondering it all, I munched on the shrimp cocktail, slurped my Coke, and ordered a small seafood pizza. It wasn't on the menu, but I remembered Jane getting a takeout version of it for me once. A million years and a trip to reform school ago.

Next thing I knew, and without any introduction, the band started playing Coldplay's "Yellow," with Heather on lead vocals.

I tapped my fingertips on the table in time to the rhythm, trying and totally failing to remember how to play *any* of it on guitar, when I glanced up to realize Kirk and Zach were staring at me.

And maybe Jeremy. With his half-closed eyes, I could never tell.

But what did *I* do? Tess nearly choked to death, and Lauren helped her when Amber and Chelsea didn't. And, okay, Lauren dissed me, but only because she didn't know all the rules that followed me even after I left Shangri-La.

But I didn't get Chelsea kicked out.

Even if I'd enjoyed every moment of it.

"They're just looking at you because they're so pissed." Amber, speaking even more quietly, kept her gaze on Kirk as she said it, but she was definitely speaking to me.

I rolled my eyes. "More likely, they're looking at me because they're guys, and I'm the only remotely cute girl within half a mile."

Amber, who'd been in the process of nibbling on a slice of pizza, dropped the slice down the front of her shirt. Her yellow, stretchy, clingy shirt now had enormous blobs of tomato sauce on each of her boobs.

Rolling my eyes, I glanced at the band. Heather stumbled on the words to the chorus of "Yellow," then fumbled with her guitar before she stopped strumming altogether.

Kirk grinned but kept playing.

Zach was playing bass as if "Yellow" was a raging heavy-metal song. Which it wasn't. Understatement.

I glanced over at the bar and caught Zach looking in that direction, too. Lauren hadn't returned.

Yep, Zach was definitely pissed. Maybe he and Lauren didn't hang out naked in wading pools anymore, or maybe they did, but he was way more protective of Lauren than Kirk and Drew were of *their* girlfriends.

Not that I gave a damn. Not about Zach or Lauren or Kirk or Drew or any of them.

I stayed until I finished my pizza, but I don't think I heard another song the band played.

♫

"YOU TOOK THE Jeep."

Cat's charms weren't all that.

I tossed the keys in the general direction of the bowl on the small chest in the front hall. Missed it completely. Shrugging, I bent down to pick them up just as Cat's foot booted them halfway down the hall.

Leaping to my feet, I waved a fist in her face. "You almost kicked my hand! What the hell?"

She didn't back up, and her eyelids didn't so much as flicker. "My aim must be off. I was going for your face."

"Girls?" Mom stepped out of the kitchen, swallowing hard and wiping what looked like frosting off the corner of her mouth. "Why are you fighting? You two never used to fight. You were such good girls."

Mom is a great lawyer, but her memory can be pretty questionable.

"Lydia stole the Jeep." Cat jabbed her finger at me, barely missing my face. "Dad said *I* get to drive the Jeep. Lydia can't."

Mom's tongue caught the last of the frosting. "I told your father that Lydia could take the Jeep tonight. She's no longer in *reform school*." She screeched that last part, so Dad must be somewhere in the vicinity. "But you can both drive the Jeep. Take turns."

Mom smiled so brightly, I could tell she was hurting. She still didn't speak to Dad without screaming, and he deserved it, but Mom didn't deserve to find out that her husband had pulled a stunt like this on both Mom and me.

"We will, Mom. Totally." I patted her arm the way I might pat a three-year-old who'd just ripped up her knee on a floor full of broken glass. Carefully. Cooing at her. "You don't need to worry about Cat and me."

"Bullshit." Cat blurted it out, caught her breath, then started shaking. "Just like always, you have Mom wrapped around your finger. I am so freaking *sick* of it."

Mom started shaking now, too. Couldn't Cat see it? For once in her life, couldn't she worry about someone other than herself?

"Jesus, Cat. She just wants us to get along." I shrugged, even though Mom had recoiled at my word choice. "I'd like that, too, you know."

Cat rolled her eyes. "What's the matter? No one else is speaking to you?"

As a matter of fact, no. But it wasn't why I missed Cat. Even living under the same roof, five feet down the hall from her, I missed my twin. So sue me.

"Girls, you love each other. You know you do." Even Mom didn't look like she believed it, though. Mom, who had a tear or two in the corner of her eye. Mom, who really *would* do anything for me.

And I mean that in a good way.

Brushing past me, Cat grabbed the keys to the Jeep off the floor. "Hate to break it to you, but maybe we never did."

She took off out the front door without her purse. Next to me, Mom called after her long after an engine rumbled and the Jeep peeled out and roared down the street.

♫

MY CHEMISTRY AND Algebra weekend homework assignments made *The Catcher in the Rye* seem like a good time in comparison.

In the old days—before Shangri-La—Cat and I would've laughed over the homework together, ignored it most of the weekend, and spent Sunday night searching desperately online for shortcuts to doing it.

Cat wasn't in any of my classes this year, even though I'd emailed her last spring to tell her what I was signing up for. Saturday morning, alone with my books, Boris, and Mary's old study aids, I finally realized that our separate classes might not be an accident.

I heard a door slam downstairs followed by the thunder of running footsteps that usually meant Liz was in the house.

Sure enough, my bedroom door banged open. Boris took a flying leap off the armoire and landed on my legs. Ouch.

"Studying?" Liz's eyebrows went up the way anyone else's would in my family if anyone else in my family was speaking to me or even gave a shit. "What are you taking?"

Laying my Chem book upside down on my bed, I shrugged. "Chemistry with Mr. Schumacher. Algebra with Ms. Patel."

Liz would've taken Advanced Chem and Calculus in her senior year of high school, but Liz was a brainiac, now majoring in biomedical engineering. I'd always taken the bare minimum to get by. That had changed in a big way at Shangri-La, and so had my grades, but we still didn't have much in common.

No matter what Mr. Fogarty kept telling me.

Liz took a few steps closer, peering at my textbooks, Mary's study aids, and the sneer on my face.

"Need any help?"

"I'm good."

Okay, not particularly, but Liz didn't need to waste her

weekend on me. She wore running shoes and workout clothes, and if I didn't know how many miles it was from her apartment in south Minneapolis to our house in Woodbury—thirty? minimum?—I wouldn't put it past her to have run all the way here.

"Are you studying all weekend?"

Was that code for asking if I really had no social life? No friends? No nothing?

All true. Bizarre but true. But only momentarily.

I shook my head. "I'll probably play some guitar."

If I practiced every day for the next five years, maybe Jazz would break down and teach me something by Green Day.

Or maybe she wouldn't.

"You're still playing? Cool." Liz said it without smirking, but it didn't mean she wouldn't laugh hysterically about it with Jane later.

"Where's Jane?"

Liz glanced back at the open door. "Like you, she's actually studying. Everyone I know is studying today. Cat, too?"

I snorted. Only if absolutely everything had changed. "I wouldn't know."

"What's *with* you guys?" Liz glanced at the foot of my bed as if she planned to sit there, but Boris bared his teeth at her. When I rubbed his back, she sat instead in the middle of the floor. I still hadn't gotten rid of Mary's ugly, disgusting, multi-stained rug. If I were Liz, I wouldn't risk sitting on it, but Liz was fearless. Stupidly, in this case. "You and Cat used to be as tight as Jane and I are."

"Times change. People change."

I hadn't, but Cat had.

Liz skewered me with the sort of intense stare that would take out a lesser mortal. Having survived a year at Shangri-La with girls who could frighten even Liz, I didn't flinch. Instead, I picked up my Chemistry textbook.

"You're seriously going to study and play guitar. Then what?"

"Study some more?"

Liz leaned back on her hands and stretched out long legs that I'd kill for. "What happened to you in reform school?"

I'd rather not think about it. Ever again. "I've been home six weeks. Believe it or not, you're the first person to ask that question."

Liz's jaw dropped. Another first.

Being Liz, she grinned and made a quick recovery. "Like they say, I'm the reigning queen of empathy in this family."

I snorted. "*No* one says that."

"They will now." Relaxing again, she studied me. "Seriously. No one has asked? Not Mom or Dad?" She scowled, although it might be because she'd finally realized exactly how disgusting the rug was, and she was sitting on it. "Not Cat?"

"No one."

Lucky thing reform school had toughened me up so much. Otherwise, the realization that no one in this family gave a shit— not when I left, not when I came back—might make me cry.

And they weren't worth it.

At all.

Liz stood up, then surprised me when she walked out of my room without a word. She *didn't* surprise me when she walked back in a minute later with one towel draped around her neck and another that she threw on the end of my bed, startling Boris into a squeak. She shrugged, which was as close as Liz ever came to asking permission.

"So tell me. What happened to you in reform school?"

I scooted back a few inches, pressing my back against my headboard. "I survived."

Silence. Liz wasn't exactly known for it.

"You *are* different." She tugged on the ends of the towel around her neck. "What I mean is, at first I didn't think so, but I've noticed."

I rolled my eyes, then blinked away a drop of moisture. "You don't need to patronize me. So I study now. I'm playing guitar. Big deal."

I also wasn't partying. But only because I wasn't invited to any parties.

Liz leaned back against the wall. Lucky thing it was already stained. Seriously, this whole room could qualify for federal disaster relief. "I'm not patronizing you. I just said you're different, and I'm glad you're sticking with guitar. Mary always said—"

I held up a hand. "I've already heard enough about Mary being a rock goddess on guitar, thanks."

"You don't know Mary." Liz shook her head but looked thoughtful. "Any more than I know you, I guess."

"She's a geeky nerd who, last time I checked, likes to tattle on everyone."

Liz barked out a laugh. "Okay, she's never completely gotten over the tattling, but we all have our faults. Even I'm not perfect. I'm sweating all over your wall."

"No shit." We both laughed. "Maybe it's time to break down and paint this room. Make it my own."

But was it mine? What would happen when Mary came home on break? Would I be relegated to the basement?

Knowing Dad, absolutely.

Liz glanced around, her eyebrows going up when she saw Mary's poster of the periodic table still taped to the wall. I hadn't bothered taking it down. It actually helped me with Chemistry. "Hey, if Cat can repaint the Jeep, I'm thinking you can throw some paint on these walls. I'll even help if you like."

My gaze left the periodic table and shot straight to Liz. I

couldn't read her. After reform school, where it could be a life-saving skill, I thought I could read anyone. But not lately. "Why?"

Liz clapped a hand over her heart. "Do I need a reason to help my sister?"

"Pretty much."

"Fine." Liz grinned. "Alex is in Connecticut, Mom can't be trusted with a paintbrush, and I want to hear exactly what happened in reform school. All the gory details."

Turning away, I stared out the window. The early-morning sun had surrendered to dark storm clouds, and the first raindrops were hitting the dirty windowpanes. Something else I needed to clean.

Okay, I needed to clean up everything. Maybe even my life.

After several moments during which Liz amazed me by not saying a word, I turned back to her. "It's your poison."

She laughed. "No, that would be Mom's cooking."

Chapter 14

*"I dare say he often hears worse things said
than I am going to say. But he is an ugly fellow!
I am glad he is gone."*

— Jane Austen, *Pride and Prejudice*
Volume II, Chapter Sixteen

LIZ FOUND TWO gallons of shockingly hot-pink paint in the basement, a remnant of one of Mom's manic phases. My nose scrunched when I saw the color, more so when Liz painted a broad slash of it on my bedroom wall.

It was blinding.

Liz's lips twitched. "Hey, I also found a really dark puke-green paint and a gallon of black. Pretty clearly *not* from a manic phase."

Biting my lip, I stared at the paint slash on the dirty beige wall. "Does she ever have a phase during which she buys light blue or purple?"

"In a word? No." Liz nodded at the paint can in the middle of the floor. "I actually like it. Bold and fun."

I was less enthusiastic. But I had to sleep here. "Would you paint your own room this color?"

Liz waved her paintbrush in the air, spraying a few drops of paint on Boris's tail. He kept whirling in a circle, trying to lick it off.

Laughing, Liz somehow managed to corner Boris long enough to wipe off his tail with turpentine. "Jane would kill me. And, yeah, I'd probably go with light blue or purple."

"Great minds think alike."

But Liz and I *weren't* alike. At all. Mr. Fogarty might be nice, but he was also wacked.

Liz set the brush on top of the still-open paint can. "So what do you think? Hot pink or drive to Menards for light blue or purple?"

She must seriously have nothing to do today. "Menards?"

"Killjoy. What are we going to do with all of this hot-pink paint?"

"Put on sunglasses and paint Mom's office?"

Liz shook a hot-pink finger at me. "I take back what I said before. Maybe you haven't changed."

I smirked. "Not in the essentials."

A FEW HOURS later, after the fumes from the violet paint that now covered my bedroom walls became too much for both of us, Liz talked me into a run to Dairy Queen, claiming she might faint if she didn't have a cherry Dilly Bar.

I couldn't shake the feeling that Dad had sicced her on me as my new guard dog, but I didn't have anything else to do, and it was better than a lock on my bedroom door. Since I *wasn't* Liz, though, I didn't get a cherry Dilly Bar.

I got a chocolate one.

She sprang for it. What the hell. I let her.

"So." Liz bit off a chunk of her Dilly Bar. "You were going to tell me about reform school."

I shook my head. "I was *going* to slog through my Chemistry and Algebra homework, then spend some quality time mangling my D chord."

She rolled her eyes. "Mary used to bitch about her D chord, too. What is it with D chords?"

I licked my Dilly Bar. "To be fair, my C chord can be frightening, too. My teacher mentioned bar chords but said she's not sure she has the courage to listen to me trying them."

"Ha ha." Liz eyed my Dilly Bar as if she contemplated stealing it the moment she finished hers. Good luck with that. "You make me glad I never tried guitar, but you're sticking with it. Lack of better things to do?"

Zing. The Liz I knew was back.

I shrugged. "It's better than talking about reform school. Believe me, you don't want to know."

"I wouldn't mind hearing."

I jerked at the deep voice behind me. Whirling in the booth, I looked up—and up some more—at Zach. His deadly serious face was an improvement over his angry scowls last night while the band played, but not by much.

"Zach?"

"I also wouldn't mind a Dilly, but I think I'll stick with cherry." He whipped his own cherry Dilly Bar from behind his back. "Join you?"

"Um."

Taking that as permission, he sat down. "You were about to tell your sister—Liz, right?—about reform school. Don't let me interrupt."

It was more than Zach usually said to me, but he also wasn't usually this cheerful. Had he gotten together with Lauren after last night's gig? Had he scored a million kisses—or more than kisses—when the only person I'd kissed in forever, and only by accident, was Drew?

I bit off a huge chunk of my Dilly Bar. It was so cold, I started to choke.

Liz and Zach both thumped me on the back. At the same time. Then both started laughing.

Liz swallowed the last of her Dilly Bar and wiped her hands, several fingers of which were still painted hot pink or violet. "I'm Liz, yeah, but do I know you? Zach?"

"I was two years behind you. Mary's class."

"I remember now. You're an artist like Cat. You were at the art show last spring."

"Cat's a much better artist, but I try. I also played in the band with Mary until she left for MIT."

The whole time he was talking, Zach methodically bit off the cherry coating on his Dilly Bar. He now had a round blob of vanilla ice cream on a stick. Bizarre. No wonder he played classical music on his car radio.

It didn't explain the Cat in the Hat tattoo, though.

"Oh, yeah." Liz lifted an eyebrow at Zach's devoid-of-cherry-coating Dilly Bar, so I wasn't the only one. "You play bass? Mary mentioned you, but I've never heard you play. How do *you* feel about D chords?"

D chords. Guitar. Shit. So much for claiming I'd played guitar for years. Of course, thanks to Cat, Zach already knew the truth, no matter what Liz and Jane claimed to Kirk.

Zach looked at Liz, not me. "On bass, chords are a different concept. I just play roots and fifths. I mean—" He broke off when we stared at him blankly. "Bass guitar is different. We don't always get a lot of respect."

Liz nodded. "I know what you mean. My incredibly inspired rendition of 'Chopsticks' on piano doesn't get a lot of respect, either."

When Zach laughed—even though he'd never laughed at a single thing *I've* ever said—I almost choked on my Dilly Bar again.

I held up a hand before either Liz or Zach, or both, could slug me.

Zach turned to me. "So you do play guitar? Or are you just starting? Jeremy said something, but then he and Cat broke up, and then last night . . ."

I frowned. "What about last night? I was there."

"No kidding." Zach licked all the way around his bare Dilly Bar, casually, and not fast enough to keep it from dripping all over the table. "But it's cool. Lauren is cool. That girl Drew goes out with . . . isn't."

I had a million questions, but I didn't plan to ask them in front of Liz. Probably not even if Liz weren't here.

She was, though. Silently watching Zach and me as if we were the best ping-pong match she'd ever seen.

But Liz didn't *watch* sports; she played them. For blood.

Like now. "Cat has played guitar forever, but she's always bitched about mangling her D chord."

I tried giving her a look.

"Do you? Play? Really?"

Zach was annoyingly persistent.

I was just annoyed. And sick of lying and bullshit and covering my ass. And possibly, despite the violet paint now covering my walls, sick of Liz.

I'd have to think about that one.

"I play, but I suck."

The moment I said it, my breath caught when I realized too late that Zach would make some perverted joke about exactly *how* I suck. Like guys did. Even in front of me.

"Taking lessons?" He nodded without so much as an eye

twitch to tell me he'd already heard I sucked. And not on guitar. "It takes a while to get good. Your sister Mary—"

"Is a child prodigy. Yeah. I know."

He shook his head. "She's good, actually, but it took a while. She joined our band when she was still busy mangling her D chord. Like you might say."

Liz patted my hand. "See? Mary sucked, too."

"I didn't say she sucked." Zach leaned back in his seat, his Dilly Bar now dripping down the front of his shirt. He glanced down, wiping off the biggest blob but leaving several smaller ones. Guys. "It takes a long time to get good. You shouldn't wait until you're good to join a band."

I thought about Cat. About how she'd sung with Zach's band and been jeered until she fainted.

I wouldn't have fainted; I would've crushed whoever pulled crap like that on me. But still.

"That's not what I hear from Cat."

Zach started licking his Dilly Bar so intently, I almost thought he hadn't heard me. Or maybe he was struggling to come up with an excuse for what they'd done to Cat, but he *looked* as if red ants were crawling around inside his shirt. "Hey, I don't like to get involved."

I snorted. "Right. I saw how uninvolved you were last night when Chelsea started cutting on Lauren."

Zach's hand tugged on the collar of his T-shirt as if it was too tight. Maybe from all those red ants crawling around and all. I bit my lip, wishing I hadn't mentioned Lauren. Wishing I knew why I cared that he was so protective of her and not, say, Cat.

I already knew he didn't give a flying fuck about me.

He sighed. "The thing is, Cat didn't join our band. That time they asked her to sing, they set her up."

Liz glanced at me and nodded.

I frowned, jabbing my Dilly Bar in Zach's direction. It's

possible a dab of ice cream hit him on the nose. "Did the whole band know? Is that why Cat and Jeremy broke up?"

"Cat didn't tell you why?"

Liz asked the question, not Zach, startling me.

I whirled on her. "She told *you*?"

She shook her head. "Not me, not Jane. But I figured you'd know."

"Not a clue."

I didn't plan to tell Zach that Cat didn't speak to me, even if he already knew. He seemed to know everything.

For once in my life, I didn't know a damn thing.

Liz and I both looked at Zach, who held up his hands in surrender. His right hand, holding his quickly melting Dilly Bar, had ice cream dripping off of it.

He licked his hand, then shrugged. "Cat told Jeremy that you *don't* play guitar, so Kirk reamed out Jeremy when your sisters told him you do."

I frowned. "Why would Kirk care one way or another?"

He looked out the window so long, I thought he wasn't going to answer. Finally, he turned back to me. "Let's just say bands are easier when love interests aren't involved."

What did *that* mean? "But I'm not—"

"Anyone's girlfriend. Yeah. That's not reassuring, as it turns out, to some of the girlfriends out there."

Including Cat?

No way. Jeremy's hair was bright green this week, which wasn't an improvement on last week's burnt orange. Cat was afraid I might want him? She was afraid I'd go after *anyone* she wanted? Was *that* why she hated me?

Was she really such an idiot?

"But you were going to tell us about reform school."

Lost in thought, I blinked at Zach's words. For someone who had zero interest in me, the guy didn't let go. "No, I wasn't."

Liz kept licking the stick from her Dilly Bar, which she'd long since finished. Finally, she set it on the table, then picked it up again and started playing with it. "I know I'm not Jane, but wouldn't it help to tell someone about it?"

I smiled sweetly at her. "Someone like Jane?"

Liz laughed, surprising me. "She'd coo and say all the right things, I admit, but she's not here."

"Don't tell me. You locked her to the fridge in your apartment so you could beat it out of me?"

Liz tilted her head. "Tempting. She *did* eat all the leftover pizza."

Zach laughed. "How about if I coo and say all the right things instead?"

I just stared at him. And kept staring.

He blinked first. "You figure I suck at cooing as much as you suck at D chords." When I bristled, he held up a hand. "Not that I said you suck at D chords."

He didn't have to. Jazz had finally shown me an easier way to play a D chord, but even that was hit or miss.

"Seriously. You don't want to know."

"Why did you cut your hair?" Liz leaned forward on her elbows, totally ignoring the fact that I didn't want to talk about it, let alone in front of Zach. At least she didn't make a crack about how vain I'd always been about my long hair, but maybe she was just waiting for the perfect moment.

My chin went out. "If enough girls try to yank out your hair by the roots, you eventually decide you'd rather give them less of a target."

I didn't add that our jailers gave us a bare minimum of bathroom time at Shangri-La, that hellhole. I refused to mention bathroom time in front of Zach. He was already looking at me as if he were wondering if leprosy was contagious.

"You weren't . . . safe?"

Liz's eyes were bright and shimmery, almost as if she might cry. Liz? Cry?

I waved a hand. "Like I said. You don't want to know. Compared to everything else that went down, the length of my hair didn't much matter."

Liz pressed her lips together. Tightly. Yeah, those were definitely tears in her eyes. "I'm so sorry."

"Your hair looks good."

Liz and I whirled on Zach. After a long, weird moment, Liz laughed first. "He's right, you know. Your hair looks good either long or short."

Hey, I had a mirror, okay? But I didn't see any point in arguing. It'd take years to grow my hair all the way back, and Zach would be long gone from my life by then.

Or much, much sooner.

He shrugged. "I don't see why so many girls wear their hair long. It must be a pain in the ass."

Running a hand through her shoulder-length hair, Liz laughed again. "You got that right. Shorter makes life easier." She turned to me. "And like your friend says, it looks good on you."

Zach wasn't my friend.

He was Lauren's friend.

I don't know why I kept picturing them together, in vivid detail, then blowing up the picture in my mind with a huge crate of explosives.

"So reform school gave you short hair." Zach took a last lick of his Dilly Bar, then used the stick to start a sword fight with Liz. No, Liz started it. Of course. "Did you get anything else good from reform school?"

I frowned. I put my haircut under the category of "How I Survived Reform School," not "Good Things That Happened in Reform School." The latter list had exactly zero items on it.

"I didn't want a haircut." Understatement. I'd cried the

whole time the barber hacked away at my hair. "The only person who saw *anything* good about locking me up in reform school for a year was my dad. Period."

I shot Liz a quick glance, daring her to argue, but she just studied me the way she'd study a rat from one of her lab experiments. None of the rats had a good life, as I recall, except maybe the one Mary rescued and kept in her room until the day Mom opened the door, shrieked, and collapsed in a heap in the upstairs hall.

Liz kept watching me for several seconds. "Mom said your grades went way up in reform school. Was it easier?"

I gave her the Glare of Death, and not just because Zach did *not* need to know about my grades. Or my hair, although that was already obvious. Or anything else about me.

Finally, I shrugged. "It was harder, actually. Everything in reform school was hard."

Understatement.

"But you never used to—" Liz broke off and glanced at Zach. "I mean, that's great. Good teachers?"

"They were all strict, cranky, sadistic assholes." A lot like Jazz, my guitar teacher, come to think of it. "What's not to like?"

Zach laughed, softly, stopping when he realized that Liz and I weren't smiling.

"Hey, good preparation for college, right? Have you taken the ACT or SAT yet? Where are you thinking about going?"

Had he not heard a word of this conversation? I'm a reform-school survivor. No college will want me. I have no future. Period.

"I haven't thought about it."

Okay, I had. Of course. Even if I hadn't had a bazillion empty hours in Shangri-La to think about college, I couldn't possibly miss all the college chatter in my classes this fall. From almost everyone except Cat.

I'd tried to ignore all of it, just like Cat ignored me.

I glanced at Liz, wondering what embarrassing thing she'd say next in front of Zach. She slid another glance at him and didn't say anything.

I pointedly checked the clock on my phone. I didn't need to check it to confirm that there were no texts, no emails, no nothing. "Oh, geez. Didn't Mom tell us to get our butts home in time for dinner?"

Liz looked horrified. "Dinner? Mom?"

I glared at her, daring her to screw up my escape plan. "She said she was making her Charlie Special."

The Charlie Special, previously known by any number of names of Jane's boyfriends over the years, was a monstrosity that might've originally been a meat-and-noodle goulash that Mom claimed was her grandmother's old recipe, but it came out gray and vile. It also tended to overwhelm the bathroom capacity in our house and, occasionally, the nearest hospital ER.

"No shit." Liz flicked a glance at Zach. "Er, so to speak."

I nodded. "So we should hurry."

"In the opposite direction." Liz finally caught the looks I kept shooting her, though, and sprang to her feet. "Hey, great to meet you, Zach. Maybe I'll catch your band sometime." She winked at him. "At least, if Kirk doesn't see me first and slam the door on my face."

He grinned at her and nodded, then turned to me. "I'd love to hear you play guitar sometime, too. Even your dreaded D chord."

"Sure." When hell froze over. "Maybe sometime."

We all walked out to the parking lot together before Zach headed to his hideous bright-orange VW Beetle and Liz and I went to the Prius. I waved good-bye to him before climbing in.

"Nice guy." Liz started the engine. "Have you known him long?"

I could tell she *meant* to ask if I've been going out with him long. Or sleeping with him long. Or whatever.

Buckling my seatbelt, I refused to think about what everyone assumed. "I don't know him at all."

"Hmm." Liz shot out of the parking lot with her usual high-speed roar. I had no idea a Prius was capable of it. "My guess? He'd like to change that."

Ha. Right.

♫

WHEN WE GOT home, Mom was too busy shrieking at Dad to notice my new violet walls or to care that Liz and I had picked up enough Chinese takeout on the way home to feed the entire offensive line of Woodbury High's football team.

Or Liz, as the case may be.

When I grabbed a small carton of rice and the entire container of seafood delight and headed for the stairs, Liz put a hand on my arm, stopping me.

"Dad could probably use a break from the shrieking. Should we all eat together?"

Mom was still pissed about all the lies Dad fed her when he sent me to Shangri-La. Mom's lungpower was amazing, but I didn't feel like rescuing Dad. He deserved it. So I kept going.

Liz's grip is ridiculously strong, though, and she bought me violet paint and helped paint my room. She also treated me to DQ, so it didn't seem like the right moment to take her down.

As if I could.

"Fine." I returned to the kitchen table just as Cat showed up, grabbed the carton of vegetable lo mein, and tried to make a similar move for the stairs.

Liz grabbed her, too. "Since when is everyone around here

so antisocial?"

"Since Lydia broke out of reform school?" Cat's claws were out, reminding me of Amber. "Why? Is this one of those special moments when we're supposed to hold hands and sing 'Kumbaya'?"

Liz frowned at her. "Cat, what's happened to you?"

She flicked a snotty look at me. I think it made at least a thousand of them. "Like I said. Lydia came home."

Liz glanced toward the stairs. Based on the decibel level, Mom and Dad were battling it out in their bedroom and unlikely to quit anytime soon. "Do you have any idea of the *hell* Lydia went through in reform school?"

Oh, great. Just what I needed. Cat hearing *anything* about reform school and telling the whole school.

Cat smirked at me. "Did you? Excellent."

Wow.

Liz wrapped an arm around my shoulders. I nearly brushed her off—I can handle my own battles with Cat, thank you very much—but my legs actually felt a little wobbly. I told myself it was a delayed reaction to the paint fumes.

Cat rolled her eyes. "Don't tell me. Lydia even has *you* under her spell. Did she tell you her so-called charms aren't working for her at school anymore? Except maybe with guys who are just looking for an easy lay?"

I sucked in a breath.

I also pictured Zach in his silly pseudo swordfight with Liz this afternoon. Was he like Drew and every other guy? Just wanting to hook up with me?

No, he had zero interest. He also had Lauren.

I glanced at the rice and seafood delight I'd set back down on the table. It wasn't too late to grab them and go as far away from here as fast as humanly possible.

But not to Montana. Or Milwaukee.

As I reached for the containers, a chair slammed down on the floor. I whirled to find Liz in Cat's face, which had gone pale, maybe because Liz had her in a headlock.

"I can't breathe."

"Like you say, excellent." Liz loosened her hold, but not much. "Maybe you'll stop talking about your *twin sister* like that."

Shrugging, I grabbed my rice and seafood delight. I was tempted to dump Cat's vegetable lo mein on the floor, but Liz would probably put *me* in a headlock. It wasn't worth it.

None of this was worth it.

"Let her go, Liz."

Liz, being Liz, didn't.

"Seriously. Please."

The impromptu wrestling match brought back vivid nightmares of bench-clearing brawls at Shangri-La, which were always stopped, but the same way the refs at a pro hockey game stop them: after letting the slugs fly for a few minutes. I felt like heaving. I'd also lost my appetite for seafood delight, which was almost unheard of.

Losing every shred of self-respect I'd ever had, I also started to cry.

Damn it.

Just like that, Liz released Cat, picked the overturned chair up from the floor, and proceeded to sit down on it. She dug into the sweet-and-sour chicken as if nothing had happened. Turning away from them both, I wiped my eye with the back of my hand, then turned back and grabbed the chair next to Liz.

Cat sat down, too. I think it had more to do with Liz's barked command—"SIT!"—than a desire to hang with her sisters.

I knew the feeling.

"So let's talk."

Liz, of course.

I raised my hand. "Don't I have a right to the assistance of counsel or at least a phone call?"

Grinning, Liz waved a rice-coated fork in the air. "There's no point in calling out for pizza, since we already have Chinese, so you don't need a phone call. But if you'd like a lawyer present, I can ask Mom to join us."

I laughed. Before Shangri-La, I don't remember anything Liz ever said being funny. After a day spent sniffing paint with her, she was growing on me.

"You really *are* falling for her crap." Cat, whose vegetable lo mein sat untouched, stuck out her lower lip. It reminded me of our seventh birthday, when Mom gave her a Barbie doll but gave me a G.I. Joe. "You drank the Kool-Aid."

"No, but I would if we had any. Especially cherry. Hey, let me check." Frowning, Liz pushed back from the table and went to the fridge. She returned with two cans of Diet Coke and one Coke. She handed me the Coke, kept one Diet Coke, and gave the other to Cat. "No Kool-Aid, sorry. Maybe Lydia's been force-feeding it to everyone she knows."

"You know that's not what I meant." Cat's lower lip was still front and center. For someone who didn't hang with Amber and Tess anymore, she sure acted like them. "Lydia waltzes back into town, acting like she still rules the world, and the whole family falls for it."

Liz pointed at the ceiling, in the general direction of Mom and Dad's bedroom, where World War III continued to rage. "The whole family, huh?"

Cat sat back, crossing her arms. The temptation to shove her vegetable lo mein in her face until she choked on it was almost overwhelming.

She must not have noticed my fingers twitching. "Fine. Dad didn't fall for it, but Mom did. So there's one rational person in this house besides me."

"You really don't get it." Liz took a long swig of her Diet Coke. "You think Jane and I fall for crap? Was it crap last spring when all those losers you used to hang out with went after you, and we helped you out? Even Mary?"

Cat shrugged. "Maybe I was wrong about Mary. At least somewhat."

"At least somewhat?"

Based on Liz's glare, I had a feeling the vegetable lo mein was going to end up in Cat's face without any help from me.

Cat bit her lip. "Fine. I didn't know Mary. But you didn't, either."

"So maybe you don't know Lydia." Liz glanced at me, offering a half-apologetic smile. "Maybe none of us do."

"Lydia is Lydia. Was, is, always will be."

"Right." Liz sighed. "So that's why you're treating her as badly as your so-called friends treated you last spring."

I watched the two of them argue, curiously detached. Actually, no, there was nothing curious about it. Detachment was the first and most useful skill I learned in reform school. It was how I survived.

After a few more volleys back and forth, Cat leaped to her feet. "That was different. I'm different from Lydia. I didn't deserve to be treated like that."

Liz's eyebrows went up. "But Lydia does?"

I'd had enough. Way more than enough. Leaving the seafood delight for another day, when I might again have some semblance of an appetite, I stood up. "Thanks, Liz. For the paint and the help and, well, for today. You can't fix everything, but I appreciate the fact that you tried."

I turned my back on both of them before another tear fell. Because Shangri-La taught me more than detachment; it taught me never to let the bastards dance on your grave.

Chapter 15

Lydia—the humiliation, the misery she was bringing
on them all soon swallowed up every private care.

— Jane Austen, *Pride and Prejudice*
Volume III, Chapter Four

I WALKED OUTSIDE after ignoring the keys to the Jeep in the chipped bowl on the front-hall chest. I needed to walk.

No, I needed to run.

Slipping back inside a house that was strangely quiet, I headed upstairs, changed into gym shorts and an old Green Day T-shirt I'd swiped from Liz a million years ago, and grabbed my one pair of running shoes from the back of my closet.

Before reform school, in the absence of a gun to my head wielded by a Gym teacher, I'd never run. Okay, it was pretty much the same scenario at Shangri-La, but the gun to my head was wielded on a daily basis, even in the worst of winter, so I'd gotten in the habit. Even so, I swore I'd never run again if I didn't have to.

Until this moment.

Outside again, I started walking down the street before speeding up to a slow jog, then eventually to a run.

I soon remembered exactly why I'd always hated it, but I kept running. It chewed into my anger and disappointment.

My disappointment in Cat.

My disappointment in myself.

But I'd rather focus on Cat.

A laugh spurted out of me, exacerbating the sting of the hitch in my side. Ouch. Running was for total morons. I'd have to mention that to Liz the first chance I got.

Laughing again, I had to stop, bend over, and wheeze a little. Okay, so maybe I shouldn't have sprinted so fast after a month and a half spent *not* running.

But like everyone said, Lydia Bennet took chances.

They had no idea.

A horn honked, making me jump. Jerking my head toward the street, I saw a bright-orange VW Beetle I'd last seen a little over an hour ago at DQ. It pulled over to the curb.

Zach rolled down the passenger window. "Hey."

"Hey." I didn't move an inch in his direction. For one thing, I was sweating like a pig.

For another thing, I was sweating like a pig.

"You're okay, right? Like, not dying?"

I rolled my eyes. "Not dying. Just out for a run."

So, as they say, only mostly dead.

"You like Green Day? It's my favorite band." Zach leaned toward me, almost falling into the passenger seat of his VW. "You know any of their songs on guitar?"

He seriously thought I could play guitar. I couldn't even nail a solo on "Twinkle, Twinkle, Little Star."

I just shook my head.

"We should play together sometime. I love 'Boulevard of Broken Dreams,' but some people think it's depressing."

I stared at him. It used to be my fave Green Day song, but he wouldn't know that. Had Liz told him? No way. It was something Cat would do.

"You hate it." He nodded but shifted back into the driver's seat a little, which was the only reason I took a few steps closer to the curb.

I shrugged. "It's complicated, but I used to love it."

Before Shangri-La. Before "Boulevard of Broken Dreams" sounded too much like my life.

"Anyway." Zach drummed the fingertips of one hand on the steering wheel, looking antsy, especially for a chill guy like him. "Sorry I interrupted your run."

I'd already stopped to suck wind, which he totally knew, but whatever. Had I gotten too close to him in this sweaty T-shirt? Resisting the urge to sniff it, I offered him a wave. "No prob. See you."

He glanced out his windshield before turning back to me. "We should play sometime. It doesn't have to be Green Day."

Right. Knowing what he played on the radio in his car, it might be Tchaikovsky.

But anything he suggested would be impossible for me, at least in front of a human being other than Jazz, who didn't count. She got paid to listen to me play.

I nodded, even though he was just being polite and we'd never play anything together. Including, unlike Zach and Lauren, in a wading pool.

He pulled away from the curb.

And slowly, very slowly, I walked back home.

MONDAY MORNING, SOMEONE must've cranked up the air

conditioning in school, because the chill in my Speech Communications classroom was subarctic from the moment Chelsea walked in and saw me sitting in the back row next to Drew.

Oh, wait. Our school *has* no air conditioning.

Without a word, Chelsea launched herself into a desk in the front row, middle. Even though the desk on the other side of Drew was free. And even though a speechless Chelsea had probably never happened in this lifetime.

Drew didn't say a word, either, but he stared at Chelsea. Kept staring. Stopping just short of drooling.

I can't believe Cat wasted so much time on him. I can't believe I wasted even two minutes *considering* him.

Ms. Ciccarelli walked in just as the final bell rang, a stack of index cards in her hand.

"Good morning." As the class settled down, she handed several index cards to the kids in the front of the room and told them to take one and pass the rest back. "We're going to do a little impromptu speaking on topics I thought would be relevant to teenagers today. Thirty seconds, a minute at the most. Whatever is on your card."

As the cards made their way to the back of the room, some kids rolled their eyes, several laughed, and a few groaned. To me, it meant a class free of actual work. Perfect.

Until I got my card.

Slut-shaming.

Jesus H. Christ.

My gaze whipped to Drew, who was grinning, and then to his card. *Legalization of marijuana.* The girl on the other side of me: *LGBTQ bullying.*

I nearly crumpled up my card, shoved it down my throat, and swallowed it. Instead, I straightened my spine and faced forward, grimly awaiting my doom.

That was the one benefit—the *only* benefit—of Shangri-La: by definition, nothing else in life would ever be harder.

Not even speaking about slut-shaming to a room full of kids who thought I put the "slut" in slut-shaming.

Lost in thought, I finally realized that Chelsea was waving her arm so wildly that if someone harnessed it, the wind power she was generating could power a small village.

"Ms. Ciccarelli? We can trade cards, can't we? Or ask for a new one?"

Grinning, I slouched back in my chair. Her card must be even worse than mine. Excellent.

"No trading, and no new cards." Ms. Ciccarelli looked like she was trying not to smirk. And failing. "Sorry, Chelsea. Every topic is relevant in today's world. I'm sure you can find something to say for thirty seconds."

"Yeah. I mean, no. I mean—"

Ms. Ciccarelli shook her head. "Would you like to go first so you can be done?"

"Um, no, but could I get a hall pass? I just realized I have to go to the nurse. I'm, like, sick."

"You and half of the class, from what I can see." Ms. Ciccarelli smiled. Kindly, even. "No hall passes today except in the event of dire necessity."

On the far side of the room, Travis clutched his chest, moaned, and dropped to the floor.

Ms. Ciccarelli actually laughed. "Nice try, Travis, but unless you want to miss football practice tonight, I suspect you're *not* requesting a trip to the nurse's office."

Grinning, Travis leaped to his feet. Bowing as half of the class applauded, he took his seat again.

Then the girl behind him, LaShonda, slumped against her chair while pressing the back of her hand to her forehead. All she needed was a fainting couch.

Ms. Ciccarelli rolled her eyes. "Seriously, class. It may be too late to audition for the fall musical, but it looks like we have several budding actors. I believe the drama club meets on Mondays after school."

I glanced again at Chelsea, who was fidgeting and sitting sideways in her chair as if she contemplated bolting. Hall pass or no hall pass.

"Chelsea? You look like you'd like to go first." Ms. Ciccarelli pointed at the podium at the front of the room, near the window, on the side opposite the door to freedom. "What's the topic on your card?"

Chelsea stood up, wobbled a bit as if her body might splatter on the floor any moment, and glanced at the door.

"The podium, Chelsea? By the window?"

The window was open, but we were on the third floor. I also wasn't sure if Chelsea's fat head would squeeze through it without help from paramedics or a Sherman tank.

Which was totally mean of me.

But we were talking Chelsea.

Finally, she wobbled over to the podium, her index card gripped so tightly in her hand that she was totally crushing it.

She glanced again at the door. Ms. Ciccarelli casually moved to stand between her and the door, even though Chelsea could probably give Travis a decent fight for his linebacker position on the varsity football team.

Also unkind of me. Oops. My bad.

"Chelsea? You just need to speak for thirty seconds." Ms. Ciccarelli looked sympathetic now. "We're just having fun with this. I'm not grading anyone."

Ha. Knowing Ms. Ciccarelli, she was.

Chelsea stared down at the podium, not at the card still clutched in her fist. "My topic is, um . . ."

"Chelsea? Please speak up so everyone can hear you."

"Oral sex and STDs."

Several guys laughed. Several girls turned bright pink.

Drew looked as if he'd just swallowed a pickle, even though his was probably the pickle responsible for Chelsea's ashen face and trembling lips.

Based on the growing laughter in the room, I wondered if Chelsea hadn't sat next to Drew today for reasons *other* than what happened at Russo's pizzeria on Friday night.

And that was before Chelsea threw up.

As Ms. Ciccarelli rushed to help her, Travis and another football player grabbed Chelsea and half escorted, half carried her out of the room.

I nudged Drew. "If this keeps up, the nurse's office might get a little crowded today."

Drew just stared straight ahead, his body rigid.

After not nearly enough time to talk myself out of it, I raised my hand. Spontaneously. Stupidly.

Ms. Ciccarelli shot me a hard look, as if preparing herself for trouble. "Lydia?"

"I'll go next if you want."

Another hard look followed by a faint nod. I set my index card face down on my desk and got to my feet. My legs didn't wobble, but that was all I could say for myself. Obviously, my brains and survival instincts, which I'd honed to the max at Shangri-La, had left the building.

When I reached the podium, Ms. Ciccarelli smiled at me. Cautiously. "Topic?"

I straightened my spine. "Slut-shaming."

Laughter and wolf whistles erupted.

Ms. Ciccarelli's smile faltered. I have a feeling she'll never assign these topics again. Ever. If she's still employed at the end of the day today.

A little nervous, I ran a hand through my hair. All these

months later, it still startled me when my hand flew out of a few inches of short, severely cropped, depressing hair instead of a foot and a half of silky vanity.

I blinked. Slut-shaming. *Focus, Lydia.*

"Even though she's not here, I'd like to thank Chelsea for starting my topic for me."

Someone hissed. Drew looked sick. Ms. Ciccarelli took a step toward me.

I shook my head.

"See, that's the thing. Like Ms. Ciccarelli said, all of these topics are relevant. If a guy talks about oral sex or STDs or slut-shaming, he'll get some pats on the back and maybe some laughs, but it's no big deal. If he *has* sex? Even more pats on the back. If a girl does it or talks about it, or even if everyone *thinks* she's doing it but she's not?" My gaze swept the room, skewering everyone. "Your basic nightmare scenario. For a girl."

Ms. Ciccarelli took another step toward me. "Thank you, Lydia. That's exactly—"

I waved her off.

"Even if a guy—" My voice cracked. Broke. Damn it. "Even if a guy, like, *rapes* a girl, the whole world calls her a slut, every other guy thinks she's fair game, and every other girl blames her and calls her things *no one* would ever want to be called. Especially in this hellhole of a godforsaken school."

I strode away from the podium, head high but looking at no one, to the sound of dead silence. Yeah, I nearly walked straight out the door. But wasn't that my point? That girls shouldn't have to take all the shit?

Like Chelsea just had?

Like I did almost every day of my life?

As I reached my desk and sat down, the murmurs started. Got louder. And continued even when Ms. Ciccarelli shushed the class and clapped her hands and finally ran her fingernails across the whiteboard at the front of the room.

Half of the class had twisted around in their seats to stare at me. And whisper. And finally talk out loud.

Then, to my surprise, they stared at Drew.

Before I could figure out what was going on, Ms. Ciccarelli somehow regained control of the class. As it turned out, slamming her hand on Chelsea's empty desk was amazingly effective.

"I'd like to thank Lydia for her brave speech today. And I'd like to thank the rest of you, in advance, for thinking about what *you* may be doing to make this school—" She cleared her throat. "A *hellhole*, as Lydia might say, for some of you. I might add that I don't think Lydia is in the minority on this, even if others may not be brave enough to say it."

Someone clapped, setting off a round of applause from most but definitely not all of the class. Drew just slunk down in his chair, looking like he'd sell his soul for an invisibility cloak.

But I wasn't brave. At all.

They had no idea.

I WALKED INTO the cafeteria after third-period Political Science, trying not to notice the murmurs when I went through the lunch line.

When I reached my old table, I would've had to be deaf and blind to miss Amber's cackle. And the fact that Kirk, next to her, didn't even try to stop her.

But maybe that was good. Maybe he was showing his respect for her by not trying to stifle her.

Or maybe he was on the verge of cutting her loose. With Kirk, and knowing Amber, I wouldn't want to place bets.

"I hear Ms. Ciccarelli called in a *pro* to teach sex-ed this morning." Amber skewered me when I paused by the chair next to Kirk, daring me to sit there. I sat there. "But aren't you overqualified?"

I patted Kirk's shoulder. "Was Amber seriously your only option? No wonder you drink."

Kirk grinned but didn't say anything.

"He doesn't want you, Lydia. Get over it."

Amber's snarl wasn't pretty. But, then, the rest of her wasn't so hot, either. I really *did* wonder how Kirk, who'd had gorgeous girls drape themselves all over him since puberty, had ended up with her.

I glanced down at my tray. The orange chicken had seemed like a good idea in the lunch line, but now it reminded me too much of Amber's face.

"Looks good." Kirk turned his back completely on Amber and jabbed a finger at my tray, even though his own tray held a half-eaten burger and fries.

Swiping a fry from his tray, I laughed. "Trade you."

On the other side of Kirk, steam was coming out of Amber's ears, nostrils, and other orifices. Across from us, Tess—silent and nervous and so unlike the Tess I used to know—just watched the three of us as she nibbled on a carrot.

"Kirk, let's blow out of here." Amber. Hyperventilating. Also not attractive, but I repeat myself. "I swear it's like something reeks."

Kirk's lips quirked. "I'm not done eating. And Lydia smells just fine."

I'd heard way too many guys comment way too personally on me before, and it usually made me want to punch the guy in question, but this time I just laughed.

I elbowed Kirk. "I owe it all to my dad's Irish Spring soap, which was the only thing I could find in the shower this morning. Nice, huh? Not too manly?"

He laughed. "You could go out for the football team smelling like that, but you're good."

With a loud scrape of her chair, Amber shoved to her feet and stalked away, even though she'd barely touched her salad.

I called out. "Amber? You forgot to take your tray. Maybe that was what reeked."

She stomped out of the cafeteria.

Surprising me, Tess didn't follow her. Of course, she might be sticking around to take notes—or even shoot a video—to report back to Amber later.

"Sorry."

Kirk. Just that. A moment before picking up his burger and taking a big bite of it.

"Not your fault." I stuck my fork into a hunk of goopy orange chicken, wondering how my stomach had ever allowed me to buy it. "Same old."

"You must be sick of it."

I shrugged. "I deal."

"You always did." Kirk glanced at Tess, probably checking to see if she *was* recording us, before turning back to me. "Hey, you know, the offer is still open to play with our band. Or sing, if you'd rather do that."

My eyebrows went up. "My sister already sang with your band. I hear it didn't go down so well."

Tess went pale. Lips trembling, she picked up her tray—and Amber's—and left our table.

I hadn't even planned it.

Kirk munched on a fry and offered one to me. "You sure know how to clear a room."

I grinned, wishing I could trade my brown rice for his fries. But gymnastics season was coming, right? If I got up the nerve to try out. I glanced down at myself. Yeah, forget the fries. I should be munching on Tess's carrots.

"So? Join our band?"

Blinking, I looked at Kirk. In the same moment, I noticed Drew at a table to my left with Jeremy. Cat sat on the far side of the room with the art geeks. I didn't see Chelsea at all.

Was I responsible for all of this?

I bit into a too-sweet chunk of chicken, accidentally grinding my teeth against my fork.

"I should've stayed in reform school."

I didn't mean to say that out loud.

"No, you shouldn't. But you *should* join our band."

I frowned at Kirk. "Why? You haven't even heard me play."

And thank God for that.

"I think you'd be good. Zach says you'd be good, too."

"Zach hasn't heard me play, either." He also thought bands and girlfriends didn't mix. But, then, I wasn't anyone's girlfriend. At the moment, it seemed like a good thing. "I'm still thinking about trying out for gymnastics."

Kirk frowned. *That* didn't happen often. "You said that before, but I thought you were kidding. Aren't you too big?"

I just stared at him.

He waved a hand, totally lacking any sort of mortification gene. But, then, he was a guy. "I mean, aren't they all like four-feet-eight?"

Was I too tall? I didn't think so. At least he didn't say I was as big as a vault. Or the width of a floor mat.

I swished my fork around in my brown rice, wondering if I *was* stupid to go out for gymnastics. As a senior. When the closest thing I'd done to gymnastics hadn't lasted long and had ultimately landed me in reform school.

"I mean, hey. You'd be good at it." Kirk polished off his burger and fries, while I'd had two bites of chicken and zero brown rice. "But you'd be even better in my band."

It was probably a tie. I'd suck at both.

When I turned to answer him, I caught him staring at my boobs and looking as if he'd like to take them for a spin.

He grinned. "Can't blame a guy for thinking you'd be good at that, too."

Actually? Yeah. I could.

♫

"YOU MUST BE thrilled. After bragging all about your sex life in one class, you had Kirk Easton practically in your pants at lunch."

Barely in the door of our house, I sucked in a breath. Cat must've spent some serious time with Liz. She could now land a knockout punch and didn't even need to use her fists.

"Hello to you, too." I dropped my backpack on the front-hall floor. "And thanks for offering me a ride home today."

"Oh, did I forget you?" Her fist curled, and her eyes glittered so fiercely that I almost wondered if she was on the verge of tears. "Sucks to be you. Maybe you'll wanna head back to reform school, where they don't even have to *pretend* to give a rip about you."

I'd handled worse. Never from Cat, though.

Grabbing my backpack, I headed to the kitchen. For a snack or an early dinner or an ice-cold beer, I couldn't decide.

Unfortunately, Cat followed me. "You still think you're so cool, even though everyone at school *hates*—"

She broke off the same moment my steps ground to a halt. Dad waved at both of us from the far end of the kitchen table, where he was in the middle of eating a banana-cream pie.

The whole pie, from the looks of it. Right out of the pie tin.

Dad. Mr. Yoga. Mr. Clean Living, except for his cigars. The

guy who sent me up the river to Shangri-La.

I headed to the fridge. Cat just sputtered.

Dad set down his fork. "Problems?"

Nothing I couldn't handle on my own. I definitely didn't need Dad's help, which tended to get me sent to Montana.

I opened the fridge, rummaged around on the bottom shelf for the last can of Coke, and almost grabbed a half-full bag of carrots that had probably been there for a year.

Leaving the carrots in the fridge, I slid the banana-cream pie from under Dad's nose, then grabbed a fork and hopped up on the counter by the sink.

Best dinner in ages. If Dad let me finish it.

He grinned, surprising me. "You saved me from myself. Thank you."

Cat crossed her arms. "Now you've even got Dad on your side? How did you pull *that* off?"

"I don't take sides." Dad wiped his mouth on a paper towel, totally missing the glob of pie on his chin. "Or I'm on everyone's side. Including Lydia's."

Not in this lifetime.

"Have a seat, girls."

I patted the counter, nearly losing my fork in the process. "Already there."

Dad rolled his eyes. "Cat?"

"I'm—" She looked ready to bolt. "I have a ton of homework."

"That must be why you drove home without waiting to give Lydia a ride." Dad nodded. "Very industrious of you, but it'll still relieve you of your driving privileges."

"No way!" Cat stayed at the edge of the kitchen, her bare toes tapping a frantic beat now that it sucked to be *her*. "It's always been about Lydia in this house, and now she comes home from reform school and it's *still* all about her."

"It's not her fault she spent a year in reform school." Dad propped his elbows on the kitchen table. His head bent, he didn't look at either of us. "It was mine. Completely mine."

Slack-jawed, I forgot all about the pie tin until it did a slow-motion flip off my lap and landed upside-down on the floor.

Time stopped. My heartbeat skidded and stuttered. Then Cat stormed off and, based on the loud thumps, up the stairs.

When Dad finally spoke, his voice was small. Cracked. Choking. "I'll never forgive myself, Lydia. I took the easy way out. Easy for me, nightmarish for you." He shook his head. "And I never asked for your side of the story."

Something lodged in my throat, and it wasn't banana-cream pie.

"You—" I waved my fork in the air. A dab of banana cream splattered against the wall. "You must've talked to Liz."

Even though he'd never talked to me.

I jumped off the counter, totally sticking my landing. "Hey, don't worry about it. You're not the first guy in my life to fuck me over."

I walked out of the kitchen, head high.

The rest of me? Not so much.

Chapter 16

*"I am inclined to think that her own disposition must
be naturally very bad, or she could not be guilty of
such an enormity at so early an age."*

— Jane Austen, *Pride and Prejudice*
Volume III, Chapter Six

I SPENT THE rest of the week sleepwalking through my classes,
although I kept up and even got ahead on homework and aced a
couple of tough pop quizzes, including one in English 12 that
took down half of the class.

Mr. Skamser put a smiley-face sticker on the top of my quiz.
I'm pretty sure it was the only smile I got all week.

Friday, in Accounting class, Lauren leaned toward me
during a rare moment when Ms. Frey was too distracted to keep
her eagle eye on us. "Going to any parties this weekend? Or do
you study all the time these days?"

I did, pretty much. And let Jazz torture me on guitar. And
slipped into the gym to work on gymnastics at odd hours when
no one else was around. And tried not to roll my eyes every time
Mr. Fogarty said I reminded him of Liz.

I shook my head. "Just not up on the gossip."

Not even the gossip about me.

"Zach said you keep turning Kirk down."

As I whirled on her, I forgot everything, even Ms. Frey. "What the *hell*? He never—"

"Lydia? Lauren?" Ms. Frey was on us like a panther on slow prey. "Is there a problem?"

I closed my eyes. Letting someone get to me was a rookie mistake. Something I'd never let happen at Shangri-La.

I opened my eyes to find Ms. Frey in my face. "No problem. I just can't believe that the guy who wrote this textbook never, uh, considered the possibility of using women in his examples. I mean, it's always Joe this or Sam that."

From the look on Ms. Frey's face, this wasn't her first rodeo. But she just smiled and went back to the front of the room. "Good point. I've just never, er, heard such a passionate objection to it."

Five minutes later, Lauren leaned my way again. I gritted my teeth.

"Zach said the band is playing tonight. Party at Kirk's house."

And Lauren was going? After the way Chelsea pounced on her at Russo's pizzeria last weekend?

Keeping an eye on Ms. Frey, who was droning on about balancing a checkbook, I whispered back. "I hadn't heard, but I'm probably not going."

I was a little surprised I hadn't heard, since Kirk and I were pals no matter how much Amber bared her fangs at me, but it didn't matter. Much. Besides, I'd already spent last Friday night watching Zach go all knight-in-shining-armor with Lauren, and I was trying to cut back on my sugar intake.

"Wanna go together?"

Frowning, I checked to make sure Ms. Frey was still talking, but I couldn't afford to go *anywhere* with a druggie. Not unless I wanted to catch the next flight back to Shangri-La. "Maybe you can ride with Zach."

"Yeah. I could." Lauren pursed her painted-black lips. "But you should go, too. We could go together."

I could even take the Jeep, since Cat's little stunt when she scooted home on Monday without me left her without wheels for the foreseeable future, as Dad had put it.

But hanging with Lauren was a big risk to me. I also didn't want to go to a party where I'd have to watch Heather playing guitar way better than me, Amber draping herself all over Kirk, and Zach doing battle with anyone who even looked at Lauren the wrong way.

I'd choose Algebra homework over that scene.

Okay, not in the absence of a lobotomy. And, okay, it'd been too long since I'd had any fun.

I shrugged. "Should I pick you up?"

SURE ENOUGH, I scored the Jeep. Cat slammed the door to her room when I asked if she wanted to tag along to Kirk's party.

But weird. I mean, I knew what happened to Cat last spring, but that was last spring. And everyone would be there tonight.

Including me.

I stood outside Cat's bedroom door. "Last chance."

Silence. It was an improvement over the barrage of swearing that ended only when she slammed the door, but it still wasn't like Cat. Or, more accurately, the Cat I used to know.

"Jeremy will be there."

I didn't even say it to taunt her.

Not that she didn't deserve it.

"He still likes you."

Okay, I had no idea if he did or why I said something nice, since God knows she hadn't said anything nice to me since I got home from Shangri-La.

She started blaring music. I didn't recognize the singer or the band, but I couldn't miss the highlight of the chorus: "Go to hell."

I laughed. At least a dozen girls at Shangri-La had told me to go to hell, and worse, but none of them had found a song to express their sentiments.

Cat must actually care.

I jogged down the stairs, still grinning.

Which, yeah, showed how much my life sucked.

Fifteen minutes later, I pulled up in front of Lauren's house. It was on the opposite side of Woodbury in a neighborhood of designer-gray lookalike houses that could definitely benefit from one of Mom's manic days and several cans of different colors of bright paint.

As I double-checked the address, I didn't see Zach's orange VW. Not that I was looking.

Before I could turn off the Jeep, Lauren came outside, then called back to someone inside the house. A moment later, she slid into the passenger seat.

She was a vision in black. Knee-high boots, leggings, whisper-thin gauzy top with a black bra underneath. More eyeliner than I'd ever seen on anyone, even at Shangri-La.

But a squeaky-clean guy who had a Cat in the Hat tattoo and drove a bright-orange VW Beetle liked her.

Huh.

She checked out my outfit, too, and frowned. "Is that what most girls will be wearing to Kirk's party?"

I glanced down at myself. Jeans, running shoes, and a mildly loose but not ratty Arctic Monkeys T-shirt, the only thing I'd ever gotten from Justin Truesdale besides a trip to jail and a one-way ticket to reform school.

Okay, I should probably burn it.

"Lydia? Am I dressed wrong?"

Blinking, I glanced at Lauren. "Sorry. No, you're fine. I guess I practiced guitar too long and forgot to get into party mode."

Actually, I didn't forget. I just wanted to pretend that Kirk's party, along with everyone at it, was no big deal. Not worth getting dressed up for.

But why didn't Lauren know how to dress for a party? Didn't she go to parties? She wasn't exactly a goody two-shoes.

Totally the opposite.

As I parked on Kirk's street and opened my door, Lauren bit her lip, glancing down at her own outfit. "You're sure?"

Weird. "Positive."

We walked into Kirk's party, which was a crazy-loud mob scene. Kirk was nowhere in sight. The band was nowhere in sight. Oh, right. I heard the neighbors had called the cops the last time Kirk had a party, so he'd probably have the band play in the basement tonight.

As if he wouldn't get busted anyway. Ha.

"Should we check out the basement?" I had to shout at Lauren, and she must not have heard, since she headed into the kitchen instead.

A moment later she pulled two beers out of a huge cooler and tried to hand me one. I shook my head, knowing it wouldn't take much to land in reform school again. Especially, despite what he said the other day, with a dad like mine.

"Oh, look. It's Lydia Bennet pretending to be a *good* girl." Amber had her claws out, and they could really use some polish. "Or are you holding out for stronger stuff?"

Shrugging, I walked over to another cooler and scored a

bottle of Coke. I toasted Amber with it. "Anything would be stronger than you. But where's Kirk? Hiding from you?"

"You are such a bitch." Turning, Amber sneered in Lauren's direction. "And I see you brought some *serious* trash to our party."

Lauren bristled, but she was also shaking. As in, nervous. Even though Zach must be here and would probably rip Amber's face off any moment.

I put a hand on Lauren's arm as I faced Amber. Casually. Knowing I could take her out at the knees without any effort. "I think you meant to say *Kirk's* party, but no. The trash was already here when I showed up."

I looked her up and down for good measure. I mean, Amber wasn't bright.

Her eyes were wild, making me wonder how much she'd already had to drink. "Kirk didn't invite you. I told him not to."

"Yeah?" I grinned. "How did that work out for you?"

"Lydia. Lauren." Sure enough, Zach appeared from out of nowhere. "Kirk asked where you guys were, so I said I'd find you. We're all in the basement."

Not Amber, obviously, but maybe Kirk needed a guard dog. Amber had the snarl and the face for the job.

She jabbed a finger in Zach's chest. "Kirk doesn't want them here."

Zach just stared down at her finger until she withdrew it and took a step backward. And another.

Her face was bright red. "He said so."

"Yeah?" Unlike me, Zach didn't even crack a grin. "I'll ask him. Just like I'll ask him what he was smoking the day he decided to go out with you. And every day since."

"You are such a—"

"—good guy? I know." Tight-lipped, Zach took Lauren and me by the elbow and led us toward the stairs to the basement.

"Seriously. Was the guy desperate? Or maybe he always wanted a dog, and his parents wouldn't buy him one?"

"I heard that!"

"Good ears. I'll bet you can even hear really high-pitched noises." Letting Lauren and me go ahead, Zach pulled the door to the basement shut.

I headed downstairs. Lauren, breathing hard, followed close behind me. From the pounding and rattling of the doorknob, Zach was holding the door closed as Amber tried to open it.

Laughing, I walked into a mostly dark basement.

At the far end, Kirk was tuning up his guitar. Alone. No Michael, no Jeremy, no Heather.

Based on all the pounding and screaming coming from upstairs, Zach might not be joining us anytime soon, either.

Kirk looked up as I headed toward him, followed by Lauren. "Lydia?" He nodded at Lauren before turning back to me. "You heard Heather was sick today? Can I talk you into playing?"

Oh. Shit.

I'd finally mastered "Knockin' on Heaven's Door." Okay, "mastered" wasn't exactly true. As Jazz kept telling me, the strumming pattern wasn't all downward strums in varying tempos that depended completely on when I had to do a D chord.

But everyone's a critic.

I gave Kirk a tight smile. "Sorry. No guitar."

He waved at the wall behind him, where five guitars other than the one he was holding were lined up in a row.

Every one of them was way more expensive than the one I owned.

I mean, not that it mattered. I could mangle a D chord on any guitar I touched. On a really bad day, I could even mangle a G chord. As Jazz put it, that took work.

"The thing is—"

"The thing is, Lydia jammed a finger on her left hand today when she was working out on the parallel bars." Zach appeared beside me, almost like magic. No, definitely magic. He'd made Amber disappear. "Or was it the uneven parallels? Is that what you call them?"

"Uneven parallels." But what I'd call *Zach* was a total liar. Or a savior. Or maybe both.

He stepped away from me, closer to Lauren, leaving me to face Kirk.

Kirk stared down at my perfectly normal-looking left hand before glancing from me to Zach and back again. "You're really going out for gymnastics? That's—"

"Totally cool, right?" Zach, looking tight with Lauren, nodded. "I stopped by school today to talk to my old art teacher, and I went past the gym. You're looking good."

Funny. I hadn't lasted twenty minutes, thanks to a group of snotty girls who refused to spot me on the uneven parallels and Coach Burns, who said I couldn't use them without a spotter.

But why Zach was lying for me, I had no idea. He didn't *really* know I couldn't play guitar. I mean, he couldn't be sure, could he?

Kirk just frowned. After an awkward moment, or several, Zach gave Lauren's hand a quick squeeze before moving past Kirk and over to the guitar stand holding his bass.

Michael and Jeremy soon thundered down the steps, but still no Amber. Michael headed to the keyboard. Jeremy just stopped and stared at me.

"Hey, Jeremy." If I had to keep giving all these tight smiles all night, at some point my face was going to freeze in a grimace. At least, that's what Dad had always said. "Cat couldn't come out tonight."

Frowning, he stomped over to the drum set. If the banging that came out of it moments later was a song, it wasn't a song I ever wanted to hear again. Or now.

"Jesus, Jeremy." Kirk covered his ears, even though he'd already put in earplugs. "If you want her back, go for it, but cut the crap."

Zach grinned at me, mouthing the word "girlfriends."

Maybe he should say that to Lauren instead.

As the band tuned up, more kids filtered downstairs until the basement was packed. I didn't see Amber or, for that matter, Tess. Or Drew and Chelsea. In fact, other than Lauren and the guys in the band, I didn't know anyone here. I mean, I *knew* them, but I didn't hang with them.

More accurately, I hadn't hung with any of them since I got home from Shangri-La.

Or they hadn't hung with me.

Straightening my spine, I walked over to the side of the room, where I leaned against the wall. Lauren stayed where she was, right in front of the band. As they started playing their first song, Hozier's "Take Me to Church," she stood alone, swaying in time to the music.

And staring at Zach.

They made an odd couple—a goth chick who maybe did drugs and a guy who had a Cat in the Hat tattoo and drove a bright-orange VW just to please his mom—but she definitely worshipped him, and he was beyond sweet with her.

And, hey, they made more sense than Kirk and Amber. And Drew and Chelsea. And Jeremy and Cat.

But who was I to judge? I'd spent most of a summer with Justin, even after everything that happened, just because I didn't have the guts to run home. Without stopping.

Justin was a player, a guy who took without giving. He'd totally sweet-talked me into actually *believing* that a guy could want to be with me for something other than sex, but I was the one who got a year in reform school. The rat bastard.

"Are you okay? You look really pissed."

I blinked, wondering when Lauren had quit staring at Zach long enough to notice me.

I didn't even try to fake a smile. "Just thinking."

She peered at me as if she could see all the way into my soul. Even though no one could. Maybe not even me.

Finally, she glanced back at the band. "They sound pretty good, but we don't have to stay if you don't want."

"I thought you'd want to hear Zach play." As twin patches of pink lit up Lauren's cheeks, I waved a hand. "It's okay. I'll hang here if you want to listen some more."

She looked again at the band. Or maybe just at Zach. "I don't have to stay. I can hear them play some other time."

She could get Zach to give her a private concert whenever she snapped her fingers, but whatever. They liked each other. Totally cool.

As she walked away, I studied the guys in the band.

Michael had sung "Take Me to Church," a song I loved until he started singing it. Now Kirk was singing "She Don't Use Jelly," even though I was pretty sure Cat told me that Kirk never sang. His voice was good—really good, actually, like his guitar playing and everything else he did except for choosing decent girlfriends. But the lyrics sounded like they'd been written by a sixteen-year-old boy who dreamed of sex but didn't have a clue, which didn't sound at *all* like Kirk.

Not that I *knew* how Kirk would be, romantically speaking, but he was way cooler than this song. Not that I was obsessing over Kirk.

For one thing, I was too busy *not* obsessing over Zach.

I'd never obsess over a guy like Zach. One, he wasn't interested. Two, he and Lauren were tight, and—unlike most guys I knew—he didn't seem like someone who'd stray. Three, he wasn't interested.

I mean, I wasn't interested in *him*. He drove a bright-orange VW Beetle, had a ridiculous Cat in the Hat tattoo, and listened to classical music instead of anything good.

Fine. Except for that, he was pretty cute.

Cool. I meant cool.

Jeremy had stopped whacking his drums and cymbals like a maniac, settling into a nice groove. His hair was purple tonight with tiny hot-pink spikes that made me grateful that Michael, who had flaming red hair, was on the opposite end of the so-called stage. Zach played at the end closest to me, in front of Jeremy on drums.

Okay, I *was* watching him, but only because he was so good on bass. I should really watch Kirk and try to figure out how he played *guitar* so well. Despite Jazz's doubts, and maybe my own, I wanted to be a great guitar player. Some day.

Kirk's fingers flew up and down the neck of his guitar in a way I couldn't even dream of, and I could usually dream of pretty much anything. At least, I had before Shangri-La. Did I dream of anything anymore?

I looked again at Zach, who I did *not* dream about. He wasn't even my type. If I had a type.

I glanced back at Kirk in time to catch the way his mouth quirked upward on one side, as if something amused him. As if *I* amused him.

"He thinks you're a total joke."

I whipped my head to the left, away from the band, and not just because one of Amber's sharp claws was digging a groove in my forearm. Grabbing her wrist, I twisted it. Hard.

She went down even harder.

The band kept playing.

As Chelsea helped her up off the floor, Drew stepped between us. "Causing trouble as usual, I see."

He was grinning, though, and totally Drew: not the

brightest bulb on the Christmas tree, as my dad would say, but cute. He moved closer, slowly, as if he wondered if I'd send him sprawling to the floor next. When I rolled my eyes, he moved all the way in and put his arm around me.

Someone in the band hit a bad chord. A really bad one. Drew squeezed my waist and moved even closer, which should've been physically impossible.

Tense, I glanced past him, but Chelsea and Amber had both disappeared.

Weird. Even for them.

"Wanna blow out of here?" Drew's mouth was on my ear as if it planned to stay there. It was wet and on the move, which wasn't exactly on my wish list. Not tonight. And not with Drew. "We could party at my house."

I liked Drew, actually. But why couldn't a guy and a girl just be pals? Or why couldn't guys see *me* as a pal and not an easy lay?

My sister Liz is totally cute, but she's always had *tons* of guy pals and, until Alex, not many boyfriends or even dates. Did she hate that just as much?

I wished I could talk to her. Like, right now.

I twisted slightly, just enough to release myself from Drew's mouth. And tongue. And various other body parts. I glanced at the band. Kirk was staring at me, but his trademark grin was gone. Because I'd thrown Amber to the floor? Or because Drew was hitting on me? None of it was my fault!

Just like that, the band stopped playing. In the middle of a song.

"Sorry, guys." Kirk looked at everyone in the crowd except Drew and me. "We need to take a short break. Be right back."

"So?" Drew's mouth, right on cue. "My house?"

"What about Chelsea?"

And what about my strong preference for guys who had a brain and not just a libido?

"Chelsea and I—" Drew shrugged. "I mean, she's not you."

I could still picture Chelsea's face in Speech Communications class right before she puked just because she had to say "oral sex and STDs" out loud. Melodramatic, yeah, but I'd also seen Drew's face. Totally guilty.

"I have to pass, but thanks." I smiled at him, trying to ease the sting. "I gave Lauren a ride here, and I need to be up early tomorrow."

"We could—"

"You could get a room." Kirk, who'd always had a bazillion gorgeous girls wrapped around him, was suddenly in Drew's face. But then he turned to me. "Did Amber ask you to help her do a flip in the air? I thought *you* were the one going out for gymnastics. If that's even true."

I flinched. "Your girlfriend was clawing my arm." I held it up for his inspection, almost wishing more blood was dripping from it, but a bright-red gash was definitely there. "She's a little possessive, huh? Do you actually *like* that?"

He pushed his silly rock-star sunglasses up on top of his head. "She's a little . . ."

He trailed off as his gaze swept the length of me, then came back up to boob level. Was this the so-called cool Kirk Easton? No wonder he'd sung "She Don't Like Jelly." Maybe it *was* autobiographical.

"She's with me, Kirk." Drew found his voice, although it cracked a little. "I think Amber went upstairs."

"Along with *your* girlfriend." Kirk turned to me, his gaze dipping again to boob level, even though I was wearing a stupid Arctic Monkeys T-shirt that was the opposite of tight. Or sexy. Or even cute. "Are you with Drew now?"

"I'm not with anyone."

"Lydia?" Lauren appeared behind Kirk but must've been too smart to get any closer, what with Kirk and Drew both baring their teeth and all. "Did you want to go?"

I glanced from her to Zach, who hadn't moved but also wasn't even touching his bass guitar. I had no idea what he was doing. Staring at the floor?

Getting out of this hot mess was the best idea I'd heard in a long time, but Lauren's question surprised me. "Don't you want to stay and listen?"

She shook her head. "I'd really like to leave, if that's okay."

"Works for me." Detaching myself from Drew, I brushed past Kirk with a completely unapologetic smile. "Sorry, guys. Feel free to keep pissing on each other, but if you get tired of it, I think your girlfriends are upstairs."

I gave Zach a wave. He just nodded, a little curt or tense or *something*, so I bit my lip and headed for the stairs. Lauren had already disappeared, but I caught up with her in the front hall.

I frowned. "Is everything okay?"

"It wasn't that much fun." She shrugged, her gaze on the floor. "Nobody said a word to me."

I patted her arm. "Zach would've talked to you all night if he hadn't been playing. And once they started playing, I couldn't hear what anyone said."

"They were talking to *you*. Everyone." Her gaze was still locked on the floor, almost as if it were the yellow brick road. I could've told her that nothing in this house was the magical path to anything she'd ever want.

I snorted. "Believe me, I wish they hadn't."

"Every guy . . . wants you."

Only in a disgusting way, and I also didn't want to have this conversation in the middle of Kirk's front hall. Or, to be honest, anywhere.

I steered Lauren outside. "It's not what you think. Like, not at all. Besides, you seem to be besties with Zach, and he's nicer than the guys who talk to *me*."

It was probably why he had no interest in the biggest slut in the entire history of Woodbury High School.

If you believed the rumors, at least.

Lauren's head was still down, her feet dragging, so I focused on getting her to the Jeep. I finally looked up, though, at the flashing lights on a couple of police cars.

Whew. We'd left Kirk's party just in time, and I hadn't had a drop of alcohol. All good.

The police cars were right next to the Jeep, though, which wasn't so good. Still, I hadn't done anything wrong, so they'd have to let us leave. I walked up to the driver's-side door of the Jeep. A cop with a buzz cut and the thickest neck I'd ever seen blocked my way.

Pointing at the Jeep, I gave him a friendly smile. "Okay if we leave? I think you'll have to move that car."

His hands went to his hips. "Is this your Jeep?"

I almost said "guilty as charged" just as Lauren, who'd gone to the passenger door, shrieked. "Lydia, your window's broken!"

Crap. Story of my life.

Chapter 17

*"At any rate, she cannot grow many degrees worse, without
authorizing us to lock her up for the rest of her life."*

— Jane Austen, *Pride and Prejudice*
Volume II, Chapter Eighteen

AS I SUCKED in a breath, I saw my fragile hopes of keeping my
Jeep privileges swirling down the drain. I headed toward Lauren
and the broken window I'd have to explain to Dad.

The cop moved in front of me, blocking me.

I sidestepped him. He matched me.

Impatient to see how bad the damage was, I shook my head.
"Someone broke the window on my Jeep. I mean, my family's
Jeep. I have to take a look at it."

"This is your Jeep?"

"My family's Jeep. My parents own it, and I've got to check
out the broken window and call my dad, so he can call the
police." I tried again to move around the cop as I pulled my
phone from the back pocket of my jeans. "Or do I just tell you?

Is that why you're here?"

Head down, I scrolled to Dad's name on my "favorites" list, even though he hadn't been one of my favorites in too long to remember. The cop reached out, trying to grab my phone, but I whipped it behind my back.

"Miss, step away from the Jeep. I need to ask you a few questions."

I waved a hand. "My dad or mom—" Wait. Strike that. Even though my mom was the lawyer in the family, she tended to freak out about things like broken windows. "My *dad* can answer whatever you need to know. I just need to call him. He can be here in ten minutes."

I looked for Lauren so I could apologize for the hassle, but she'd totally disappeared. I knew she was antsy to leave the party, but she didn't have to freak about it.

Even I wasn't freaking, and I had the broken window.

The veins in the cop's neck bulged like a heart attack or aneurysm waiting to happen. "I need you to come with me."

Talk about creepy. I shook my head. "No offense, but I'm not going anywhere with you. I'm calling my dad. Someone broke my window, and my dad's going to freak."

Another cop joined us, a slim, pretty woman who made me want to ask who cut her short hair. She looked nearly as lacking in humanity as the male cop, though, so this didn't seem like the moment. "Are you Lydia Bennet?" She glanced at a small notebook she carried. "Were you with Lauren . . . Kjelstad?"

I blinked. She totally butchered Lauren's last name, trying to pronounce the "j" in it, but that wasn't what made my jaw drop. "Yeah, I'm Lydia, but how do you know my name? The Jeep should be registered in my mom or dad's name."

She glanced at the male cop, who nodded, then turned back to me. "You can call your parents. Please tell them to come here as quickly as possible."

Both my parents? Mom? Thanks, but I didn't have a death wish. *And how did these cops know my name?*

"My mom's out of town, but I'm sure my dad can come."

While the female cop gave me the evil eye, I pulled my phone from my back pocket. Holding it tightly in case one of the cops made a grab for it, I called Dad's cell phone.

He picked up on the first ring. "Is everything okay?"

So much for cheerful parental greetings.

"Um, Dad?" Both cops were listening, but I resisted the strong urge to turn my back on them or, say, run like hell. "Someone broke a window on the Jeep, and the cops want you to come. Like, right now."

Dead silence. Just as I pulled my phone away from my ear to see if we'd gotten disconnected, I heard Dad sigh.

"Where are you?"

I gave him the streets at the intersection near Kirk's house. I almost told him not to bring Mom, but the cops were listening intently. Besides, Dad tended to do the opposite of whatever I asked. I closed my eyes and hoped for the best.

"I'll be right there." Click. Yeah, Dad still had a cell phone that snapped shut. Dinosaurs R Us.

Slipping my phone in my back pocket, I gave the female cop a tight smile. "He's coming."

I glanced at Kirk's house, a few houses up the street from where the Jeep was parked. Unlike ten minutes ago, I didn't hear loud music or any other noise, but a few dozen kids were on Kirk's front lawn and sidewalk, and some even closer, checking out what Lydia Bennet had done *this* time.

Not a damn thing.

Had one of them broken my window? Or had the asshat who broke it already split? Just like Lauren?

I didn't see Kirk or any of the guys in the band, who were probably still in the basement. Finally, I spied a girl half hidden behind a tree in the yard across the street from me, her arms wrapped around her waist.

Tess.

The moment I caught her eye, I expected her to run. She didn't, but she took another step behind the tree as she kept staring at me. Bizarre.

She'd probably already posted a video of the whole thing online, along with a ton of other kids. Just like at that strip bar in Milwaukee last summer.

Remembering only too well, I felt my cheeks flame.

"Miss?" The female cop had a hard edge to her voice, and I could tell she didn't fall for anyone's bullshit, but with a soft touch on my arm she turned me away from the crowd. "Let's wait on the sidewalk for your father."

It registered, finally, that I was still in the middle of the street, where anyone could run me down. Based on the passenger window of the Jeep and Amber's claw marks on my arm, I was surprised no one had. Yet.

Shaking more than I wanted to think about, I walked behind the Jeep and onto the sidewalk, where I caught my first glimpse of the broken window.

"Jesus."

Whoever broke the window had used a baseball bat or worse. I also spied several dents that hadn't been on the side and hood of the Jeep before, and that included all the dents Cat and I put there before we had our driver's licenses.

Feeling tears welling in my eyes, I bit my lip.

The female cop watched me but didn't say a word. The male cop was still in the middle of the street, talking to someone on his cell phone.

Finally, a green Honda Civic cruised slowly down the street toward us. Seeing someone in the passenger seat, I bit back a curse. When Dad parked a few cars behind the Jeep, though, Liz hopped out from the passenger side.

Thank God.

As she strode toward me, wearing a ragged pair of jeans and a Rolling Stones T-shirt, I wished for a moment that Jane had joined Dad for this rescue mission. Jane would be dressed impeccably and speak so soothingly that the cops would fall all over themselves to do what she asked.

Seeing Liz, the male cop ended his call and tried to intercept her. She waved him off. Dismissively. I glanced at the female cop, still tight at my side. Her lips were pursed.

I'd never been happier in my life to see Liz.

"Hey, I just want to see my sister." Liz was still trying to get past the male cop. I could tell from her scowl that she was tempted to take him down, but so far she was restraining herself. "You called us here, right? We're here."

The male cop stayed next to her as she came up and hugged me. For the first time in my life.

Then she glanced at the Jeep. "Jesus!"

The female cop cracked a sliver of a grin. "That's what your sister said."

Dad joined us, finally, his mouth a grim slash, his eyes tired. Let's just say he didn't hug me.

His eyes swept the side of the Jeep. When he moved closer to it, the male cop rushed forward. "Sir, you can't touch the Jeep. It's evidence."

Dad rolled his eyes. "I think the evidence is obvious. A bashed-in window and other damage to the body that none of my five daughters put there, despite their best attempts over the last few years."

He grinned at Liz and me. Or maybe just at Liz.

"Sir, there's nothing funny about this situation." The male cop totally had a pole up his ass. "Are you Lydia Bennet's father?"

Dad's dark-blond eyebrows rose. "Yes, I'm her father. All

day today."

The cop looked pissed, but Liz was bouncing on her toes and grinning. To her, this was probably just another sporting event.

"Of course this isn't even remotely funny." Dad took a step closer to the cop. Then another step, until he was in the guy's face. "Some jackass beat the hell out of my Jeep, but you're so busy harassing my daughter and insisting that I come to the scene of the crime that you can't do your job."

The cop glared right back at Dad. "My job, sir, is to arrest your daughter for possession of the drugs we found in plain sight in the vehicle."

What?

In the sudden and jaw-dropping silence, the cop puffed out his barrel chest. "Since she's a minor, we wanted you here, but the drugs involved mean we can't release her to your custody."

"Drugs?" Dad glanced at me.

"I don't do drugs." I don't know why I bothered saying it, since Dad obviously took the word of the cops over me. Did he think I smashed in the window, too? "I've never touched them. Ever."

After a year at Shangri-La, I didn't even shake as I said it.

Dad looked at me again, more intently, for what felt like forever. Finally, he looked from the male cop to the female cop, his gaze stopping with her. Good decision. "The drugs aren't Lydia's. Or anyone else's in my family."

The female cop just gazed back at him, but the male cop waved his arms, apoplexy style. "The drugs are on the front seat of the Jeep, confirming tips we received. Marijuana, cocaine, crack, and pills that appear to be hallucinogens."

Dad rolled his eyes again. "Did the tips mention the broken window? Did you happen to *see* the broken window?"

"Sir, that's not dispositive."

The female cop moved forward, stepping between them. "Mr. Bennet, I'm Officer Lewis, and this is my partner, Officer Andreassen. The callers both mentioned the Jeep, the drugs, and the fact that Lydia Bennet and—" She whipped out her notebook again. "Lauren Kjelstad." Butchered it again. "Both callers identified the occupants of the Jeep as Lydia and Lauren. If Lauren is the young woman who returned to the vehicle with Lydia, I will note that she ran from the scene."

"Lauren?" Dad's brow furrowed as he caught my eye. "Who's Lauren?"

I shrugged. "Just a girl from school. I gave her a ride to Kirk's party, and we were about to head home."

Dad glanced at his watch. "So early?"

"The party was a bore, and a couple of girls were harassing me." Frowning, I turned to the female cop. "Were the calls from girls? Like, teenage girls?"

Amber? Chelsea? Or Tess, who was no longer in sight?

"Did Tess do this?" Liz's fists were clenched. "That little shit."

"My first guess would be Amber and Chelsea." I hadn't turned into a snitch at Shangri-La, even though the place had been infested with them, but I was *not* going down without a fight. I turned to Liz, holding up my arm. "Amber actually clawed me at the party, and she and Chelsea are afraid I might steal their boyfriends. Their totally lame boyfriends."

At this point, I definitely included Kirk in the "lame" category.

"All I can confirm is that the callers sounded female." Officer Lewis exchanged a look with the male cop. "They identified Lauren—" She paused, then apparently decided not to attempt her last name again. "Well, as a drug dealer. They also said Lydia had spent time in reform school and that Lauren provided drugs to Lydia during class a few weeks ago." She looked up at Dad, who looked stricken. "We have to take this information seriously."

"Even if it's completely untrue." I shook my head, seeing a tall metal fence again in my near future. "And both girls said the same exact thing? Did they also mention the fact that they bashed in the freaking window?"

"The window is irrelevant." Officer Andreassen's neck was bulging again. I hoped he *did* have a heart attack or stroke and drop on the spot. I'd kick him where he lay. "The evi-dence—"

Officer Lewis held up a hand, cutting him off. She then walked over to the Jeep and peered through the now-permanently open window. Her jaw clenched.

"Mr. Bennet, would you and your daughter agree to have her submit to a drug test?"

Dad looked at me, frowning, probably because he figured I'd fail a drug test.

"Fine by me." I nodded at the woman. "Drug, alcohol, anything you want."

When Liz caught my eye, a question in hers, I shrugged. She didn't believe me, Dad didn't believe me, and both cops would string me up by my toes if given half the chance.

Been there. Not my fault that time, either.

This time, though, I'd fight. No one I knew was going to rescue me, and I was pretty sure Amber and Chelsea set me up. Let them and everyone else at that stupid party rot in hell.

Sorry, Zach.

Liz pointed at Kirk's brick three-story house, surprising me. Liz was no snitch, either. "My guess is that the so-called tips came from girls at a party at that house. I would also guess that, unlike my sister, most of the kids at the party would *not* willingly agree to a drug or alcohol test."

Officer Lewis frowned as she pulled out her walkie-talkie and barked orders into it. Hearing "PBT" and "party" and "minors," I grinned. So shoot me. Two cops hustled out of the patrol car farthest from us and took off across the street. To Kirk's house.

Officer Pole Up His Ass turned to me. "We'll deal with that situation, but it doesn't change the facts. There is a significant quantity of illegal drugs in this vehicle, and you've acknowledged that you were driving it."

"When I drove it to the party, there weren't any drugs in it." I waved a hand at the wrecked Jeep. "While I was at the party, someone bashed in the window, then *obviously* set me up by sticking drugs inside. You won't find my fingerprints on the drugs. Or Lauren's."

But Lauren *had* taken off, which wasn't good. Despite her reputation, though, I was pretty sure her biggest crime tonight had been having the bad judgment to catch a ride to the party with me.

Officer Lewis turned to Dad. "Sir? With your permission, we'll administer a drug test to your daughter. Unfortunately, all we can do here is a PBT, a preliminary breath test that detects alcohol but not drugs. We'll need to do the drug test at the hospital."

Dad looked like someone had gut-punched him. Like, say, me.

"Dad, it's okay." Liz left my side to walk over and slug him on the arm—her unique way of comforting someone—even though no one tried to reassure *me*. "But you screwed up in Milwaukee. Don't let it happen twice."

When Dad's lips pressed together, I remembered exactly how he looked in Milwaukee after Justin and I were arrested . . . and wished I didn't. Phil Donnelly, a criminal-defense lawyer in Mom's law firm, had done most of the talking, but Dad had told the judge to send me away.

Like, say, to Montana.

Then and now, the so-called evidence was against me.

Then and now, Dad never bothered to ask me if I was guilty.

♫

AS DAD BRUSHED past Liz and walked over to me, I stared at the ground. Glass had flown everywhere. Some little kid was going to run around barefoot and rip up his or her feet.

"Lydia."

I didn't look up.

"Lydia, I let you down in Milwaukee. I never will again." Dad's voice broke, but I'd *seen* the look in his eyes when the cops mentioned drugs. No matter what he said right now, he'd believed them. "I'll call Phil."

Finally meeting his gaze, I held up a hand. "I don't need Phil. I'm innocent. Just let them give me the tests."

Officer Pole Up His Ass shook his head. "The tests will show only whether you have drugs or alcohol in your system. They won't change the fact that you were in possession."

"Frank." Officer Lewis cut him off, which seemed like a great idea. "Let's get a fingerprint analysis on the drugs. And, actually, we didn't find Lydia in possession of anything. The drugs are in the vehicle. She isn't."

"Trin, we have to follow procedure."

"I am." She turned to me. "If you and your father will accompany me to the hospital, your sister can follow in your other car. Wait." She walked over to the nearest police car, rummaged in the trunk, and returned with a handheld breathalyzer and a small flashlight.

A minute later, I'd blown a zero on the breathalyzer, and she'd tested my eyes with the flashlight. Liz stood next to Dad, both of them watching it all.

I wished Dad liked me the way he liked Liz.

I wished he trusted me.

But wishing had never gotten me anywhere except a stint in Shangri-La.

"Lydia? You okay?"

My head whipped up at the sound of Zach's voice. Kids were streaming out of Kirk's house, some of them climbing out of windows to avoid getting busted. A lot of them were huddled across the street now, watching me just like Tess had earlier, but Zach was the only one who actually crossed the street for a close-up look at my latest humiliation.

I met his gaze, head high, fiercely. And wiped the back of my hand across my face, refusing to cry.

It was too late to refuse to be embarrassed.

"Lauren texted me." Perfect. He was digging my hole deeper, but he wouldn't know that. "She tried to come back to Kirk's house, but Amber wouldn't let her in."

Officer Lewis, who'd been paying way too much attention to Zach, frowned. "Lauren? Amber?"

Zach stuffed his hands in the front pockets of his jeans. "Yeah. Lauren's my friend. Amber isn't."

As Officer Lewis jotted something in her notebook, I looked at Zach. "Where did Lauren go?"

He shrugged. "She called my mom for a ride. Boy, will I hear about *that* when I get home."

I told myself that Zach and Lauren were tight, and they were neighbors, and they'd known each other forever. So of course she was tight with his mom, too.

I still wanted to hit something.

Zach slanted me an oddly embarrassed grin. "I wanted to make sure you were okay." He glanced at the broken window on the Jeep. "Lauren mentioned the window. Man, that blows."

I just nodded. Thank God Lauren hadn't mentioned the

drugs. Had she seen them? Was that why she took off?

"Lauren thought—" Zach broke off, maybe because both cops, my dad, and Liz were all hanging on his words. He nodded at Liz, then looked back at me. "She thought Amber and Chelsea might've done it." He glanced at Officer Lewis. "I mean, I have no idea. I'm not accusing anyone."

"Good to see you again, Zach." Liz grinned at him. "Did you pass the breath test or climb out a window?"

Officer Pole Up His Ass frowned. "Miss, this is no time to joke. We're looking at—"

"Frank? Talk to you a moment?"

Officer Lewis pulled her partner several yards down the sidewalk away from us.

Liz immediately came over to me. "If you ask me, this would be an excellent time to cut and run."

"Liz." Dad frowned at her. That had to be a first.

Zach just laughed, then took another look at the broken window before turning to me. "Seriously. Are you okay? You don't look like yourself."

What was I supposed to look like? A hardened felon?

I shrugged. "The cops found drugs in my Jeep, and someone told them they belonged to Lauren and me."

"Lauren doesn't use drugs."

But I did?

Wait. Lauren didn't use drugs?

"She parties, sure." He glanced over at my dad, who looked numb, then back at me. "But, like, just the occasional beer. You know?"

I knew she'd had a beer tonight, which might explain why she took off when she saw the cops. But she'd tried to give me drugs in class that day. Or were they drugs? Had I jumped to conclusions just like everyone always did with me?

Seeing my frown, Zach shook his head. "She told me she

tried to sneak some chocolate to you in class one time, even though you can't bring food to class." Seeing and totally misinterpreting the stunned look on my face, he laughed. "She hates to get in trouble with teachers. Even though she does all the time."

Officer Lewis rejoined us. "Lydia, you can go home now. We have no probable cause to believe you're under the influence of drugs or alcohol, but we'll need to gather evidence from the Jeep before releasing it to you." She glanced at my dad. "Is that okay, Mr. Bennet?"

He looked like a deer in the headlights, but he nodded.

She turned back to me. "I need to get the names of the friends you mentioned. Amber and Chelsea? Tess?"

"They're not my friends."

She smiled. Slightly, but still. "It doesn't sound like it, but it would help if I could contact them. We'll likely have more questions for you later, too."

I wasn't going to jail.

At least, not right this moment.

I didn't know anything about Chelsea except her name, but I pulled Amber's contact info from my phone and gave it to Officer Lewis along with my own contact info. After a moment's hesitation, I gave her Tess's info, too. But I told Officer Lewis I really had no idea about Tess, only that she was friends with Amber and Chelsea and that she'd been standing behind a tree across the street, watching me.

Officer Lewis frowned. "When? Just now?"

I shook my head. "Earlier. When I first came out and saw the Jeep."

Nodding, she scribbled something in her notebook, then flipped it shut. "Thanks. I'll be in touch."

♫

I WATCHED BOTH cops walk away, toward Kirk's house, which still had kids streaming out of it. Kirk was on the lawn now, looking like he was arguing with Amber while Chelsea looked on. I didn't see Drew or, for that matter, Tess.

"Officer?"

Both cops turned back to me.

I pointed out Amber and Chelsea to Officer Lewis, totally ignoring her partner. They both started across the street.

Zach tilted his head, studying me with a serious look on his face, but he didn't know Amber and Chelsea the way I did. He also didn't have Amber's claw marks in his arm.

When he started to say something, Liz shook her head. "If they're innocent, they'll be fine. But I have a feeling those girls aren't often compared to Mother Teresa."

I punched her arm, partly because she'd expect it, but my knees were still shaking. Someone hated me enough to set me up with something this serious. To lock me up. What had I ever done to them?

What had Cat done to Tess last spring, though?

"Do you need a ride home?" Zach kept studying me, but I couldn't read him. Was he disgusted? Like everyone at school on Monday, would he believe I did this? "Or do you need to go with your dad and sister?"

Dad waved his keys in the air. "We'll take Lydia home."

Where he'd probably lock me in the basement. Forever.

"Actually, the back seat of Dad's car is totally full of crap. Right, Dad?" As he shook his head, Liz nodded. "So if you could give Lydia a ride home, Zach, that would be cool. She's too big to sit on my lap."

Catching sight of the bright-orange Beetle right in front of

Kirk's house, where all hell was still breaking loose, I started to think a ride with Dad—even in the trunk—might be a better idea.

Dad cleared his throat. "Lydia, we should go home."

"Zach will give her a ride. He's a good guy."

Liz gave Zach a thumbs up, but he didn't exactly look thrilled at the thought of going *anywhere* with me. Despite his offer.

Besides, Dad looked a little apoplectic. I turned to Zach. "Hey, I appreciate it, but my house is in the opposite direction from yours, and you probably want to get home."

"I said I'd give you a ride."

"But—" *But you don't want to.*

He shook his head. "My gear is in the front *and* back seat, but it sounds like my car has more room than your dad's. You don't even have to sit on my lap."

Zach. Making a joke. Wow.

That was a joke, right?

"Fine. Go with your friend." Dad didn't look pleased, but being jabbed in the side by Liz couldn't be pleasant. "But be home by nine."

It was already eight forty-five.

Liz's eyebrows danced. "Eleven."

This time, Dad jabbed her back. "Ten."

"Thirty."

I rolled my eyes. It would take ten minutes, max, for Zach to drive me home and then take off with a roar two seconds after I opened the passenger door and climbed out.

Before I could explain Liz's pathetic sense of humor to him, though, he started walking toward his car without waiting to see if I followed.

Should I?

When he offered me a ride, he was just being polite. He

obviously had something going on with Lauren, who was practically part of his family. He didn't even try to pretend he thought I was a *nice* girl. Unlike, say, Lauren.

"Lydia?" Ten feet from me, Zach stopped and turned around, looking impatient. "Your dad already left. Unless you'd rather walk home, I'll give you a ride."

Great. He looked totally disgusted. Maybe even pissed. Just like everyone I knew.

"Do we have to listen to classical music?"

He stared at me a long moment before his lips twitched. A miracle. "You've had a shitty day. Maybe just this once I'll break down and play Green Day."

My eyebrows went up. "You will? Seriously?"

"Hey, you never know."

With Zach, definitely true. I never knew.

Chapter 18

*Lydia led voluntarily to subjects which her sisters
would not have alluded to for the world.*

— Jane Austen, *Pride and Prejudice*
Volume III, Chapter Nine

AFTER SHOVING HIS bass and amp in the tiny back seat of the
Beetle, Zach waved a hand at the front passenger seat.

It was piled high with CDs.

"Oh, yeah. Sorry." He scooped them up, or most of them,
and deposited them on the floor of the back seat.

Reaching down, I grabbed the few he'd left behind. The
Killers. Beethoven. Benny Goodman. Lady Gaga.

Lady Gaga?

After Zach sat down in the driver's seat and saw her CD in
my hand, he shrugged. "I play anyone who has talent."

I climbed into the Beetle, too, and buckled up. I had my
doubts about Beethoven, but I had to admit Zach had eclectic
taste. "The Killers?"

"They're sick." He slid their CD from my grasp, pulled it

out of the case, and inserted it in his CD player. So much for Green Day, but at least it wasn't Beethoven or Mozart or anyone else who lived before the earth's crust cooled, which probably included Benny Goodman. "Okay if I play it?"

I nodded, not really caring. I'd be home in ten minutes. It might take Zach longer than that to find Green Day in the massive pile of CDs in his car. Hadn't the guy ever heard of an aux cord?

As I leaned back in my seat, he started the engine. Eardrum-shattering music—the Killers, apparently—erupted from the radio.

I blinked. Okay, this was pretty good.

Before I could settle in to the first song, though, he started punching buttons. "Let me play my favorite song of theirs. 'Read My Mind.' It reminds me of you."

And it was his favorite?

What about Lauren?

Shaking off that thought, I listened as Zach pulled away from the curb and headed down the street. Sure, he was going in the opposite direction of my house, but he probably didn't want to try a U-turn in front of all these cops.

I loved the melody, the rhythm of the song, and couldn't help tapping my fingertips on my thigh. It totally drew me in. When I listened more closely, though, I frowned. I slid a sideways glance at Zach, whose gaze was focused straight ahead.

He still wasn't heading toward my house, but that didn't matter as much as the words of the song.

Words like "a subtle kiss" and "a big trapeze."

A big trapeze?

Thoughts of Justin, and the circus troupe I joined for about two minutes, and Justin again, flooded my brain. Wisconsin Dells followed by Milwaukee followed by the Montana outpost of Reform Schools R Us. One long nightmare.

This song reminded Zach of *me*.

"Read My Mind"? He definitely couldn't.

I stared out the window, partly to avoid his face and partly to memorize my surroundings in case Zach's actual plan was to dump my bludgeoned, lifeless body in a ditch somewhere.

Because he didn't seem to be driving to my house.

A silent five-minute drive later, he swung into the parking lot at Dairy Queen, parked, and turned off the Killers. Thank God for small favors.

I frowned. "Hungry?"

"I think the food at Kirk's party consisted of a single bag of lime-flavored tortilla chips. I hate lime."

He climbed out of the Beetle, so I did, too. For lack of better things to do.

"He had plenty of beer."

Zach waited for me, then walked across the lot to the door, which he held for me. "I don't drink."

My eyebrows rose.

He shrugged. "I don't need alcohol to have a good time, and it's illegal, and my mom—"

"—would be pissed."

He shook his head. "Not pissed. Disappointed."

My parents had spent their lives being disappointed in me. No, probably just Dad. Mom still had my back when it counted, which was often, even if she hadn't been able to prevent or cut short my stint at Shangri-La.

We reached the counter, where a fresh-scrubbed worker batted her eyelashes at Zach and acted as if I didn't exist. Smiling possessively, she held up a cherry Dilly. "The usual?"

Zach thanked her, then turned to me. "What would you like?"

I'd like it if my stomach stopped jumping, but the Jeep and the broken window and all those drugs kept flashing through my brain on a never-ending loop.

"A small Coke? But I can get it."

"My treat." He ordered a Coke for me, a Sprite for him, and a chocolate Dilly Bar. When he handed me the chocolate Dilly, the girl behind the counter looked like she'd just swallowed battery acid. "I hate to eat alone, so you'd be doing me a favor."

Ha. Right.

But I seriously had no idea if my stomach would tolerate the Dilly or send it right back up, possibly in Zach's face.

As I sipped my Coke, he led me to a cozy corner table. Okay, the ten million kids in soccer jerseys and cleats who surrounded us made it less than cozy. Not that it mattered. This wasn't a date.

Understatement.

I had no idea what to say, which had never happened to me with any guy I'd known before Zach.

But I didn't know him, and he didn't know me. If he did, "Read My Mind" would *not* remind him of me. At least, not the part about the trapeze.

"Why did that song remind you of me?"

Damn. My mouth really needed a lock and key. Ever since Milwaukee and Shangri-La, though, I despised locks and keys.

Zach, who was busy nibbling the cherry shell off his Dilly Bar and leaving the ice cream virtually untouched, didn't seem to have heard my question.

I looked at my chocolate Dilly, felt my stomach do a half-hearted somersault, and took a sip of my Coke.

"Thanks." I nodded at the Coke and the Dilly, even though the odds of me eating the Dilly Bar were slim to none. "I mean, if you're going to kidnap a girl, this is a decent place to bring her before dumping her dead body in a drainage ditch. You know, last meal and all. Very sporting of you."

Zach nodded. "Problem is, I forgot to put a shovel in my

car. The bass and amp took up too much room."

He had a sense of humor. Oh, wait. Of course he did. He was out with me in public.

Not that he was really out with me.

"So. The song? Why did it remind you of me?"

He kept nibbling for several seconds as a dark-red flush crept up his neck. "Oh, you know."

"I don't, actually." I'd also have to look up the lyrics the moment I got home. "Tell me?"

He studied his Dilly, which was now bare of its red shell. "The whole thing about reading your mind. I'll bet no one has ever read your mind, even if half the guys you know think they can."

My jaw dropped.

He waved his Dilly in the air. Luckily, it hadn't yet melted enough to fly off the stick. "I don't mean it that way. I just—"

He took a bite of his ice cream.

I didn't touch mine.

He pointed at my Dilly Bar. "It's going to melt. Didn't you want a Dilly?"

No, but I picked it up anyway. Peeled off the wrapper. Took a tiny bite. Swallowed. Managed to keep it down. Barely.

"Look."

I didn't. Not at him, anyway.

"Lydia."

I still didn't.

All around me, a gazillion pint-sized soccer players were whooping it up, squealing and laughing. I glanced at my Dilly, then set it down on the wrapper and stood up. "Thanks, really, but I'm kind of in the mood to walk home, and it's still decently light out."

It wasn't, actually, but I'd call Liz the moment I walked outside and beg her for a ride. If I had to, I'd even beg Dad.

Zach grabbed my hand.

I glanced down at it, at him, coldly, waiting for him to let me go.

"The thing is—" Nope, he wasn't letting go. "Every guy thinks he owns you. Or *wants* you. That's why I got pissed tonight. At Drew, at Kirk, even Michael."

I snorted. "Michael has never even looked at me, but *you're* tired of crap like that? Welcome to my world."

He tugged on my hand, gently, until I finally sat down.

Totally against my will.

"I heard what happened to you." Zach finally let go of my hand, leaving it cold. In more ways than one. "I'm sorry."

Just like that, eating the Dilly Bar seemed like a good idea. It might keep me from shoving it in Zach's face.

"Yeah?" I aimed for blasé, which felt even harder than my D chord. "In Milwaukee? Old news."

Even if it still felt fresh, and horrifying, to me.

"No." Zach waited until I met his gaze before continuing. Let's just say it took a while. "When you were a freshman. After the homecoming game."

My breath caught in my throat. Tiny black splotches danced before my eyes. Waving them away, I looked out the window, as far away from Zach as I could without my head spinning on my neck. "I don't know what you're talking about."

"Anyway, I'm sorry." Zach took several licks of his cherry-coating-bare Dilly, then a bite. Another bite. A huge one. "If I'd heard at the time, I would've done something, even though I was just a sophomore."

"You didn't know me."

I sucked a big gulp of my Coke, choking on it until a tween boy behind me shrieked that I was choking to death and several hands—all of them probably sticky as hell—thumped me on the back.

After Zach got rid of the kids, or mostly, he shrugged. "I knew who you were. And everyone knew the star quarterback of the football team."

I pushed to my feet again, too fast for Zach to stop me this time. "I have to go."

"Can I have your Dilly?"

My eyes flew wide. "You're kidding."

"Yeah." Just like that, Zach was at my side, but holding my chocolate Dilly Bar. "I mean, you get first dibs. And I can't carry the sodas, too."

I glanced back at our table but kept walking. Out the door. Past Zach's bright-orange Beetle. Headed for home or hell or wherever.

I didn't much care.

"I'll walk you home, but I do have Green Day in my car."

I snorted, even though icicles of long-ago pain kept nailing me with every step. "That's what you promised, but you *played* the Killers. They couldn't possibly read my mind."

And neither can you.

"And neither can I."

Jesus. Could he?

Zach slowed his pace to match my faltering steps. "But I'd like to."

"Why? Because I'm friends with Lauren?"

This time, Zach's steps faltered. In fact, he tripped over a rock on the sidewalk that, in fairness, I really should've pointed out to him.

"Lauren?"

I rolled my eyes. "Your girlfriend?"

"She's my friend. One of my best friends, actually, since we were little kids."

I didn't want to have this conversation. I also didn't want to walk home, but I couldn't call Liz for a ride if Zach planned to stay glued to my side.

For reasons I couldn't begin to understand.

"Anyway. I heard the rumors about you, and I remembered what everyone said Blake bragged at the time."

Zach was intrepid; I'd give him that.

"Please. Stop." I held up a hand, using it as an excuse to turn back to Dairy Queen. One way or another, I was getting a ride home. ASAP. "It was a long time ago, and it wasn't true, but everyone thought what they thought."

Even my own sisters. Liz had graduated that year with Blake, Mr. Star Quarterback. They weren't friends, but as far as I knew he'd left Woodbury High with his testicles intact. If Liz had known the truth, he wouldn't have.

At least, I'd always hoped so.

"Lydia, I remember the look on your face. For months afterward."

So not true. I'd pasted a cocky grin on my face the next day and every day since.

Until Milwaukee. When I grew up.

I shook my head. "I don't know what you thought you saw, but it doesn't matter. Besides, you never said anything."

"I didn't know you." Reaching the rock he'd tripped over a few minutes ago, Zach kicked it. "I didn't know Blake, either, but I know his college football scholarship fell through for reasons other than his academic eligibility."

We kept walking in silence.

Wait. What?

"You did something?"

Next to me, he squirmed. "Um, my mom might've. I mean, I'm not sure. But she—"

I skidded to a halt. "You told your mom? Even though you didn't know me or know what really happened?"

His mouth twisted. "Yeah. Maybe I can't read your mind,

but I would've had to be blind not to see the look on your face when you thought no one was looking. Back then, and ever since."

It was too much—way too much—and I refused to cry.

I'd cried myself out three years ago, or so I hoped. I'd also thought I was the only person in the world, besides Blake, who knew what happened that night. The big senior football star had flirted with me after the game—me, a lowly freshman with a crush and an inflated ego—before sweetly offering me a ride home and then driving to a dead-end road.

The rest was history. And I couldn't change it.

But I could lash out at Zach.

I patted him on the arm as a knife twisted inside me. "Hey, I totally get it. Now you know why all the bad boys want me, even if you don't. Which is a total relief. You're not my type."

I took off, grateful for running shoes and the fact that I'd logged a lot of miles in the last week in addition to all the time I spent sweating all over the uneven parallels. I might not make the team, but I could run like hell when I needed to.

Right now, I needed to.

Before Zach saw the tears rolling down my cheeks and tried to read my mind.

I MADE IT a block before he caught up to me.

Damn it.

"You're not my type, either." He was breathing hard, which made me happy. A little happy. "But you're *really* not Drew's or Kirk's type."

He ran just so he could slam me like this? Actually *ran*?

I jammed my hands on my hips, something Liz usually did

right before taking down pretty much every guy—besides Alex—who'd ever crossed her path.

It probably explained why Liz got all the varsity letters and Jane got all the boyfriends, but I didn't want to be Jane. Not that I wanted to be Liz, either.

I met Zach's serious gaze and raised him one. "What is it you want? To *protect* me from every guy on the planet? Thanks, but not necessary."

Not since Shangri-La, definitely. Except for Drew, who was going out with Chelsea and therefore desperate by definition, no one was lining up to go out with me or even just hook up with me, which was a relief.

Mostly.

Zach held my chocolate Dilly up to my nose, nailing me with it. "You forgot your dinner. *Someone* needs to make sure you eat."

"I already did." Just like that, my stomach erupted in a growl reminiscent of a herd of water buffalo. Crap. Feeling like an idiot, I laughed along with Zach and grabbed my Dilly out of his hand. "But for the record, I'm not hungry."

"Then give me back the Dilly."

As he took a step toward me, I shoved him backward. "Not on your life."

He grinned, but that's when it got weird.

He didn't hit on me.

Didn't try to pull me into his arms, didn't try to kiss me, didn't give me a lame-ass smoldering look, didn't even say something flirty or suggestive.

Oh, right. He was with Lauren.

Even if he'd said he wasn't. Hadn't he?

"You don't really want to walk home, do you?" He tilted his head, studying me. Nope, not a drop of smoldering. "When at least two Green Day CDs are sitting in my car?"

"So you say." I glanced down at my Dilly, which was on the run to melting all over my hand. Rolling my eyes, I handed it to Zach. "But you don't have to give me a ride."

He inhaled half of it in one bite. "You didn't have to give me your Dilly."

I snorted. "Self-preservation. You would've tackled me for it."

But he still wouldn't have tried to kiss me, let alone go for more.

"You don't know that." Zach finished the Dilly with his second bite, but his hand was a mess of melted ice cream. He licked it. "But sure. It's possible."

Without another word, we turned back toward Dairy Queen. He pointed out a rock on the sidewalk before I tripped over it. He was a better person than I was. So sue me.

We reached his Beetle and climbed in, even though his hands had to be beyond sticky and even though the space inside his car felt too confined. Too—I don't know—embarrassing.

He had a tiny bottle of hand sanitizer in the glove compartment. As I stared, he put a dab on his hands and offered the bottle to me with a lift of his brows.

"Hand sanitizer?"

His mouth quirked. He'd smiled more tonight than in the entire time I'd known him. "My mom."

He didn't even blush. At this point, I just laughed.

Twisting, he reached down to the floor of the back seat and dug through the huge pile of CDs. "Found 'em."

He handed me two CDs, *Dookie* and *Insomniac*. How did he know they were my all-time faves?

It was almost like he could read my mind.

Ha.

Wordless, I handed one back to him. Equally wordless, he started the car, popped the Killers out of the CD player, and inserted *Insomniac*.

Then he pulled out of the DQ parking lot. This time, he headed for my house.

Just when I wished he wouldn't.

♫

TEN MINUTES LATER, he pulled up in front of my house.

In mildly shocking news, Dad wasn't waiting at the front door with a shotgun.

"Green Day, as promised. Your house, as promised." Zach gave me a crooked smile. "Sorry I didn't drop you in a drainage ditch, which sounded like a big fantasy for you, but I'll be better about the shovel next time."

Next time?

"Um, thanks." I fidgeted in my seat but didn't unbuckle. A guy drove me home on a Friday night and didn't have the faintest interest in kissing me, let alone doing more. What was I supposed to *do* with a guy like that?

Zach unbuckled me. "It's not even ten. Maybe your dad will let me live."

"You never know." Still, I didn't open my door. I leaned ever so slightly in his direction, but he didn't take that hint, either.

"The thing is . . ."

My gaze flew to his eyes, which were so serious. And dark. And, okay, gorgeous. "Yeah?"

He swallowed hard, his Adam's apple bobbing wildly. "I think every guy in the world has wanted to kiss you—and maybe more—and half of them say they *have*, but I don't think it's true."

He really did pay attention.

But what did he want? Guys all wanted *something*, didn't they?

"The thing is, I'd like to be friends."

Oh. Wow.

Nodding, I bit my lip but didn't say a word. The huge lump in my throat pretty much prevented it.

"We can work on your D chord, move on to bar chords, and maybe put a band together."

"Wait." I held up a hand, even though words were still beyond hard. "Last time I checked, you're already in a band."

He laughed, softly. "Not after tonight. And I'm thinking I can steal Heather and maybe even Jeremy away from Kirk."

I frowned. "Not Michael?"

"Michael thinks you're hot."

Not as far as I could tell, but whatever. "Jeremy doesn't?"

He wagged a finger in my face. "My guess? Neither does Heather, but you can't have them all. Besides, Jeremy still likes your sister."

"Even though he dumped her?"

He rolled his eyes. "You really *don't* talk to her, do you?"

"Not lately."

"So you can work on that *and* your D chord. And gymnastics." He shook his head. "In case I ever need to catch you again, though, please don't work on your running."

I couldn't figure him out. At all. "Why would you want to catch me? Your Dilly Bar is totally safe from me. I mean, probably."

He laughed. "For a smart, savvy, streetwise chick, you have no idea."

Then, for the briefest moment, he touched his lips to mine.

"I—" Was that a "friends" kiss? Was it even really a kiss at all? "I thought you wanted to be friends?"

He grinned and climbed out of the VW, then walked

around to my side and opened my door. "I want that, too."

Chapter 19

Wholly inattentive to her sister's feelings,
Lydia flew about the house in restless ecstasy.

— Jane Austen, *Pride and Prejudice*
Volume II, Chapter Eighteen

CAT'S BEDROOM DOOR was closed when I went upstairs, but I approached it with a combination of mild dread, two cans of soda, and a package of mint Oreos. Her favorite, not mine.

I knocked.

She didn't answer, not even to curse at me.

I glanced down at the Oreos, wishing I'd grabbed the berry ones, just as Cat's door swung open and hit the wall.

"Another conquest, I see." Her eyes were suspiciously red and possibly damp, which didn't seem like the hard-as-nails Cat she'd become. But like Zach said, I hadn't talked to her—really talked to her—in forever.

That was mutual.

"Conquest?" I didn't gratify her by touching my lips. Besides, Zach hadn't really kissed me, had he? I mean, not really?

269

"Hey, Jeremy is still pining for you, not me."

She tried to slam the door on me. Lucky thing I'd left my running shoes on, because it would've hurt.

"I'm not talking about Jeremy."

Or *to* Jeremy, apparently, but whatever.

I held out the mint Oreos, even though I was starting to think she owed *me* the peace offering.

When she eyed the Oreos but didn't cave, I tucked both sodas under my arm, ripped open the package, and popped an Oreo in my mouth.

Mint. Seriously. A total waste of calories.

I nodded at my old room. The remnants of my old *life*. "Can I come in?"

"Why?"

I sighed. "Because it's been too long?"

Her mouth twisted. Just when I thought she was going to try slamming the door again, harder this time, she stepped away from it, letting me inside.

I couldn't accuse her of being gracious, but it was a start. Maybe.

I handed her a Diet Coke and the whole package of mint Oreos, keeping only the Coke for myself. Popping the top on it, I walked over to Mary's old bed, which had ended up here, and dropped onto it, then scooted backward to lean against the wall.

Cat's pissed-off gaze never left me, but she didn't say a word.

I waited her out. Yet another life skill I'd mastered at Shangri-La.

Finally, she looked away from me and out the window, into the inky-black night. "Liz said you went home with Zach. Didn't that piss off Kirk and Drew and a million other guys?"

Like, say, Jeremy?

I took a long swig of Coke, but it didn't soothe my dry throat, not to mention my restless legs, which kept bouncing on the bed.

"I didn't go home with him. We stopped by DQ so he could grab something to eat." His Dilly *and* mine. "Then he gave me a ride home. Liz told him that the back seat of Dad's car was too junked up to leave room for me."

Right on cue, Cat snorted. "Like I believe that."

"Liz said it, not me, but Zach believed her and offered me a ride."

"He's going out with Lauren." Cat's mouth twisted with her usual contempt of late. "Not that you've ever worried about stealing another girl's guy."

Zing.

"He just gave me a ride." The Cat I used to know would've believed me, since I'd always been honest with her—and probably only her—but the angry girl sitting with her arms wrapped tightly around herself was a stranger. "Besides, he's tight with Lauren, but I don't think they're a couple."

Or else he was a total creep. Hadn't I already met every creep in Woodbury? Couldn't it *finally* be my turn to meet a nice guy? Was that too much to ask?

From the look on Cat's face, it was too much to ask.

"I hear Kirk's party got busted."

I tilted my head. "Liz told you?"

She nodded, her mouth pinched. After the shit Tess and Kirk had pulled on her last spring, I would've thought she'd be a little more gleeful.

"Did—" She broke off, grabbed a few Oreos, and stuffed two in her mouth, swallowing hard. "Did Jeremy get out okay?"

Ahh.

I shrugged. "I'm guessing anyone who wasn't drinking got out okay. Would Jeremy have been drinking?"

She shook her head, but the pinched look didn't go away.

Long pause. I almost grabbed a few Oreos, too, before

remembering that they were mint and I wasn't desperate.

"So you weren't with Jeremy."

I rolled my eyes. "Why would I be with Jeremy? Last time I checked, he liked *you*."

Although, okay, maybe not lately.

She stuffed a few more Oreos in her mouth, nearly choking on them. I didn't leap up to thump her on the back.

"I . . . broke up with him."

No shit, Sherlock. "Why?"

For a long moment, or maybe a million of them, I didn't think she was going to answer. No surprise there. At least, not since I got home from Shangri-La.

Finally, she mumbled something.

It didn't used to be this hard. "What?"

"When Kirk asked you to be in the band, I figured you might want to add Jeremy to your list."

"My list? What list?"

She waved a hand. "You know. Your list of guys. Guys who want you."

My list. Before everything changed. Before Shangri-La. I would've laughed if it wasn't so stupid now. Or maybe if Justin's name hadn't been on the list before I left with the circus for Wisconsin Dells and one long nightmare.

I tipped back my Coke only to discover that I'd already drained it. "I never slept with any of those guys. And you had a list, too."

This time, she *did* choke. "Mine never had more than two or three names on it, and I made them up. Yours had ten or twenty."

"So?" Pulling my knees up to my chest, I studied her. She'd lost weight in the last few weeks, most of it from her face. Her cheeks looked hollow, her eyes lost. "I never slept with any of them. Or, you know, did anything. I mean, not really."

Cat knew that, didn't she? She'd been the only one who knew. Plus, as it turned out, maybe Zach.

"What about Justin?" She sucked in a deep breath. "You bragged so much when you came home from Milwaukee."

Looking out the window, I blinked hard against even the *possibility* of tears. "I'd rather brag than dwell on the bad stuff."

Cat stared at me, obviously puzzled. Totally unlike the Cat who'd known me so well, or so I thought.

Finally, she tossed aside the package of Oreos and shot me a snotty look. "No matter what, you've always come out on top. What could be so bad?"

A lot of things. Things that, remembering, still made my skin crawl. Things a lot worse than whatever made Cat dump and then pine over her drummer boyfriend, but I didn't say that.

Instead, I bit my lip until I tasted blood.

After turning to wipe it with the back of my hand, I glanced sideways at Cat. Could I trust her? Doubtful in the extreme.

But what the hell.

"The short version? My so-called wild sexual escapades consist of being raped by two guys. One in ninth grade." I stared at her until she pursed her lips and nodded. "Then when I screwed up with the circus—" Understatement, but Bunny's husband *did* egg me on and hadn't been quite so pure of heart as I let Bunny keep believing. "I didn't have anywhere to go, and I knew Dad would be pissed. And Justin seemed safe."

He'd also told me he loved me.

Unlike all the times that guys in high school had said that to me, when I'd laughed and told them to find another sucker, I'd believed Justin.

But I still wanted to wait. As it turned out, he didn't.

Next thing I knew, Cat was next to me, on Mary's old bed, hugging me to within an inch of my life. I almost couldn't breathe. Vital organs were probably being pulverized.

It felt good.

"Justin raped you? Did you tell Dad? Or the judge?"

I laughed, somehow managing not to choke on it. "Dad, who'd already decided to ship me out? The judge, who told me he'd seen too many girls *just like me*, who never turned out well? Why waste my breath?"

"Because it was your *life*?"

Honest to God, I had no idea whether Cat was being supportive, or telling me I was an idiot, or even if she gave a rat's ass about anything other than mint Oreos. Which, let's face it, bordered on putrid.

I picked at a ball of lint on the bedspread. *My* old bedspread. I left it behind when Dad moved me to Mary's old room. I had my pride, yeah, but I also had a revulsion for the hot-pink daisy print Mom had bought without asking during one of her manic phases.

Avoiding Cat's gaze, I shrugged. "As it turns out, my life doesn't matter to a lot of people."

Including, lately, my own twin.

She didn't exactly disagree. "Not even to you?"

More than I'd admit, but less than I'd wish upon my worst enemy. Okay, except for Amber and Chelsea. I'd wish the fires of hell upon them . . . and throw in some gasoline for good measure.

Head down, I pulled at a thread on my old bedspread, tugging at it until I unraveled an entire seam. Oops. "I don't think it much matters what I want."

Or, despite Zach's kiss, who I maybe want.

Because maybe he *was* with Lauren. Or wished he were. Or, in any case, didn't wish he was with me. Maybe he'd kissed me to win a bet or a dare or something.

He wouldn't be the first guy who had.

"So you're not with Jeremy?"

My head flew up, my gaze shooting to Cat's face. It wasn't angry anymore. It looked . . . bleak.

What had *happened* to Cat? "If I still had a list, and I don't, he's not on it. Not now. Not ever. But I'm pretty sure he's on *your* list, and you're on his."

Getting up, Cat retrieved the Oreos and waved them under my nose, then started mainlining them. Mint Oreos. Ugh. "His list is probably a mile long."

Right. The guy who once dyed his spiked hair black and yellow, reminding me of a bumblebee, and dyed it an especially revolting mix of pink and orange for a few days last week. Yeah, girls were lined up all along the halls of Woodbury High to go out with him.

In Cat's case, love *was* blind. Or at least color-blind. Which was kinda sweet, actually.

I grinned at her. "I'm pretty sure he has *exactly* one name on his list."

Her hands twisted so tightly in her lap, I half-expected a few fingers to break off. "He doesn't even speak to me."

"Weird. Last time I checked, you weren't speaking to *him*."

"I-I didn't want to lose him to you."

"So you threw him away before you *could* lose him to me?" I rolled my eyes. "Not your brightest move ever. And to think Mr. Fogarty gushes over you so much."

Her lips twitched, almost reminding me of someone I used to know. Cat. "I shoveled for him last winter when it was a million degrees below zero."

"Give or take."

"Give or take." She grinned. For the first time since I returned home, it didn't remind me of piranhas at feeding time. "So maybe I should talk to Jeremy?"

I snorted. "Unless you're a total idiot, yeah, and you're not a total idiot. Except, of course, in your love for mint Oreos."

Her grin faded, taking mine with it. "The thing is, I don't want to be your sidekick."

I blinked. "My sidekick?"

"You know." This time, *she* picked at my mangy old bedspread. At this point, nothing could make it much worse. "I'm your twin, but somehow I always came in second." Her lower lip quivered, which stung more than if she'd screamed at me. "Everything we did was always your idea and what *you* wanted to do, like I didn't exist. Everyone followed you. They worshipped you. Blindly."

They'd definitely gotten over *that* while I'd been gone.

I sighed. "I don't want a sidekick. Or a follower or a worshipper or whatever." I bit my lip, wondering why I'd *ever* wanted that. But Cat was right: I had. Totally. "Truth is, I'd really just like one thing."

Cat eyed me, but for the first time since I got home, not with contempt. "What?"

"A friend?"

SATURDAY CAME AND went without a word from Zach. Not that I expected anything. If Shangri-La taught me anything, it was to keep my expectations low.

Like, at zero.

Social media lit up, though, with big news: the police had busted Kirk *and* his parents for the party. Even better, they'd busted Amber and Chelsea for vandalizing the Jeep and planting the drugs in it, for making false claims against me, and for possession.

They *hadn't* charged them with being worthless human beings, but like Liz said, that would be piling on after the tackle.

Why Liz makes sports analogies to anyone in our family other than Dad is beyond me.

Although I not-so-secretly cheered the news about Amber and Chelsea, I had no idea how the cops had gone after them so quickly. And apparently, based on the gossip, with a ton of rock-solid evidence.

Sunday morning, as Cat and I both slumped over Mom's questionable scrambled eggs after a long night spent watching old *Star Wars* movies and catching up, our doorbell rang.

Neither of us moved. No one moved.

Finally, with a loud sigh, Dad set down the sports section of the newspaper and groaned to his feet.

Half a minute later, he returned to the kitchen and pointed at me. Period.

Zach? Had he actually stopped by?

Before I'd even showered?

Damn!

I ran a hand through my hair, remembering too late that I no longer had enough of it to mess up, let alone snarl.

Still, I was wearing sweatpants and a baggy T-shirt and no bra. As my mind scrambled for traction and got none, Cat tossed one of Liz's hoodies at me. I threw it on and zipped it all the way up to my neck.

Okay, not quite all the way. Maybe Zach wouldn't notice my bare face if he saw a *little* skin, right?

Except that we're talking Zach. Who's impossible to read.

Finally, I stumbled to the front door. On a positive note, Dad had left it open. On a not-so-positive note, he hadn't bothered to invite Zach inside.

"I'm so sorry you had to—"

My heart racing, I skidded to a halt when I looked outside. Zach wasn't at the door.

Tess was.

After what she'd done to Cat last spring, no wonder Dad hadn't let her in. But let's get real: he probably wouldn't have let Zach in, either.

Tess's back was to me as she stared across the street, where Mr. Fogarty was outside, pushing his manual lawnmower around his yard and, based on his purple face, likely to have a coronary any minute. I groaned, psyching myself up to go over and mow it myself as soon as I got rid of Tess.

"Uh, Tess?" I paused, waiting for her to turn and face me. Finally, she did. From the look on her face, reluctantly. "What brings you here?"

She wasn't wearing makeup, either, which was startling for Tess, who'd always tried to look perfect. Basically, like my sister Jane, even if Tess had gone back to her natural brown and wavy hair from her dyed version of Jane's blond and straight.

She stared at me, obviously noting my lack of makeup, my slobby attire, and the fact that I maybe hadn't washed my hair since Friday.

Actually, we looked pretty similar.

"I'm . . . sorry."

I frowned. Had Tess done something to me, too? Shouldn't people at least take turns?

"Sorry? Why?"

"A million reasons." She laughed, but not really. Okay, that *was* like Tess. "I don't even know where to begin."

I was still holding the screen door open, which meant Mom would start shrieking at me any moment. Pulling our front door closed behind me, I stepped outside and plunked down on the steps. After a long pause, Tess sat next to me.

We'd been friends once. Close friends. Tess had always been the third wheel to the Lydia-and-Cat show, which had probably driven her crazy. No, based on the crap she pulled on Cat last spring, it had definitely driven Tess crazy. But the three of us had been tight. Super tight.

Before my life went all to hell.

Before Tess tried to send Cat's life to hell right along with mine.

Still, we *had* been friends. Close, tight, share-everything-but-guys friends. So I didn't just spit in her face and stomp back inside my house.

But, yeah, I was tempted.

Instead, I stretched out my legs and wiggled my toes and didn't look at her. "Whatever it is, just say it. Even if you helped Amber and Chelsea with their little stunt Friday night. Believe me, nothing anyone does to me shocks me anymore."

Not after a year dealing with the nasty pieces of work I met at Shangri-La.

Instead of answering, Tess gnawed on her lip. From the chewed-up, swollen redness of it, she must've spent the last twenty-four hours treating it the way a dog goes after a bone.

"Tess? Seriously. Tell me."

I looked out at the street, finally realizing that her cherry-red Firebird wasn't parked at the curb. God knows Tess wasn't the type to bike. Or run. Or even walk.

She swallowed hard. Opened her mouth. Swallowed again. "I was a total jerk to Cat last year."

I shrugged. "So I hear. But you should apologize to Cat for that, not me. I wasn't even here."

"If you'd been here, you would've taken me down even more fiercely than your sisters did."

Hard to believe, since Liz was one of the sisters in question, but I nodded, acknowledging her compliment. If it was a compliment.

She waved a hand, almost as if erasing her remark. "Okay, I maybe deserved it. But it didn't make me feel like stopping Chelsea and Amber when they went after *you* this semester.

Including—" She straightened her spine, as if she was gearing up for battle. What battle? Not mine. "Friday night."

Despite myself, my gut twisted when I remembered the broken glass and other damage to the Jeep. Not to mention the look of grim acceptance on Dad's face when he assumed that, yeah, I *had* gotten caught with drugs.

But I didn't say anything. What was there to say? The cops had caught Amber and Chelsea, but half the school would still think Lydia Bennet was guilty as hell. As always.

"But I turned them in."

One of Tess's feet tapped against the step so hard and so fast, it mesmerized me. So much so that I almost didn't hear what she said.

I frowned. "You—"

"I turned them in." She nodded. "They came upstairs from the basement at Kirk's house, bitching about you. Loudly. Next thing I knew, Chelsea whispered something to Amber, and they both laughed and went out to Amber's car together."

Amber had her own car? Did *everyone* I know own a car? When I no longer had even a battered old Jeep to fight over?

"I mean, her mom's car." Maybe Tess *did* still know me. "I had a bad feeling, so I followed them. When they got some stuff out of the trunk and headed toward your Jeep, I slipped behind a tree across the street." Tess looked at me, but her eyes didn't meet mine. "You saw me there, but they didn't."

My jaw dropped. Tess and Amber had always been as tight as Cat and I used to be. Rule number one of friendship: no ratting your friend out, no matter what.

Okay, that's actually rule number two. After no stealing your friend's guy.

Tess was shaky, so I touched a hand to her arm. "Did you tell the cops what you saw?"

A tight nod. "I even shot a video and gave it to them. You

know, just in case Amber's dad tried to talk his way out of Amber getting busted."

I almost laughed. Tess's mom might not pay much attention to her, but she was the reigning queen of getting Tess out of trouble. Or she had been until the school suspended Tess last spring for what she'd done to Cat.

I gave her a soft smile. "Thanks."

I almost said I owed her, but the debts were piled so high on both sides that I didn't feel like adding another one to the pile.

She shook her head. "You didn't deserve that."

"No." I hesitated a moment, then broke down and hugged her. To the extent her rigid spine allowed it. "But I sure hope college doesn't suck this bad."

She laughed, the sound more than a little rusty. "If we get in."

"I guess we'd better start praying, huh?"

Her lips twitched. "I have a feeling prayers won't be enough to help Amber and Chelsea."

I offered her a high-five. "Works for me."

Chapter 20

*She began to comprehend that he was exactly the man
who, in disposition and talents, would most suit her.*

— Jane Austen, *Pride and Prejudice*
Volume III, Chapter Eight

MONDAY MORNING, THE whole school buzzed with the news
of what Amber and Chelsea had done. Kirk got the usual cheers
and slaps on the back for throwing a party wild enough to earn a
police raid, but Amber and Chelsea were missing in action. If the
rumors were true, they'd been suspended indefinitely with little
hope of returning to school. Ever.

I should really tell them about this great school I knew in
Montana.

Oh, wait. With any luck, I'd never see them again.

I walked into Speech Communications class, saw Drew
sitting alone in the back of the room, and almost grabbed a desk
in the front. He looked so sad, even though getting rid of Chelsea
should make any rational guy wildly *happy*. After hesitating a
beat, I headed to the back and sat next to him.

When he leaned toward me, reeking of cologne, I cursed

myself.

"I'm sorry."

That's all. No flirty twinkle in his eye, no not-so-secret glance down my shirt, definitely no touching or panting or drooling.

I almost patted his arm, like I'd done with Tess yesterday, but I didn't want to give him false hope. Okay, based on the kicked-puppy look on his face, that was pretty egotistical of me. But still. Drew had gone out with Chelsea until about two seconds ago, which had to be the definition of stupid.

So, instead, I gave him a bright, asexual, don't-even-think-I'm-interested smile. "Not your fault."

"No, it was." Slouched in his chair, he ran a hand through his longish hair. "Chelsea thought I wanted you, and she can be a little insecure."

Not to put too fine a point on it, but Drew *had* wanted me. The way Cat used to want Drew. The way I maybe, possibly, wanted Zach.

Who probably didn't want me. I mean, not really.

I almost told Drew he'd dodged a bullet by getting rid of Chelsea, but this didn't seem like the perfect moment.

So I opted for something more innocuous. "Hey, did you make it out of the party without getting busted?"

Just like that, his face went from sad to sheepish. "As it turns out, Kirk's house has this little room in the basement with a secret panel. Just like in the movies, you know?"

I laughed. "I'm surprised Kirk didn't use it. How many of you hid in there? And for how long?"

"Forever." He shuddered. "Jeremy and Zach weren't drinking, so they could walk out the front door, but Michael and I used it. And as many girls as we could squeeze in. You know, just to do them a favor."

He winked at me, and I rolled my eyes. So much for missing

Chelsea.

Then he looked at me a little more intensely. "So, uh, you and Zach?"

I blinked. Everyone knew *everything* in this school.

Except, too often, the truth.

"After the Jeep got wrecked, I needed a ride home." When Drew flinched, I just shrugged. "So Zach gave me one."

"Are you two—"

"Good morning, class." As Ms. Ciccarelli strode into the room, looking like she'd just drunk fifteen cups of coffee, all conversation screeched to a halt.

Right that moment, I liked that about her.

Drew kept giving me these questioning looks, though, and maybe sneaking a peek or five down my shirt. So much for missing Chelsea.

He didn't ask about Zach again, though, not even at lunch, when my old table suddenly had plenty of spare room. Cat and Jeremy sat at one end of it, holding hands. *That* didn't take long. But before I could pat myself on the back for my good deed, Lauren walked by, head high and totally blowing me off.

Even though she hadn't gotten busted when the police spotted the drugs in the Jeep.

Even though it wasn't my fault that she had to call Zach's mom for a ride home.

"Lauren?" As I called her, a couple of girls at my table made faces as if she was beneath them. Maybe even beneath *me*, if such a thing was possible. "Hey. Lauren. Wait up."

She walked even faster, disappearing around a corner before I could grab my lunch tray and follow her.

"I hear she's pissed about you and Zach." Kirk, next to me, leaned close and rumbled the words in my ear, which might've been sexy a week ago. Definitely a month ago. But it wasn't now, not even remotely. Weird. "But you're not actually going out with him. Am I right?"

"You're right." Unfortunately.

"Sorry about your Jeep, by the way." Kirk shook his head. If I didn't know him so well, I'd almost think he cared. But I did, and he didn't. "Amber never did think. You know?"

She'd probably sold her soul to go out with Kirk, the coolest guy in school. Hadn't she been thinking then?

I didn't ask him.

I also didn't ask if Amber was, by any chance, currently rotting in jail. Had she and Chelsea turned eighteen yet, locking them into adult-court rules? A girl could dream.

But I must've dreamed so vividly that I missed whatever Kirk said next. Until he repeated himself, his mouth pressed even harder against my ear.

"You? Me? Friday?" It seriously felt like a wet centipede crawling around my earlobe. Ick. "Or sooner? Like tonight?"

The smile I gave him was apologetic. The rest of me wasn't. Not even remotely.

"I have a guitar lesson tonight." And, Jazz willing, any other night Kirk wanted to go out with me. "But I'm mostly busy with gymnastics. Tryouts are next week."

"So you're really doing it. Guitar *and* gymnastics?" Kirk stared at me, hard, as if he actually wanted to look into my soul or at least read my mind. Good luck with that. "Or you just don't want to go out with me?"

Wow. Those words had probably *never* come out of Kirk's mouth. Not in this lifetime.

I batted my eyelashes at him, mostly for the benefit of the small crowd we'd drawn. "What girl wouldn't?"

He rolled his eyes. "Don't tell me. You?"

I always had. I mean, Kirk *was* cool, despite the silly sunglasses he wore when he played in the band, despite helping Tess humiliate Cat last spring, and despite putting up with a snake like Amber for so long. Despite everything.

But did I still want him? No.

Maybe I wanted something more than the coolest guy in school. Maybe I'd like a guy who was honest and decent and, for better or worse, didn't fall for my bullshit.

Unfortunately.

♫

LAUREN ARRIVED LATE for Accounting class, so late I'd long since figured she wasn't coming.

After handing Ms. Frey a tardy slip, she headed for a desk on the far side of the room from where I sat.

"Lauren?" Ms. Frey cleared her throat when Lauren didn't stop. "Your assigned seat is on the other side of the room."

Lauren sat down anyway. "I need a new desk. The, uh, feng shui over there isn't working for me."

A few girls laughed, half of the room started murmuring, and a dozen kids stared at me. No one had accused me of pinning my own drug crimes on Amber and Chelsea, though, so this was pretty mild compared to what I'd geared up for today.

Okay, so my standards have slipped.

A lot.

"Nice try, Lauren, but you can either sit at your usual desk or you can go to Mr. Paymar's office. Your choice."

"You call that a choice?" Lauren stood up and grabbed her books. "I'll go see Mr. Paymar."

Ms. Frey frowned but didn't say a word. Unlike everyone else in the room, she also didn't slide a curious glance at me.

The door slammed hard behind Lauren.

Five minutes later, Mr. Paymar opened it, then escorted a sullen Lauren inside. He smiled at Ms. Frey. "I believe you're missing one of your students?"

"As luck would have it, yes." Ms. Frey pointed to Lauren's usual desk next to mine.

After a mulish glare in my direction, Lauren sulked all the way to her desk. She dragged it sideways, making a harsh scraping sound against the floor, until it was a foot or so farther away from me.

Ms. Frey didn't say a word.

And Mr. Paymar didn't budge from his position at the door.

Finally, when the air was so thick with tension that I could've choked on it, Ms. Frey nodded at Mr. Paymar, who left. As if nothing had happened, she then explained the instructions for today's pop quiz on balancing a checkbook.

I aced the quiz, but I couldn't stop wondering if I'd *ever* ace the concept of being friends with other girls without them inevitably hating me for stealing their guys. Even when I *didn't* steal their guys. In Zach's case, I definitely hadn't.

Or if I had, I wish he'd at least let me know.

AFTER THE FINAL bell rang, I walked out of school with Cat. According to Dad, we'd be lucky if the Jeep got fixed by the end of the week, so we had to walk back and forth to school until then.

But we'd be walking together. Talking again. Friends again. Almost like old times, despite a few awkward silences, but in some ways better. Equal. Not just my sidekick and me.

"Uh, Cat? Give you a ride?"

So maybe I shouldn't have encouraged her to get back together with Jeremy.

I shooed her away, though, shaking my head when Jeremy

belatedly offered me a ride, too. "I'm good. You guys go."

I watched them stroll hand in hand over to Jeremy's car, which was old and ugly and didn't look like it could actually make it the mile to our house. I mean, not that they'd care if it did. Cat looked thrilled, Jeremy even more so.

I was happy for them. Mostly.

Hitching my backpack higher on my shoulders, I headed toward home. Head down. Lost in thought.

A block from school, an engine rumbled, followed by a horn honking. Startled, I almost tripped. When I saw the bright-orange VW Beetle, I almost tripped again.

So much for the sense of balance a gymnast needs. Maybe I should find a different sport. Checkers?

"Hey."

I walked over to Zach's car but didn't open the door, let alone climb inside. "Hey yourself."

Leaning toward me, Zach pushed open the door.

I still didn't get in.

He sat back in his seat, his hands drumming a beat on the steering wheel. "I heard about Kirk's girlfriend. And Drew's." He didn't grin as much as *I* had when I heard the news. "I also figured your Jeep might still be a mess and wondered if you needed a ride home."

I bit down so hard on my confusion, I tasted blood. What was *with* Zach? Did he have a hero complex? A martyr complex? A pissed-off girlfriend named Lauren?

I inched closer but still didn't get in. "Don't tell me. You're afraid I'll *run* home and get even faster?"

"Busted."

We just stared at each other, not laughing or grinning or batting our eyelashes at each other. In my case, also not necessarily breathing.

I blinked first. "So what's up, really? Lauren spent all day wishing I were dead, and all I can figure is that it has something to do with you."

I swallowed hard, mildly shocked that I'd said it, but my days of stealing guys from other girls—accidentally or not—were over. Especially when the guys in question always wanted me for something other than holding hands and talking.

Which, let's face it, they all did.

Zach's eyes searched mine, but I'm pretty sure they didn't find anything. "Can I give you a ride home?"

"If you answer my question first." I crossed my arms. "Maybe."

"Like I already told you, I'm just friends with Lauren."

I snorted. "Does Lauren know?"

"According to my mom, no."

Zach wasn't looking at me anymore. The stack of CDs on the front passenger seat of his VW claimed all of his attention. Not that he was moving the CDs to the back seat, like he had Friday night. No, he rummaged through the pile until he grabbed a CD, opened the case, and popped the disc in the CD player before punching a few buttons.

Hearing the opening to "Boulevard of Broken Dreams"— ever since reform school, *not* my favorite song by Green Day—I almost laughed.

But I didn't. "Is that supposed to be about me? Or you? Oh, wait. Since I'm on foot, I guess *I'm* the one walking alone."

He slid me a grin and patted the passenger seat. The piled-high-with-CDs passenger seat. "But you don't have to."

"You still didn't answer my question."

"Fine." He grabbed a handful of CDs and dumped them in the back seat, then another. And another. When the last ones hit the floor behind him, he met my exasperated gaze. "I'm not going out with Lauren, and never have. But we've been close since we were toddlers, so I watch out for her. Maybe she took that the wrong way." He gritted his teeth. "According to my mom."

The death glares I'd gotten from Lauren all day would definitely agree. "And?"

"And?" He tapped a beat on the steering wheel in time to "Boulevard of Broken Dreams," which was still playing. It was a long song. And sad. Today, it put me on edge. "I take care of my friends, and Lauren's a friend. So are you. And, yeah, I don't want you getting any faster."

I was probably too fast for him already, in more ways than one, if he believed all the rumors. But he said he didn't believe them.

Hard to believe.

I sighed. "What *do* you want?"

Another few beats on the steering wheel as he stared out the windshield. Really, he should've been a drummer.

Finally, he looked at me. "I'd like to go out with you. I'd like to kiss you again, for longer than a millisecond but not so long that your dad dumps my dead body in one of those ditches you're so fond of. And I'd love it if you got in my car before the entire student body of Woodbury High School drives by."

"You're pretty demanding. Needy, even." I climbed into the passenger seat anyway.

"So I'm told. But usually by my mom."

He eased away from the curb, cautiously, unlike every other guy I knew. And unlike me.

Trying to picture us together, I laughed, but it caught in my throat when I pictured Lauren today. All day today. "What about Lauren?"

"Swear to God, I've never even kissed her." He made a half-hearted slash across his chest. His legs might be so long and skinny that I felt demoralized every time I compared them to mine, but his chest was nice. Okay, his legs were, too. "I didn't even kiss her in eighth grade when she claimed she was the only girl in middle school who'd never been kissed."

I grinned, remembering those days. Lauren must've had even more guts in eighth grade than I did, which said something. When I opened my mouth to say just that, though, Zach pulled to the curb in the middle of nowhere and turned to me. "I also didn't kiss her Friday night, when I got home after dropping you off. She was waiting up for me. On my front steps."

I frowned. "Did she ask you to?"

"Yep."

Had she already heard about Zach and me? Wait. There hadn't been anything to know!

"And . . . you said no?"

"Worse." One corner of his mouth twisted. "Since Lauren and I *have* been friends since forever, I told her I maybe kinda liked you."

He hadn't even told *me* that. I mean, not really.

I held up a hand. "Let me guess. It didn't go over too well."

Based on all the death glares today? Understatement.

"Like I said. My mom told me I was a complete idiot."

"For telling Lauren? Or for not kissing her?"

He laughed, surprising me. It also didn't make me wildly eager to meet his mom. I mean, as if I would. Guys didn't tend to bring me home to meet their moms. After I shoved them off me, I was usually lucky if they brought me to *my* house.

Come to think of it, Zach and I were still parked on a random street somewhere in the middle of Woodbury. Thank God I'd worn shoes I could walk in today. Or, if I needed to, run.

Zach stopped laughing. Surprising me more than a little, he grabbed my hand.

"My mom just said I needed to be clear with Lauren. Oh, and to quit mumbling Lydia-Lydia-Lydia *all the time* and ask you out already."

Maybe I *would* like his mom.

"So." My brain shorted out, making me forget whatever I was going to say. Or ask. And hopefully not beg. The fact that Zach was playing with my fingers might've had something to do with it. "Do you—"

"Will you go out with me?" Zach's eyes met mine, and I was lost. In a good way, I think, but I'd felt like this only twice before, and let's just say it hadn't ended well either time. "I was going to suggest Russo's, but it kinda sucked the last time we were there."

"No kidding." And he'd given Lauren a ride home. "But you don't want to go to a movie?"

In my experience, which was vast and mostly awful, guys *always* wanted to go to a movie on their first so-called date with me. And sit in the back row. And make out during the previews. And try for a home run not long after that.

Zach frowned. "We can't talk in a movie. You don't want to talk?"

My breath caught. I wasn't sure I *could* talk, so I nodded. "Russo's would be great."

"Tonight? Or are you busy with guitar or gymnastics or trying to avoid getting dumped into ditches by creepy bass players?"

"Tonight?" I squeezed his hand, which was still holding mine, and sent up a little prayer of thanks that I *hadn't* booked a last-minute guitar lesson with Jazz. "If you're the creepy bass player in question, I'm totally free."

We sealed it with a kiss. It lasted way longer than a millisecond but not so long that my dad showed up and dumped Zach into a ditch. Or the cops arrived. Or my mom found out and starting shrieking in my ear.

So, yeah. As kisses went, it was pretty perfect.

Chapter 21

"My sisters may write to me.
They will have nothing else to do."

— Jane Austen, *Pride and Prejudice*
Volume III, Chapter Eleven

FOUR WEEKS, THREE days, and exactly zero movie dates with Zach later, I took an even wilder than planned flip off the top bar of the uneven parallels and—miraculously—earned a roar from the crowd when I stuck my landing.

I was still wiping chalk off my taped hands, most of it onto my leotard, when ear-splitting squeals warned me that my mom had broken loose from my dad's promised chokehold on her and was running in my direction.

Grinning, I shook a finger at my dad, who still sat halfway up the bleachers. Probably out of a sense of self-preservation.

Smart guy. Unreliable but smart.

"Lydia! That was so *perfect*! Amazing! Incredible!"

Not even remotely, but I was happy anyway. I'd earned a spot on the gymnastics team, despite a few bitchy girls who'd whined to Coach Burns about me—and who lost their spots on the team as a result.

And I could play a decent D chord now. Most of the time.

And Zach really *was* starting a band with me, Jeremy, Michael, and Heather. And maybe even my sister Mary, whenever she came home on breaks from MIT.

And Zach and I were together, really together, even though our so-called dates mostly consisted of playing music, holding hands and smooching and not much else, and arguing over whether he *could* "read my mind" like the Killers sang or whether he just happened to make a lot of lucky guesses.

He made a *lot* of lucky guesses.

Like right now. He guessed really, really accurately that he should drag my dad down from the bleachers before my mom had a high-pitched coronary right in front of all of my gymnastics teammates.

Before Zach and Dad could make their way here, though, I gave my mom a gigantic hug. Because she *had* always been there for me. In a wild, screeching, totally unpredictable way, but she'd been there. Even at the worst times of my life.

Okay, often with her credit card.

"Lydia?" Coach Burns eyed Mom's high heels and the floor mat she was probably putting holes in as we spoke. "Great job, but can you take this off the mat?"

I steered Mom off the mat and away from as much of the crowd as possible, but another small crowd quickly gathered around us. Dad. Zach. Cat and Jeremy. Liz and Jane and their guys. Mr. Fogarty, who was still clapping. Lauren, who stopped hating Zach and me after she started dating a really sweet college friend of Zach's who had more tattoos and piercings than I'd ever seen up close. Even Mary, who'd made a surprise trip home from college just for my first gymnastics meet.

And Rachel Langdon, Liz's BFF since the dawn of time, who

shocked my whole family when she showed up hand in hand with Wild Bill Cooper, the biggest weirdo on the face of the earth, and softly announced that she was pregnant.

Yeah. Like, eight months pregnant.

"You were the best." Zach, despite the constant threats my dad made to toss him into a ditch and leave him for dead, put his arm around me. "Even on the balance beam."

"Slight problem: I don't do the balance beam."

Except really, really badly. And when no one else was around.

"But you'd be the best if you did."

I rolled my eyes. "So much for honesty in a relationship."

"Hey, honesty can be overrated." Liz stepped closer, getting in Zach's face until he let go of me so she could give me a bone-squeezing hug. "For instance, Alex *never* tells me what he really thinks of my sweatpants."

As Alex's eyebrows danced, Jane held up a hand. "He doesn't need to. Even Charlie says they belong at the bottom of a landfill."

"Hey! I never said that." Charlie, Jane's blond cocker spaniel of a boyfriend, who was quite possibly the sweetest guy on the planet, shook his head. "I said they looked like something my grandmother wore. In the nursing home. I meant it in a good way."

Liz slugged him anyway.

Mary, whose boyfriend Josh hadn't been able to make the quick trip home from MIT, gave Charlie a high-five before offering me one, too. "You were even better than me on the bars. Or parallel thingies. Or whatever you call them."

"No shit, Sherlock."

As Cat and I said it in unison, we looked at each other and grinned. I happened to glance over at Dad just then, though, and caught him with tears in his eyes. But not from allergies or anything like that. Serious tears.

Dad.

My dad.

I tilted my head, a question in my eyes, but he just shook his head and walked away.

I followed him all the way to the far side of the gym, near the exit to the parking lot.

Somewhat shockingly, no one else in my family tagged along.

"Dad?"

His back was still to me, as if he was headed out without so much as a simple "congrats," let alone a much-needed increase in my allowance. I mean, let's get real: all those dinners at Russo's with Zach were costing serious money, and I still felt squeamish about a guy paying and expecting results. Even though it was Zach. Or, okay, maybe because I knew he was saving up for a new bass guitar.

Just when I thought Dad was going to walk out on my big night, he turned and faced me. The tears were streaming down his cheeks now.

Clearly, he spent too much time with Mom.

"I'm . . . so proud, sweetie."

He probably hadn't called me "sweetie" since I was three or four, which was another clue. Of what, I wasn't sure.

"Uh, thanks?"

"And you did it—" He swept a hand through the air, at the gym and the uneven parallels and mats and everything. "You managed to do *this* after everything that happened to you. After everything I did to you. After I cost you a year of your life."

"Oh, Dad." I actually threw my arms around him, also probably for the first time since age three or four. "Yeah, you totally did."

He flinched. As in, the way he would if he'd just taken a

mortar round to his chest.

I shrugged. I wasn't going to lie, but I'd also moved past it. I mean, as much as I could. "But I should've told you how it was. What Justin did."

And what Blake, Mr. Star Quarterback, did to me freshman year. Because Dad would've done something. Maybe something stupid, or possibly illegal, but he would've done something. And then maybe he wouldn't be crying right now.

And maybe neither would I.

He brushed a hand roughly across his cheek, exactly the way Liz did on the rare occasions anyone caught her crying.

"I suspect it's too late now, but I want you to know that when you looked me in the eye and told me those drugs in the Jeep weren't yours, I believed you." He cleared his throat and took a swipe at his other cheek. "And if I could give you back that year, I would. A thousand times over."

I looked down at my feet, which were bare and a little cold, and then back at him. "It made me stronger."

"It's a strength I wouldn't wish upon you." He tapped my nose, maybe to distract me from the fact that he was still crying. Like, seriously crying. His yoga training was making him *way* too sensitive. "But, yes, you're strong. Like Liz."

Laughing, I flexed my mostly nonexistent bicep. "Yeah, that's what everyone says."

"You are." He smiled as his flow of tears finally slowed to a trickle. "Actually, so are Jane and Mary and Cat. Each of you, in your own way, has become a strong woman, and I'm very proud." Okay, the tears started again. His *and* mine. "But you may be the strongest of all."

Stronger than Liz, our family's fearless Amazon? Startled, I blinked, but then nudged him with my elbow. "Let's not tell Liz, okay? She'll put me in a headlock in the middle of the mat just to prove you wrong."

"It's our secret." He held out a hand, shaking mine, before drawing me into another hug. "After all, she'd probably knock me to the mat first, and all the yoga in the world hasn't made my back strong enough to take a blow like that."

I laughed. "Fair enough."

"Oh, and Lydia?"

I looked up at him—with respect, even—which was something I hadn't done for a long time. "Yeah?"

"Tell Zach to quit worrying about me leaving him for dead in a ditch somewhere. I'd be much more creative than that."

I nodded, knowing Dad would never actually do anything to a guy I liked. Especially one who drove a bright-orange VW Beetle just because his mom had picked it out. "I'll let him know. Maybe."

Laughing, we walked arm in arm back to the rest of my family and friends and Zach. And to my future.

It looked pretty freaking amazing.

ABOUT THE AUTHOR

MARY STRAND practiced corporate law in a large Minneapolis law firm for sixteen years until the day she set aside her pointy-toed shoes (or most of them) and escaped the land of mergers and acquisitions to write novels. The first novel she wrote, *Cooper's Folly,* won Romance Writers of America's Golden Heart award and was her debut novel.

Mary lives on a lake in Minneapolis with her husband, two cute kidlets, and a stuffed monkey named Philip. When not writing, she lives for sports, travel, guitar, dancing (badly), Cosmos, Hugh Jackman, and ill-advised adventures that offer a high probability of injury to herself and others. She writes YA, romantic comedy, and women's fiction novels. *Livin' La Vida Bennet* is the fourth and final novel in her four-book YA series, The Bennet Sisters.

You can find Mary at www.marystrand.com, follow her on Twitter or Instagram (@Mary_Strand), or "like" her on Facebook (www.facebook.com/marystrandauthor).

Website: www.marystrand.com
Newsletter: http://eepurl.com/M0EwH
Facebook: www.facebook.com/marystrandauthor
Twitter: http://twitter.com/Mary_Strand
Instagram: http://instagram.com/Mary_Strand

Also by Mary Strand

Pride, Prejudice, and Push-Up Bras
(The Bennet Sisters, book 1)
Triple Berry Press, 2016

Being Mary Bennet Blows
(The Bennet Sisters, book 2),
Triple Berry Press, 2016

Cat Bennet, Queen of Nothing
(The Bennet Sisters, book 3)
Triple Berry Press, 2017

Cooper's Folly
Bell Bridge Books, 2014

CPSIA information can be obtained
at www.ICGtesting.com
Printed in the USA
BVOW06s0216120218
507873BV00001B/37/P